MY

BROTHER'S

KEEPER

A DCI ROHAN ROY CRIME THRILLER

Book 1

M.L. ROSE

CHAPTER 1

Nine-year-old Johnny looked around him fearfully. The dense trees stood silent with their thick, cracked brown bark, rising tall into the dark sky. Green undergrowth came up to his waist, covering the ground as far as he could see, which wasn't far, as the trees, packed together like matchsticks in a box, blocked most of his view.

"Dolly?" he called out; his voice wobbly. Dolly was the family's mischievous black Labrador, who had run into the bushes. "Dolly, where are you?"

Nothing but silence answered him, and a whisper from the trees, far above his head. The wind gathered pace, brushing through the skeletal October branches, the sound of it like a chorus of discordant, cold voices that murmured in his ears. Johnny shivered, hair rising on his neck.

"Daddy?" He shouted. "Daddy! I can't find Dolly."

Johnny heard footsteps trampling behind him. A frisson of fear ignited in his guts as he turned around quickly. A grey coated man was walking towards him, and he relaxed when he saw his father, Duncan Reid. His father's face was like thunder, mirroring the grey sky above.

"I told you not to go running after Dolly!" Duncan said. He got to his son and bent lower to face him. "Stop running after her. We'll find her, don't worry. But we go together, okay?"

Johnny nodded, relieved that his father was here. "Okay, Daddy."

Duncan took his son's hand, and they stepped over the thick shrubbery and twigs. "She's chasing some rabbits. I just hope she's not fallen in some hole." He murmured the last sentence under his breath, to himself. He didn't want Johnny to get worried. Like Johnny, he loved that dog, but she was always getting herself into trouble.

After a few more steps, Duncan stopped. Ahead of him the knot of trees got thicker, and the shrubs rose higher. He needed a machete to hack through this crap, and he certainly couldn't do it with his son in tow. Not that he had a machete to start with.

He cursed the dog in silence. He should never have taken her off the leash. But they were on the hill, in open land, and though it was isolated, he came here often with the family. Mandy, Johnny, and him, with Dolly. This place was free of the other dogwalkers in this area. They were in Wyming Brook Nature Reserve, an area that was at the border between south Sheffield, and the beginning of the vast mountainous area of the Derbyshire Dales.

Johnny tugged on his hand. "Daddy, what shall we do?"

Duncan needed to make a decision. It was three in the afternoon on a Sunday, and Mandy would want him back soon. She was making a roast. Duncan did a 360, and all that met his eyes were fern leaves, foliage of various sizes, and the numerous trees that effectively blocked further advance with a child in tow.

And yet, he needed to find Dolly. Where could that dog have gone? Not far in this thicket. He cast his gaze around but couldn't see anyone else walking their dogs. It was remote here, and there wasn't any other living person around for miles. Maybe he shouldn't have come this far for a walk.

"I'll tell you what. Let's go back to the car. You have a biscuit, while I look for Dolly. She can't be that far ahead."

There was a stubborn look on Johnny's face. His eyebrows lowered, and his lips followed.

"No. Coming with you." He tightened his grip on his father's hand. Duncan sighed. Admittedly, he had his doubts about locking Johnny in the car. But that was better than being out here in the middle of a forest.

"Let's go on the path and walk around. Dolly's probably back there anyway."

"Yes," Johnny brightened.

They walked back to the path that was a couple of hundred yards from the edge of the hill. The dirt track skirted the woodlands, and its trail bent up ahead, disappearing from view. Straight ahead the hill sloped down steeply, through bracken and bush, all the way to the outskirts of Sheffield. The city lay nestled in the palm of the valley, the peaks of the Derbyshire Dales undulating to the left. A few lights glimmered, and smokestacks blew smoke out into the frigid air.

Sheffield looked beautiful from this distance, its houses and streets sneaking into the slopes of the craggy hills that towered over this side of it. Duncan came here at night sometimes, when he wanted to walk and think alone. The lights far down below made the long walk worthwhile.

Johnny skipped ahead of his father, then broke into a run, shouting Dolly's name. Duncan shouted back, telling him to slow down. Johnny didn't listen. Duncan walked quicker, then almost tripped over on his shoelaces. Cursing, he looked down to find them undone.

"Wait," he called out to his son, but Johnny was already just a flicker of movement on the extreme right, curving around the bend. He shouted something, his words lost in a gust of wind. Duncan tied his laces quickly and broke into a run himself. Johnny was a good runner; he had broken a record in a four-hundred-metre sprint at school. He was much faster than his dad. Johnny's nimble legs scampered down the track. Duncan ran past his parked car, craning his neck to the right, but his line of sight was hampered by a thick screen of conifers.

"Johnny!" he shouted, picking up pace. The path took a sharp right, and Duncan panted as he came to a sudden stop. The track straightened and went in a straight line as far as his eyes could see. There was no one on the track. No sigh of Johnny. He called for his son but heard nothing except the whistling wind. Shaking his head, Duncan half walked, half ran, jerking his head around. After a few minutes, he stopped and frowned.

Where could Johnny have gone? He went to the bushes, and without wading into the undergrowth, strained his eyes. He called his son's name again. He walked forward a while and repeated the process. Nothing.

Duncan felt the first stab of panic lance across his chest. He quelled the surge by shouting Johnny's name again, and rationalising to himself. The boy had seen the dog, and then gone back into the woods.

Yes, that's what Johnny had done. He had to have, otherwise…

No, no. Duncan set his jaws, and shook his head. There was no other alternative. It was stupid. He was being stupid. There was no one else here, only the three of them. His only fear was that Johnny had fallen and hit his head on some log on the forest floor.

Duncan ran in a straight line, jerking his head to the left and right, then realised it was futile. Johnny had definitely gone into the woods. After the verge where people parked their cars, there was a thin line of trees before the hills sloped down.

Johnny wouldn't be there, but another stab of fear almost crippled Duncan. What if that stupid dog had gone there, and Johnny followed? Shouting hoarsely now, Duncan stormed to the trees near the edge. A quick look around told him there was no dog, or boy hiding there. It was still daylight, and he was thankful. He went as far as he dared, leaning against a tree, looking down at the void below. It was a gentle slope, and he could climb down it easily enough, if necessary. A quick scan told him there was no sign of Johnny.

Duncan got back on the path, his heart hammering at a nuclear rate, breath coming in short gasps. He checked the car once, as it was nearby. Nothing. It was locked. He ran forward a little, then retraced his steps, and went back inside the forest. He found his way back to the spot where he had seen Johnny last. He screamed his son's name again. His anguished cry was picked up by a forlorn wind and scattered between the trees.

Duncan stepped forward, his heart in an ice-cold grip of fear. Then he heard a sound. A snapping of twigs, feet moving on the ground. And they were little feet, making small sounds. It came from behind a tree up ahead. His soul sang in relief. Johnny was hiding behind a tree. Thank God...

He surged ahead, crashing through the undergrowth, and swung around the big birch that blocked his way. He stared at the ground. Dolly, the black Labrador looked up at him, tongue lolling out. Duncan gritted his teeth, shut his eyes, and muttered a curse under his breath.

"Where's Johnny?" He bellowed, his roar scaring Dolly off. She scampered away, tail between her legs. Duncan followed, a dead black weight now lodged against his throat, extending its malicious fingers into his lungs, squeezing breath out. He couldn't think or speak. Like a madman, he thrashed around in the forest, screaming his son's name out till his voice broke.

Dolly knew something was up, and came up to him, whining. She followed him back to the car. That was Duncan's last hope. Johnny got lost but had the sense to come back to the car. He told him that anyway, every time they came here. Go back to the car if you get lost.

The black Honda Civic stood there in silence. There was no sign of Johnny. Panic bulged in Duncan's chest, and a sickness flooded his belly. He ran up and down the track again, searching, screaming, crying. Then he fell to his knees on the grass verge, eyes shaky, chest tight with a crushing pain. With ice cold fingers, he fished out his phone and dialled 999.

CHAPTER 2

Detective Chief Inspector Rohan Roy crouched by the door of the house. Dawn was just breaking, but it was dark enough that no one could see him, or his team, in their black tactical gear.

He was by the front fence, and, when he peered through the bullet proof glass of his goggles, he could see the dilapidated front door, green paint flaking off it. The bay window was boarded up with plywood. Upstairs, the windows were intact, but shut, with curtains drawn. Like the other houses on this street in Newham, East London, the place had seen better days. The brickwork was crumbling, and large patches of damp spread down the front. There was a stench of rotting something, either food or a dead animal, or, he shuddered to think what else.

"Zero to Romeo One, are you in position?" Roy whispered on the microphone attached to his helmet.

"Yes, guv, all set," came the weirdly cheerful voice of Detective Sergeant Darren Maddison. Darren and two others were watching the back.

"I'm going in. Stand by."

Roy was an AFO, or Authorised Firearms Officer in the London Metropolitan Force. He gripped the Glock 22 tightly and moved like lightning. The door looked flimsy but proved to be tougher than he had imagined. One solid kick from his size twelve boots made it wobble, but it didn't give way. He took three steps back, then kicked it again, and it shuddered. He hurled himself at it with his shoulders, aware he was going to fall in now, and if there was a bullet headed his way, he was toast. So be it. He had a helmet and bulletproof vest on.

He crashed inside, the door slamming open. He lost his balance, but put his back to the wall, and went down on one knee.

"Police!" He shouted, as if that was necessary. He was hardly breaking into Buckingham Palace. But protocol ruled police life these days.

From upstairs, he heard a crash, then muffled voices speaking fast, at least two of them. Two doors lay on his left, both shut. A kitchen door was right front. The stench of rot was a pulsing wave emanating from the kitchen. He gagged, then held his breath as he kicked down both doors. He shouted, "Police!" twice before he entered and checked both rooms. Both were bereft of furniture. There was no carpet, and half the floor was missing in the second room that opened onto the garden.

He heard the scampering feet of DC Kilpatrick, also an AFO, right behind him. Kilpatrick bounded up the stairs, followed by another two uniformed members.

Roy tiptoed around the half-excavated floor, taking a look to ensure there was nothing under it. Only the rafters on the floor, and decades of accumulated dirt and muck. He kicked down the garden door, the glass panels smashing, showering his helmet with fragments. He stepped out on the patio, clocking the garden shed to his right. A sixth sense made him look up, and he flung himself to the side as a man came sailing down from upstairs and fell to the floor with a loud thump. He literally missed Roy by inches. He scrambled to his feet and lunged forward, heading straight down the garden. But Roy, despite his heavy, six-foot-three, frame, managed to get fingers to the man's ankle, making him trip. He went sprawling on the grass and Roy jumped on his back. The man grunted in pain, and Roy cuffed his hands swiftly.

"Where are they?" he said to the man, fire and brimstone in his voice. The man fired out a couple of expletives in a language he didn't understand. Roy raised the man's head by pulling on his hair. "Nice to meet you too. Now, where are they?"

The man uttered more of the same garbage, and Roy slapped him once, and narrowly avoided a gob of spit. He slipped off a plastic tie from his chest rig and tied it around the man's ankles. He left the guttersnipe writhing on the ground and shouting curses.

"I'll get a translator, pal. Don't fret."

He went to the garden shed and cupped his hands over the glass window. Nothing inside but old garden gear. He kicked the door down and looked inside for good measure.

"Guv! Up here!"

One of the rear bedroom windows was open, and Kilpatrick was shouting down at him. Roy took one look at the man on the ground. He wasn't going anywhere. He dashed inside and bounded up the ramshackle staircase. Dust flew around him as his feet pounded the threadbare carpet on the narrow landing. Two bedrooms and a bathroom opened up in front of him. Kilpatrick was in the first bedroom ahead of him. He heard the other two uniforms in the bedroom behind, shouting and restraining a man. He could check, but he knew Kilpatrick had called him for a reason.

CHAPTER 3

Kilpatrick had his back to him, and he moved so Roy could see. There was a mattress on the floor, with no bedsheets, only a duvet without a cover. On the mattress lay several children, all of them awake. They clutched each other in terror, their staring, wild eyes fixed with fear. They had learnt not to make a sound, and to cry in silence. A searing pain lanced across Roy's heart, slicing it in two.

"Take off your helmet, and step back," he instructed. Kilpatrick did as told. Roy did the same and went down on his knees.

"It's okay," he said, in what he hoped was his most reassuring voice. His helmet and goggles were off. The grimy-cheeked, and torn-clothed, skinny children stared at him. All of them held each other, because they had no one else.

"We'll look after you, okay?" He smiled. "You're safe now." Turning, he said, "Get blankets. Ask the uniforms to get some food and drinks from the corner shop." He spoke over his shoulder to Kilpatrick, who left promptly. On the landing, the uniforms pulled out the second trafficker, who was quieter than his friend downstairs.

Roy searched the room. He felt the children's watchful eyes on him. There was a wardrobe, and he opened it

14

cautiously. Two pairs of terror-struck little eyes focused on him. They flinched back against the woodwork. A boy and a girl. Seven to ten years old, if he had to guess. The girl had green eyes, and pale brown skin. Her long hair was dank and straggly. The boy had grime on his cheeks, dark eyes, and black hair. Streaks of tears lined both their faces. Their eyes were on the verge of popping out.

"Friends, okay? Buddies?" Roy forced himself to smile. "Don't worry."

He looked around at the other children on the mattress. All of them were pre-pubescent. Their skeletal forms remained huddled close together, watching Roy. He got up, unable to look them in the eyes for long. That familiar squeeze around the base of his neck, tightening his windpipe, was back. He got up and looked out the bay window. The bastard was still downstairs, writhing around. He had DS Darren Maddison and another uniform constable for company now. The window was open, and Roy leaned over.

"They're up here. Get the thermal gear from the cars, now."

"Yes guv," Darren nodded, looking up.

Roy sat down cross legged, facing the children like he was their teacher. He fought the clawing in his heart, silenced the desperate voices and their whisperings.

"Now," he said brightly. "Who speaks English?"

The silent faces stared at him. One girl in the front was the first to move, brushing hair from her face. All of them remained silent, even the two who had now crawled out of the wardrobe.

"Me, Roy," he said pointing to his chest. He smiled, then pointed at the girl. "And you?"

He knew there was no point. These little souls had been separated from their families. Bundled in vans, trucks, shipping containers, hurled across seas. What could he hope to get out of them?

His eyes moved from one tragic face to another. He wanted to give them a giant hug, hold them close and say it would all be okay, but he knew they were scared of all adults. Kilpatrick appeared with a bundle of blankets. They handed them out and helped the children to cover themselves. One of the uniforms came in with drinks and sweets.

Roy pulled out a twenty-pound note and stuffed it in the uniform constable's pocket.

"One of the men wants a lawyer," Kilpatrick said. His face spoke more than his words ever could. He shook his head.

"Does he now? Did he speak in English?"

"Only two words. Want lawyer."

"I'll give him lawyer." Roy rose swiftly and marched out of the room. The last uniform constable was watching over the two handcuffed and ankle tied men in the front living room. Roy heard a volley of curses as he opened the door, aimed at the constable. The men were sat up against the wall, on the bare floorboards.

Roy put both hands on his waist, trying to contain the seething ocean of hatred spilling inside him.

"Who wants a lawyer?" He asked. One of them spoke.

"Me. Want lawyer."

Roy knelt on his right knee, getting closer to the man. His breath was foetid, teeth yellow, and he stank like he hadn't showered in weeks.

"What's your name?" The man snarled. "Where are you taking the children?"

"Want lawyer."

"We tracked you from Calais to Dover. Where are the children from?"

Roy knew the answer. These poor, innocent souls were from some sad, broken, war-ravaged corner of North Africa, the Middle East, or Eastern Europe. But what he wanted to hear it from this horrible excuse of a human being.

"Want. Lawyer." The man raised his voice and spat on the floor.

Roy saw red. It happened so quickly he couldn't stop himself. His right hand shot out and grabbed the man by the collar, then both his hands were on his neck. He shoved the man on the floor, gripping his neck tightly. The man fought.

"Lawyer, eh? Get past me first, you…"

"Guv. Guv!" Darren was in the room, pulling at his shoulder. "Not again, guv," he said in a lower voice, intended for his ears only. "Stop it."

Roy snarled once, then let the man go. He stood, wiping sweat from his brow. Darren stood in front of him, shielding the two men from his view.

"What now, guv?" It was a rhetorical question, aimed at calming things down.

Roy let out a shaky breath. "Child Services here?"

"Just pulled up."

"Good. Let them work first. Put these two in the car and we head back to the nick, after the kids have gone."

CHAPTER 4

"It's still an assault. And he's spoken to his solicitor, who wants to lodge a complaint against you."

Rohan Roy's boss, Detective Chief Superintendent Arla Baker, had a resigned look on her face. Her dark hair was pulled in a tight ponytail. Her lips were pinched and there was a hard look in her glinting eyes. Beneath high cheekbones, her cheeks caved into thin lips and a prominent chin. She was still an attractive woman, but he always got the feeling she made herself look less pretty at work on purpose. Most senior detectives were men, and Arla Baker wanted to be accepted as an equal. He respected that.

But right now, his angry antenna was buzzing like a bee.

Roy couldn't believe his ears. "What for? For refusing to tell me how he destroyed the lives of innocent children. This is the biggest load of bollocks I've ever heard."

Arla Baker had a reputation for being headstrong herself, and Roy had seen her fling herself at a criminal once, with nothing but her bare knuckles. He thought he saw the flicker of a smile in the corner of her lips, then it vanished.

"You should've waited. We need to follow due process, regardless."

"Due process didn't save those kids, did they? We did. My team and I. If we had waited, these men would now be out of London, changed vehicles, and we would lose all trace of them."

Detective Super Baker sighed and folded her hands on her lap. She stared at him without a word. Oh no, he groaned inwardly. He knew that look. Not that folded hands in lap, I will stare you down no matter what, look. The I am majorly pissed off and am about to make your life considerably more difficult, look.

Arla Baker had worked hard, and high kicked many arses, to get where she was today. She didn't tolerate fools, and she never minced her words.

Roy looked to the ceiling, then closed his eyes. "Come on, Ma'am. You would've done the same."

"With the same result, Rohan. That's why I don't pull stupid stunts like that," her voice was like steel. "A disciplinary hearing, a complaint with the IPCC, all for some scumbag who's not worth wasting time on. I had it myself, and I'm trying to protect you from it, but do you listen? Chance would be a fine thing."

He spread his hands. "You want me to apologise? Write a letter? Fine, no problem."

Arla frowned and put her elbows on the desk. That was even worse than her previous look. Roy knew he should shut his big gob, but it was difficult at the best of times.

Besides, Baker was his guvnor, his mentor over the years, and she knew him best.

"You didn't have authority to take a team with you. You didn't ask for clearance. But you know what? I overlooked all of that. I covered for you. Yes, Commander Johnson asked me. I told him I gave the order. So how about you cut the crap, Rohan? Shut your face and sit the fuck down."

Roy rolled his eyes but pulled up a chair. "Thanks, Ma'am." He knew taking an AFO team on a raid was a big deal, but the situation demanded it. He told her, and she glared at him.

"You don't have to tell me that."

Arla shook her head. "The funny thing is you're a lot like me. But I'm getting tired of watching your back, Rohan. You're a brilliant investigator. One of the best I've ever trained. But you really need to stop running around like a loose cannon. You didn't even call me last night to let me know."

That he hadn't. He didn't want her to ask for more intel. He didn't want to let these bastards slip through his fingers. And he didn't want her to know what he was thinking, but he had a feeling she just might.

"And that paedophile whose face you cracked open. He was in hospital for a month, getting his jaw rewired."

Roy grimaced. "He deserved it." As soon as the words left his mouth, he regretted them. Arla Baker leaned back in her chair, and it was her turn to look at the ceiling for divine inspiration, it seemed.

"I know that," she said quietly, "but the defence don't see it that way, and it makes the prosecutions, our job, harder. I don't have to tell you that."

Roy sighed. "Yeah, I know."

"Look, I think things are getting on top of you a bit. Why don't you take a break? Go somewhere and relax for a while."

He narrowed his eyes and looked at her suspiciously. "How? I've got active cases. I can't just up sticks and leave."

"I think you need a break, Rohan. You've been working night and day. These Albanian human traffickers took up a lot of your time. I told you not to do the surveillance yourself, but did you listen? Nope. You carried on with two hours' sleep at night. It's not good. You're burning out."

"I'm fine," he said, hating how defensive he sounded. Baker raised an eyebrow in reply, and he looked away. She knew too much about him, that was the problem.

"I think you should be somewhere relaxing. Not too far, but out of London."

"Ma'am honestly, I'm fine. Let me see this trafficking case through. I deserve to be part of the prosecution. Besides, I have to pay rent. My landlord won't exactly clap me on the back and wave goodbye, is he? I have to break the contract."

"I spoke to Commander Johnson. The Met will cover the rent while you're on secondment."

"Secondment?" He frowned. "Hang on. Has this been planned in advance? What's going on?"

A knot of tension was curling tighter in his guts. Was the London Met trying to get rid of him?

Baker sighed. "I know a Detective Superintendent in Sheffield. One of his DIs is off sick, maybe permanently. He couldn't disclose details. In any case, they have a vacancy. And you need a break. He asked me if I could think of a suitable replacement." She stopped and gazed at him expectantly.

"And you thought of me? Which part of me screams Northern to you, Ma'am? Sheffield is way up there. And it's going to be freezing cold."

Baker rolled her eyes. "Stop being melodramatic. As it happens, Sheffield is a fantastic city. A third of Sheffield is in the Derbyshire Dales mountains. It's the perfect mix of city life and the great outdoors." She smiled, and Roy didn't like it one bit. It was like a shark grinning before it gnawed at a swimmer's leg. "You're going to love it."

"With all due respect, Ma'am, you sound like a travel rep, and I'm going to hate it. I don't need the great outdoors. I've got too much to do here. I still need to follow up the leads on…" He drifted into silence, his eyes flickering down to the floor, a cloud settling on his mind. Detective Super Baker also sensed it.

"It's about that, as well."

Roy's head jerked up straight. His eyes bore into Baker's. "What do you mean?"

CHAPTER 5

Arla Baker's voice was low, her eyes fixed on Roy's.

"A nine-year-old boy's been abducted. Father and son were out walking their dog on the hills near the city. The boy's gone, and the abductor left a ransom note, saying he would be in touch. The ransom note was stuck to a white lily."

Words, sounds, voices scattered and drummed inside Roy's mind like a screaming train inside a tunnel. A kaleidoscope of anguish and regrets. His throat became tight, and his lungs followed, air expelling like he'd been hit in the guts with a jackhammer.

Baker's face swam in his eyes, blurred, as a sudden veil of memories obscured everything. "It's the same MO. Different location, though. Not sure if that makes a difference. Men like him can move around."

Arla Baker's voice seemed to come from a distance, with a strange echo. Roy shook his head, as if that would dispel the barnacles in his brain. And they were barnacles with roots that reached long, dark fingers into the bottom of his soul. They made him what they were. Those rotten fingers squeezed his heart now, and he couldn't bear it. He stood, and paced the room, trying not to gasp, and failing miserably.

Baker gave him some time before speaking. "You okay?"

"I'm fine." He passed a hand over his face, feeling the two-week stubble. He was trying to grow a beard. His hair was receding, so he thought facial hair was a distant alternative. And apparently, some women liked it. Whatever. He needed hair.

With his back to Baker, he put his forehead against the door, gathering his thoughts. He was exhausted from the dawn raid, and the subsequent paperwork. Right now, his mind was flying around like a bunch of birds in a cyclone. He needed to get a grip. His eyes squeezed shut as he tried to force out the pain and misery. Then he turned around.

"Did he leave a name? A number to call? Anything?"

Arla Baker shook her head. "No. Sorry."

"Handwritten or typed note?"

"Handwritten, block caps in black fountain pen ink. He knew the boy's full name. Johnny Reid. The father, Duncan Reid, found the ransom note and the white lily attached to the car's wiper."

"Same MO," Roy whispered. "But why now?"

Twenty-seven years ago, his brother had disappeared. Robin was eight, and Roy was fourteen at the time. The two brothers had gone out playing in the fields, next to a long stretch of woodlands. Robin wanted to play hide and seek. Roy couldn't find him. He searched as long as he could, then went back home in tears. His parent called the police immediately. The next morning, a ransom note, fixed to a white lily with a paper clip, appeared on their doorstep. The ransom note was bogus, and a distraction.

Robin's disappearance sparked a nationwide manhunt. But Robin was never found. Six months later, a boy called Mathew Ripley was taken, in the same manner. He was out dog walking with his mother when he was snatched.

Four months later, another boy called Jack Peters vanished on his way back from school. All three boys were taken within a three-mile radius of where Rohan's family lived.

This time, the police tracked a man who had lured Jack into his white van. They got him on CCTV outside the school. After two weeks, the trail led them to a derelict house in the outskirts of Godalming, in Surrey. Mathew Ripley and Jack Peter's bodies were found in shallow graves in the garden of that house.

But the abductor had vanished. He was never found, and neither was Robin.

England was turned upside down in the subsequent search, hampered by a media frenzy. The press dubbed him the Lily Man.

"I don't know," Baker said quietly. "Twenty-seven years is a long time. Sit down, Rohan." Her voice was gentle now.

He shook his head. He leaned against the door; hands folded behind his back. "The Lily Man. We thought he was dead. But the witnesses said he was young back then, in his mid-twenties. He'll be in his early fifties now. It's possible it's him."

"Unless it's a copycat. The Lily Man had quite a reputation. Some sick bastard might want to emulate him."

Roy sat down. His listless eyes roamed around the room, and finally came to a rest on Baker's face.

He didn't have to say the words. She knew it, and he could see it in her eyes. Robin was dead. His remains were never found, but everyone knew that, after one week of an abduction, the child was likely dead. The Lily Man had killed all the boys he took, and Robin wouldn't be an exception.

But that didn't mean the pain had ever gone away. It never would.

He inclined his head towards Arla Baker. "When can I leave?"

CHAPTER 6

Roy wished he hadn't left so late. It was half past four already. He had barely slept last night, and now he had to look forward to the pleasure of being stuck in never ending traffic for the next four hours.

He went home to his one bed ground floor flat in Balham, got changed and had a quick shower. He chucked his stuff in a duffel bag and got into his car. Then he realised he had forgotten his toiletries, so he went back to get them. His twelve-year-old VW Passat groaned to life, which was a miracle in itself. The car broke down more times than railway workers went on strike these days. He was about to drive out when he thought he might as well pack his running gear. If what Arla Baker had said was true, Sheffield might have some nice running tracks. So, he went back a third time, growling and cursing.

As he walked out the door, his eyes fell on the shelf below the mirror in the hallway. There was a photo of Robin and him, arms around each other. It was taken so long ago he didn't even remember the date. It was on a train, and they were going down to Dorset for the summer holidays. His mother had snapped the photo.

He picked the frame up and swallowed the heavy weight in his throat. Robin had been a sweet little boy. A forgotten sunlight enclosed them both in a halo, and they were smiling, eager for days of laughter and sunshine. A dark cloud covered him suddenly, and the pain surged back, a black wave that lapped around his insides forever. He blinked, then put the photo frame in his jacket pocket.

He looked more knackered than the door he'd kicked down this morning. His light coffee-coloured cheeks caved into a squarish chin. His hair was all over the place, he needed to get it cut. He did a rough comb with his hand, aware what Anna, his teenage daughter, would say if she saw him now.

Let me comb your hair for you. It's easy, you don't have much.

He hadn't seen Anna for more than a week and missed her. As he locked the door, thoughts of Anna made him smile. Fifteen in six months, and already getting close to six feet, and his shoulder height. Very tall girl, but always his little one. He slammed the car door shut, realising he needed to send her a text, or call to let her know he wouldn't be around this week. He did that quickly, as soon as he was behind the steering wheel. Anna lived with her mother, and she stayed with Roy on alternate weekends.

This time, before he started the car, he checked his stuff. It was all there. He'd even taken his passport. Finally, he set off, joining the phalanx of traffic on the South Circular, heading to the M25 motorway. But before he got there, he had to stop off at Chiswick. It was 5 pm already, and he knew the traffic would only get worse. But he had to stop at the Nursing Home in Chiswick, he had no option.

Sunrise Nursing Home occupied a spot on the Thames riverside. All the abandoned warehouses and wharves had been converted into eye-wateringly expensive flats. Looking after the elderly was clearly big business as well, or Sunrise wouldn't exist in such a premium spot. Roy looked after his parents the best he could. They were broken after Robin's disappearance, and they would never heal. The lack of closure was even worse, a living nightmare that tormented every day of their lives. Roy felt the knife twist as he parked, then walked up the drive.

His parents weren't in the lounge, and a carer told him they were in their room. Roy went up to the second floor and knocked on their door. He didn't hear a sound, so he pushed the handle and went in. The suite of two interconnected rooms was big, and overlooked a garden, beyond which the Thames curled around the Chiswick bend.

Rohan's mother, Maya, was asleep on her bed. He went to the other room, and found his father, Neil, awake, sitting out on the armchair in front of the window, staring at the view outside. The sky was still bright. Sailboats of white clouds moved lazily across the deep blue shade. A group of rowers made an arrow of movement on the placid Thame's breast.

Rohan crouched by his father's side and put a hand on his forearm. Neil startled, then recognition flashed in

31

his eyes. Neil's memory had faded, and he had trouble recalling faces. His lips moved, and then he frowned.

"It's me, Dad," Roy said. "How are you?"

"Robin?"

Roy felt a vice-like grip seize his heart and plunge it into a bed of hot coals. He blinked, then rubbed his father's forearm.

"No Dad, it's Rohan."

Neil looked surprised, then he slowly nodded. Saliva drooled from the corner of his mouth, and Roy picked up a tissue and wiped it. Neil took the tissue from Roy's hand. "Thanks. I'm fine, you know. Nice to see you."

"Good." Roy pointed at the bowl of fruit on the portable table in front of the armchair. "Why don't you have some?"

Neil looked at the fruit bowl as if he was seeing it for the first time. "Oh yes. I will. Robin left them earlier today. Did you see him?" He locked eyes with Roy, who couldn't hold his father's gaze.

"Robin wasn't here Dad." His words were hollow, empty, and he wondered why he even bothered saying them.

"He was. He came with the fruit, and also left some flowers. There, look." Neil raised a shaky hand and pointed a gnarled finger at the fresh bouquet of flowers by the bedside.

Roy had sent them. "Glad you like them. Take care, Dad." He kissed his father on the cheek, then got up. He pondered his next words. A force inside him said he needed to say it, but a forlorn sense of futility overrode that feeling. Why was he even here?

"See you later, Dad." He smiled at his old man, who looked up at him.

"Where's Robin?"

"I don't… I'm going to look for him, Dad." His lips trembled, and he shook his head, then turned away. When he looked back, Neil had resumed his glassy-eyed stare out the window.

"Rohan, is that you?" Maya's voice came from the other room. Maya was far more alert than Neil. Roy went over to her bedside. He helped her to sit up, then pulled up a chair. He poured her a glass of water from the bedside table and Maya took a sip.

His eyes fell on the red jewellery box. It was open, and inside the soft white felt interior, lay a replica of the gold chain that Maya had presented to both her sons. Roy still wore his. Robin had one too, and after he disappeared, Maya made a replica that she always kept close to her. She said it meant she could keep an eye on Robin, wherever he was.

Roy's heart ached as he watched the gold chain. He wanted to close the box, put a lid on the cauldron of hurt and pain that shrouded their lives. But he knew Maya didn't want that. That chain reminded her of Robin, and this was her morning ritual. She woke up, opened that box, then muttered a prayer. She kept it open all day long and put it under her pillow when she slept at night.

"I can feel him," she told Robin once. "He's in the bed, next to me. My son's here."

Roy's lips trembled, and he turned away, then passed a hand over his face. He needed to get a grip.

"What's the matter?" Maya asked. "Why did you turn your back?"

Roy swivelled round quickly, and smiled, then sat down. "Nothing. Just working on a big case, and something came to mind. How are you?"

They talked for a while. Maya had retained her memory, and could also move around more, with walking sticks. Roy mulled it over for the hundredth time. Should he tell her? What good would it do? Both his parents were on antidepressants for life.

Would raking up the past do any good?

In the end, he decided against it. If he caught the Lily Man, and finally discovered Robin's remains, then he would tell her. He carried Robin's dental records and preserved DNA sample with him. That was one thing he would always be grateful to the London Met for. They let him keep his brother's forensic identity.

"I'm going to Sheffield for a few weeks, Ma. I'll call, and we can do Facetime."

"Have you found someone there? Who is she?" Maya squinted at him. She had all her marbles intact. He hated not telling her the real reason.

"No, not yet. I'm going to work there."

"Oh." The lines of disappointment on Maya's face grew deeper. "You need to find a good woman. Settle down."

Amen to that, Roy thought to himself in silence. "Maybe one day, Ma. It will happen." He smiled, but Maya was clearly not reassured. She looked out the window.

"How's Anna?"

"Good," Roy smiled. He showed his mother a picture of Anna, posing with her hockey team after they won a match. "Getting to my shoulder height now."

"Yes," Maya smiled with delight. "I haven't seen her for so long. Please bring her."

"I will. Sorry, you know it's not easy, and I've been so busy."

"You need to look after yourself better."

"I am. I promise. It's all going to be ok. Anyway, I'm looking forward to going up North, after a long time."

"Oh good. Nice to have a change, isn't it?"

"I guess it is."

CHAPTER 7

If this was a change, Roy thought, then he was better off not having one. He was resigned to the M25 being a slow caterpillar of traffic. But even on the M1 North, one of the main arteries that connected London to the far north, the long line of red lights and exhaust fumes stretched as far as eyes could see.

Roy hated London's traffic, and now it seemed he had taken it with him when he left. He wound the window down, and the air stank of exhaust fumes. He was stuck behind a lorry as well, which belched out acrid black smoke every time it lurched forward. All four lanes were packed. But at least, it was moving. Roy massaged his forehead, the ache behind his eyes growing, spreading deeper into his skull.

He popped open a Pro Plus packet, the caffeine fix he carried around with him, and downed it with his third coffee of the day. He wasn't a big coffee drinker, but he needed it today. That double caffein boost was working, the only problem was his bladder was also getting fuller by the second. And it didn't seem like he could stop for a break anytime soon.

Two and a half hours after he left southwest London, the tangle finally eased up. He sped past Luton and Dunstable, on a home run towards Leicestershire and the Midlands. He wasn't a stranger to this route. When he was young, his parents had settled in a depressing industrial dog shit town called Scunthorpe. Sunny Scunny, they called it. They didn't stay there for long, and his parents had relatives in southwest London. Roy remembered the travels up and down the M1, a black asphalt river of light at night, and how the big fat yellow summer moon bounced along the hills as they drove, keeping him company.

There was no moon now, and the hint of cold in London slowly got more frigid the farther he rolled up the M1. Soon, the lights of Leicester and Nottingham had flashed by, and the road started to undulate, rising high above ground.

It was from this vantage point that he saw the giant cluster of lights that was Sheffield. It was how he recalled seeing the city when his father drove down the same road, many years ago. Another memory stabbed his heart. Robin used to fall asleep on these journeys, leaning against him, then eventually falling on to his lap.

Roy tightened his grip on the wheel and gritted his teeth together. That void opened up again, a never-ending chasm. It came and went in a flash, reminding him of its presence. He focused on the road and dared to look to the right for as long as he could. Sheffield was far below, spread out in a glittering carpet of yellow, orange and red. The lights sneaked in between the foothills of the Peak District mountain range that lay to the city's left. He indicated, then took the exit that would take him down to the panoply of lights.

It was almost 9 pm and traffic was light in the city. Roy had stopped earlier and relieved his bladder. He had also stocked up on more coffee and biscuits, and the resulting palpitations were making him sweat and breathe like he'd just run a mile.

He wound the window down, expecting the greasy, diesel laden fumes of the city, and was pleasantly surprised to find them absent. There was a freshness in the air, and he wondered if it was the breeze that filtered down from the hills, refreshing the city's streets. He could smell exhaust, but it wasn't the caged in, suffocating stench of motors that clogged roads, and nostrils, in London. It was the absence of wheezing, gridlocked vehicles that pleased him the most. He zoomed down to the Southeast Sheffield station of South Yorkshire Police. The car park was barricaded, and he had to lean out the window, and press the buzzer. He announced his name and rank, and the barricade lifted. White vans with the logo and badge of South Yorkshire Police were parked everywhere. Roy spotted a number of cars that looked similar to the unmarked CID vehicles that he was used to and parked his decrepit rust bucket next to them.

The station was a modern building, low metallic roof that sloped down like a hillside, and cream coloured stone blocks for its walls. It was four stories high, and, with the outbuildings, took up a block of the southeast city centre. The reception area had green plastic seats in rows, with a few people sitting on them. One man was lying on the floor, obviously drunk, and oblivious to the world. He had handcuffs on and was clearly waiting to spend a night in custody. It wasn't crowded, but neither was it empty. Two uniformed PCs stood at either end of the seats, keeping an eye on the punters. They glanced at Roy as he walked in, and their gazes followed him as he walked up to the main counter desk

The uniformed duty sergeant at the desk looked sleep deprived. He was a few stones past being fit, and a wobble of fat descended from his chin to the collar of his uniform. His eyes were red-rimmed, and he yawned.

That makes two of us, Roy thought. Without a word, he placed his warrant card on the desk, and the sergeant lowered his head, frowning like he was inspecting a new form of life. Then his spine straightened, and the boredom vanished from his face. "You alright, guv. This way, please."

He pressed a buzzer underneath the counter, and the glass panelled steel doors at the far end of the room, behind the row of green seats, slid to one side. One of the PCs went and stood next to it. Roy nodded and walked down to it. When he stepped inside, the PC pressed a red button on the wall, and the doors slid back. He was in a corridor with grey lino on the floor, grey painted walls, and panelled cardboard covered ceilings. Posters of crime statistics and wanted individuals were stuck on notice boards clipped to the wall. There was a slightly musty smell of an area that wasn't ventilated well, mingled with the odour of old files, books and that office smell that seemed the same in every police station.

He walked into the open plan detective's office. A plastic see-through wall separated the desks from the walkway that circled around the large office. In the bullpen, most of the desks were empty, which was not surprising, given the hour. He walked up to a group of three detectives. One of them, a blonde-haired woman, had her back to him. The two men looked up. All three wore the plain suits of detectives.

Roy showed his warrant card. "I'm DI Roy. Is D Super Nugent here?"

The three of them looked at each other. Then the woman got to her feet. "DS Sarah Botham," she extended a hand, and Roy shook it. "The Super told us you were coming so we stayed behind."

Sarah was five-five to five-seven, petite, and she had a mass of skin-coloured freckles on her nose and upper cheeks. Her large, sea green eyes dominated her face. There was a firm set to her lips, and her jaws ground together as she met Roy's eyes.

"This is PC Rizwan Ahmed," Sarah introduced the young Asian man with a light goatee beard, who looked nervous. There was also mild fascination in his eyes as he pumped Roy's hand. His hand was slim and cold, and they disappeared in Roy's bear grasp.

"Nice to meet you, guv. Heard a lot about you."

Roy raised an eyebrow. "Not as much as I've heard about you."

Rizwan's smile faltered, and his Adam's apple bobbed up and down. His looked at Sarah askance before speaking. "Sorry? You heard; you mean…" He tried to stutter a reply and Roy put him out of his misery.

"Only messing, son." He stuck his hands in his suit pocket and shrugged. "I know we're all knackered so trying to keep this interesting. Nice to meet you as well."

Rizwan grinned, then tugged at his collar. Sarah looked even more unimpressed, Roy noted. In fact, rather a stormy cloud had descended upon her attractive features.

"And this is DC Oliver Walmsley," she said, staring straight at the brown-haired man, who was in his late twenties, about the same age as Rizwan.

They shook hands. Oliver's hair was gelled back, and he wore a nice suit, and shiny shoes. He looked more like an estate agent than detective constable. His brown eyes matched his hair, and he smiled at Roy.

"Long drive?" Oliver asked. "You must've left London at peak time."

He spoke with a Yorkshire accent. Roy hadn't heard it in years, and it harkened back to his distant childhood. A strangely comforting sound.

"That I did. No time to waste in this case."

"You got those girls back two years ago. The Mason case, down south. Did well there."

Roy and his team managed to find two abducted girls, and the man who took them. The case received the usual media storm and had thousands of civilian volunteers who offered their help. The girls had been abused, but Roy found them alive in a garage in East London. Their kidnapper, Jim Mason, was caught in a high-speed car chase. Roy's name appeared in the papers. "Flattery won't get you anywhere," Roy said. "But thanks anyway."

Oliver cleared his throat, his confidence a little dented. "You're welcome. Looking forward to working with you."

He was a good kid, Roy thought. A bit of pride over appearance never harmed a detective, but Oliver overdid it. His heart was in the right place. Roy had a sixth sense about his juniors, and these two seemed alright. He couldn't quite put a finger on Sarah as yet.

"In the Mason case, everyone chipped in. It was teamwork. Glad it worked out in the end. Can't give up hope, you see."

He glanced at Sarah, who remained stone faced. Roy wondered if it was something he said.

"Johnny Reid was abducted yesterday, right?"

She glanced at him, her eyes cold and hard. "Yes. It was reported at 3.45 pm. Crime scene was established by 4.30 pm. Scene of crime was up there by 5 pm, but light hampered their work. They resumed work today. Nothing to report as of yet."

Roy shook his head. "That's one day lost. We need to get a move on. Who's in charge of your team, by the way? I mean, who's the DI?"

All three of them stared at him, and it twigged. That would be me.

"Right then." The bright lights were hurting his eyes, and the headache was worse now that the caffeine buzz had regressed. "Nice to meet all of you. Is the Super here?"

Sarah walked off and called behind her back. "This way."

"She always this friendly?" Roy muttered under his breath, and Oliver caught it.

"She's alright. She was good mates with the previous DI," Oliver whispered.

"He's on indefinite leave, I heard."

Oliver nodded, and didn't elaborate further, as Roy had expected. Arla Baker had filled him in, anyway. Donald Wiggins had a serious case of PTSD. Roy had some experience of that particular dark hole, and it wasn't nice, to say the least. He wished DI Wiggins all the best.

Sarah rapped on the door, and a muffled voice asked them to enter. Roy was amazed the Detective Superintendent was still here at 9.30 pm, but he understood the case demanded overtime from everyone. They crowded into Superintendent Michael Nugent's office. Rizwan shut the door.

Nugent was a short, stodgy man with a barrel chest that strained the buttons of his shirt. His cheeks were reddish from meat and booze, and his dark eyes glinted. He was on the wrong side of sixty. His black, bushy eyebrows lowered, then straightened as he gazed at Roy, ignoring the others.

"Rohan Roy?" His voice was raspy and gruff, and Roy now knew what the suffocating, cloying sweet smell in the room was – air freshener meant to disguise cigarette smoke. Nugent must smoke out the window, which was now shut. The Super's yellow stained nails and dark lips corroborated that guess.

"Yes sir."

"Let's get one thing clear. I don't need any fancy southern detective telling me what to do on my patch. Your job is to find that missing boy, and then get back where you came from. Got it?"

"Crystal, sir. To be honest, I'm sure you've got a good team here, and I don't want to get in the way." He met Nugent's eyes. "I'll find somewhere to sleep tonight, then be on my way in the morning. Wish you all the best." He smiled widely, then turned to leave. He stopped at the door and turned.

"Oh, and I'm not some fancy southerner. Not sure what that means, anyway. I grew up in Doncaster, as it happens. Not that it matters, but just so you know. Sir."

He opened the door and walked out.

CHAPTER 8

Roy gnashed his teeth together as he stalked down the corridor. A voice called his name, but he ignored it. Someone ran past him. It was Sarah Botham. Her sprightly figure was rigid, and her eyes bright. She spread her arms out, stopping just short of his chest. He towered above her.

There was an urgent tone in her voice. "Please stop. The Super wants to see you."

"I can't do my job with limitations. He's put me on watch already. This isn't going to work."

He went to move past her, but Sarah stood in his way. "Please, sir. A little boy's life is on the line, and so are our jobs. We need your help." She dropped her voice to a whisper.

Roy frowned. "What's happening with your jobs?"

Sarah weighed things over in her mind. "Cost cutting," she said finally. "A third of our jobs are going. And we don't have a DI in our team now. If we don't get this boy back, we might well get shunted into other departments."

Roy knew how this went. These detectives had worked hard to pass exams and gain experience and now they'd become glorified secretaries at some bigwig's office in the Constabulary. Some gormless management consultant would call it restructuring the force. Every time he heard that R word, he wanted to restructure their faces with his fist. He had lost count of colleagues who were "retired" from front line police work, the job they loved.

He mulled it over, then shook his head. "I'm sorry." He hooked a thumb behind his back. "He's got it in for me already. One slip up and he's going to bury me. I can see it happening."

"DCI Roy," Nugent's deep voice rumbled down the corridor. Sarah looked past him, and Roy went still. His fists clenched in his pockets. Then he turned.

"Sorry we got off on the wrong foot. Come in and I'll explain." Nugent stood by the door of his office. He indicated with his head, then waited.

Roy blew out his cheeks, trying to make his mind up. He felt sorry for Sarah and the others. He also desperately wanted to find the boy. But he didn't need attitude, and he sure as hell wasn't going to be the SIO in name only, and a puppet in the Super's hands. Well, he might as well see what Nugent had to say. He walked back to the office, Sarah hurrying behind him.

Rizwan and Oliver stood in one corner, both looking nervous. Sarah shut the door behind them. Roy stood in the middle of the room; feet spread.

"Sit down," Nugent growled.

"I'll stand if that's OK with you. Sir."

Nugent grimaced, opened a drawer, then slammed it shut. If Roy had to guess, his money would be on Nugent looking for a packet of fags, then deciding against it. He sat back in his chair and glared at Roy.

"Not sure if the others told you, but our budgets are under pressure from the top brass. Wiggins was a good man, and his loss has deprived us of a DI. He's gone off on full salary sick leave, and now we have to pay for you as well." Roy said nothing. Nugent continued. "I didn't want Wiggins to go. I also have a replacement, but it turns out the Chief Constable is pals with your boss in Clapham. Detective Superintendent Baker, is that right?"

Roy nodded in silence. Nugent's upper lip curled up in a snarl. "So, the Chief Constable has a word with your boss, and you turn up. I know you done well getting those girls back." His voice softened a touch. "But Wiggins, my man, was also good."

"I don't want to step on any toes," Roy said plainly. "And obviously, I didn't know about any of this."

Nugent grunted. "I have to follow orders." He looked at Roy. "I don't have anything personal against you."

Roy held his eyes. "Noted, sir. I don't have anything against you either. But I won't be told what to do. I need to run this investigation in the way that I see fit. I need to have authority to pull in members of the uniform team, forensics, cybercrime, financial crime, gait analysis, the whole lot. And I don't want to have to ask you at every step. Wastes your time, and mine."

"Got it." Nugent said. Something in his attitude told Roy he still wasn't happy about the situation. "Right. Let's get started." He looked at Sarah, who opened her mouth to speak. Roy raised a hand and she stopped.

"Just so we're clear, sir. I need to treat the department like my gaff, as they used to say in Doncaster. Is that alright?" A smile hovered on his lips at the decades-old memory. Maybe no one said that anymore. He was hoping the point would get through to Nugent, and it seemed to.

Nugent's caterpillar eyebrows did a wiggly dance, then descended over his eyes. "You'll have control over your investigation, Roy, like you asked for. Not sure what you mean by treating it like your gaff."

"As in, people here know that I'm in charge. They ask me for anything to do with the case."

Nugent opened the drawer again, and this time, pulled out a packet of Marlboro Reds, took one out and tapped it on the desk. "I cleared that already, didn't I?" he drawled slowly.

"Just making sure we're on the same page, sir." Roy turned to Sarah. "Go on then," he smiled. "What have you got so far?"

"I'm popping out," Nugent raised his cigarette to indicate he needed a smoke. "Let me know if anything happens."

They filed out of Nugent's office with him. "Where's the incident room?" Roy asked.

"This way," Sarah walked down the corridor, past the bullpen, and turned right. She pointed to a closed office door. "This will be your office, I think. But I need to ask the Super first."

"Was your previous DI in there?"

Roy saw a strange light flash in Sarah's eyes, then flicker all over her face. She went stone faced again, with a grim line in her jaws.

"No," she said shortly. She wouldn't look Roy in the eye, but her manner was easier than before. "This way, guv."

The corridor got wider, and there was a large, thick door that bore the logo of Incident Room 1. Inside, there was a long central table that seated about twenty. A big screen was attached to the far wall, and two projectors hung from the ceiling. There was a desk near the screen with a laptop, printer, and fax machines. The wall opposite was divided into windows that now had blinds drawn.

"Is this where the multi team meetings are held?" Roy asked. All three heads nodded.

"Guess I'll do the same then, first thing tomorrow. Now, tell me what you got from the uniforms and forensics." He pulled up a chair and sat down. Oliver perched against a sideboard, Sarah and Rizwan pulled up chairs to face him.

Sarah said, "Four uniform teams scoured the area today. They found nothing. The boy ran away from his father, and just vanished. Duncan Reid, the dad, thinks he went into the woods, and someone grabbed him there."

"Show me a map."

Oliver did the honours. On his phone, he zoomed into southwest Sheffield and Hunter's Bar, then handed Roy the phone.

"That's where the family live, near Endcliffe Park. Mr Reid took the A57 down to Wyming Brook Nature Reserve, about half an hour drive. He's been there before to walk the dog."

Oliver guided Roy on the map to the Nature Reserve. It was remote, and right on the border where Sheffield's eastern margin merged with the Derbyshire Dales. Roy had never been but heard about it. The Dales were South Yorkshire's main tourist attraction.

"Forensics? They didn't find anything in the whole day they spent there?"

"They took samples from where the boy had been. The ground where he stood. He left some tracks on the dirt. But it's not much to go on. No blood splatter, no torn clothes, no signs of a physical struggle anywhere."

"And Mr Reid is clean? No PCN's, not on the CSODS?" That stood for the Child Sex Offence Disclosure Scheme, UK's child sex offender's register.

"Nope," Sarah said. "Neither are the immediate family members like his brother, and Mrs Reid's brother and sister."

50

"Grandparents?"

"Mr Reid's father is dead, but his mother had regular contact with Johnny and his sister, Amanda. Mrs Reid's parents both alive. They visited two weeks ago. None of them are on the CSODS, nor do they have a police record."

Roy took out his black leather notebook and scribbled. Duncan Reid had a brother, and his wife had a brother and sister. He put question marks next to the words. Then he put the notebook back in the inner jacket pocket. "What about the media?"

Oliver fielded the question. "The Super will hold a conference tomorrow afternoon. Well, that's what he said anyway. It depends on any new evidence in the morning."

Roy nodded. "In some cases, the children return. They're abused, then either sent home, or dropped off nearby. With any luck, we have that scenario, and then we can go after him with a description from the child."

He glanced at all three members of his new team. "Any member of the press approached you? Offer you money for a story?"

Sarah replied. "Not as yet, guv. But we know the family have spoken to parents at the school. Word has spread. People arrived at the Wyming Brook Nature Reserved this afternoon, offering help. We had to hold them back to protect the crime scene."

"It's only a matter of time. There's going to be a massive media scrum. I suspect by first light tomorrow there will be reporters camped outside. If past experience is anything to go by, either the family, or friends, have already started a social media campaign with Johnny's photo."

Rizwan said, "That's what the FLO said, guv. I haven't seen it myself as yet. Apparently, Mrs Reid's sister has done a post and sent it to the school parent WhatsApp group."

"There you go. I promise you by tomorrow the media vultures will be there." Roy sighed. "I want to go and see the family."

Three blank faces looked back at him. Sarah was the first to answer.

"Now, guv? Kind of late, isn't it."

"Trust me, Sarah, when your child goes missing you don't care what time of day or night it is. It's a non-stop horror show, and it's on repeat every second of your life. Please make the call." He looked at the two men. "One of you must have their number."

Rizwan got his phone out and scrolled through. "I've got it." He called them and got through immediately.

"No… nothing new has come to light. But Detective Inspector Roy would like to see you. No, you haven't met him as yet." Rizwan spoke for a bit longer, then hung up.

"They'll see us, now."

"I thought they would," Roy said, rising.

CHAPTER 9

Sarah drove in one of the unmarked CID cars that were parked next to Roy's beaten-up rust bucket. Roy sat in the front. As Sarah accelerated down the road, he realised how nice it was to be in a car that didn't shudder, creak, and belch out smoke like a dragon farting. He needed to get a new car, like he needed to change a few other things in his life.

He took out his phone and checked the page that he maintained. It was a homepage for Robin, with some photos of him as a child, and also age progression photos that police artists had done for him. Robin's case remained lodged with the police, but, like many other missing people, it had gone cold. Roy checked to make sure there were no new comments, or visitors, then he shut the phone.

The residential streets followed from the lights of the city centre. The yellow-orange glow of the streetlamps hurt Roy's eyes and made his headache worse. He closed his eyes and woke up when the car came to a halt. Sarah was looking at him funny, and he rubbed his face.

"Sorry, did I pass out?"

"Just for a few ticks, like," Sarah smiled for the first time. "Won't hold it against you."

"Note to myself," Roy grumbled as he got out of the car. "An overdose of coffee and Pro Plus doesn't last long." He yawned and stretched his long, six foot three frame. He also realised he was famished, but that could wait. Everything could wait till he had seen the Reids.

He was pleased to see the lack of reporters. It was one of the reasons he wanted to speak to the parents tonight. Get their measure before the chaos started tomorrow.

He tried to calm the marching drumbeat of his heart and failed. Endless memories assailed his mind, like shrapnel from an explosion. He remembered the police detective who came to question him, and his parents. So long ago, but each second, each word, was engraved on his soul like bullets finding their mark on a bullseye.

"Guv?" Sarah was standing in front of him again. Roy smoothed down his hair and nodded curtly.

"The FLO's gone home I assume?" Roy meant the words as a deflection, because Sarah had that quizzical, searching look in her eyes.

"Yes. She had the option of staying the night, but Amanda Reid's sister's staying over."

Rizwan knocked on the door. The front room light was on. The front garden was small, a square patch of grass with a waist high tree in the middle. The grass was overgrown. There was a shed, which had a padlock on it. It looked large enough to contain a bike.

The outside light came on, and then the door opened. A man stood there, blinking at them. Then he stood to one side. He appeared to know Rizwan and the others. Roy hung at the back, aware familiarity with the police mattered in these situations.

The house was simple, but smart, a large four bed, bay fronted family home. They followed the man into the first room, which was a living room with three sofa sets, and a TV in the corner. Shelves on the wall on either side of the TV held books and framed family photos.

A woman was sat on the edge of a sofa. Her spine was ramrod straight, a stricken look on her face. Her eyes were red rimmed, and her hands twisted on her lap. She locked eyes with Roy, and he felt the burn of her panic hit gaze. She was the boy's mother; he didn't need to be told. He had seen that look before. He leaned forward and shook her hand.

"DI Rohan Roy. I'm in charge of finding Johnny. We won't leave any stone unturned; I can promise that much."

He knew his words sounded hollow, but he meant every syllable. He held her gaze for a fraction longer than necessary, and a light flickered in her eyes as the tip of her nose turned red. She struggled to contain her emotions, and her head lowered. She reached in the pocket of her jeans and pulled out a tissue to dab at her face.

Duncan Reid sat down on the sofa next to his wife. Roy shook hands with him as well. The grip was limp and lifeless, and he barely looked Roy in the eyes. He stared at the carpet, a hunted expression in his eyes.

"It wasn't your fault," Roy said. "You did everything you could."

Duncan raised his eyes slowly and looked at Roy like he was seeing him for the first time. Roy knew how he felt. How the first hours and days were like. Numb, comatose, buried under an avalanche of guilt and regret.

I know how you feel.

He could never say the words. But there was a desperate need in his heart, the feeling crawling out and settling on his skin like acid, burning into the bones.

Duncan's eyes were crimson hued, like his wife's. They met Roy's briefly before they flickered back to the ground. His cheeks were sunken with a few days' worth of stubble. There was also a smell emanating from him, like he had hadn't washed, or changed his clothes since the incident.

"I know you've been through this already. And I'm sorry for coming this late. But tell me, in your own words, what happened yesterday."

Duncan took his time. Roy noted the lack of touch, or proximity, between husband and wife. Duncan sat next to Amanda, but not close. Amanda also avoided looking at Duncan.

Roy didn't want to read too much into it. It was perfectly normal for parents to act weird at this time.

"It's half term, so Johnny and I decided to go a bit further out to take Dolly for a walk. We've been to Wyming Brook before, he likes the place."

"What time did you leave the house?"

"Around 1 pm. The plan was to be back by 5 pm, in time for dinner." Duncan's Adam apple bobbed up and down, and he wrung his hands together. "But the dog got lost. We went looking for it, and Johnny ran ahead. I lost him for a while, but then found him in the trees. It's quite wooded up there, but there's also rocks, and a big reservoir."

He paused to gather his thoughts, it seemed. He still wouldn't look at anyone in the room. "We came back out on one of the main paths. I had parked my car there as well. It wasn't the usual car park, mind. But you're allowed to park there. I wanted to be a bit further from the other dog walkers and tourists, it's just a bit nicer."

"So, you didn't see that many people?" Roy asked. Duncan met his eyes, then shook his head.

"Wyming Brook can get crowded sometimes, although it wasn't that bad yesterday. But it was quiet where we parked." He closed his eyes, and a tormented sigh shook through his body. "That was a mistake. Even going there was a bloody mistake." He clenched his jaws, then slammed a fist on his knee. "Damn it."

"You did what thousands, maybe millions of fathers did yesterday with their children. Don't beat yourself up. Carry on," Roy's voice was gentle. "You came out on the path, then what happened?"

"Johnny ran forward. The path curves around, leading to the rocks. I wanted to stop him, but he's quick. He went around the bend and then…. I searched everywhere. I even went to the rocks, but they're too steep to climb. I looked in the woods, but…" his words faded, and he looked at the floor.

"On your way there, did any car follow you? Anything that you noticed on the roads?"

"No."

"Over the last few days or weeks, have you seen anyone outside your house? Any new neighbours?"

Duncan looked at his wife, who shook her head.

"What about outside the school? When you pick Johnny up, have you noticed anyone hanging around?"

Again, husband and wife stared at each other, then both shrugged. "Nothing out of the usual, no. Not seen any bloke hanging outside school."

"Has Johnny been in touch with anyone else apart from his school crowd, and you?" Roy clarified. "By that I mean any other family members as well?"

Duncan frowned, and Amanda cleared her throat. "Yes. My sister's boyfriend, Keith Burgess." She glanced at Duncan, who nodded.

"Yes, Keith's been helping me with some housework. We're redecorating the bedrooms upstairs. New paint and the like. He was here over the last couple of days.

He's good with Johnny, we played football in the garden."

"We will need his contact details." Roy glanced at Sarah, and he could tell from her face she didn't know about Keith.

"Anyone else been in touch with Johnny?"

"My parents," Amanda said. "That was almost a fortnight ago. They're mostly housebound now, so I take Johnny over when I get a chance. It's weekly actually, but the last two weeks were busy with school breaking up. They wanted to see him this week." A sob caught on her throat, and she covered her mouth with a hand.

Duncan sat like a statue, not making a move to comfort his wife. "Johnny's not seen my father recently. He lives farther out, in Skegness. I did plan to take him there for the half term."

"How was Johnny doing at school?" Roy asked. "Both academically, and with friends."

"Alright, as far as we know. The teachers never said anything. And he wasn't bullied or anything, if that's what you mean. He was happy."

Roy detected a defensive note creep into Duncan's voice. He turned to Sarah. "Have scene of crime been to Johnny's room?"

Sarah nodded. She flicked her eyes to the door, and Roy followed her gaze. A woman was standing there. She wore tracksuit jogging bottoms, and a loose vest. Her shoulder length brown hair was wet and combed. She crossed arms across her chest and looked at them inquisitively.

Amanda said, "That's my sister, Fiona. She's staying with us for a couple of days."

Fiona was in her mid-thirties, Roy guessed. She didn't wear any make up, and clearly wasn't expecting visitors.

Roy asked, "Good evening. My name is DCI Rohan Roy. Is Keith Burgess your partner?"

Fiona frowned. "Yes. Why do you ask?"

"No reason at all," Roy said in his most soothing voice. "We just want to speak to anyone who had contact with Johnny in the last few days, which includes all his family members. Often, a child will say something that sticks in the mind or prove valuable in hindsight."

"Keith isn't here," Fiona said brusquely. "I came to stay from today. I think Keith was here yesterday?" She looked at her brother-in-law, who nodded.

Duncan said, "Keith helped to strip the wallpaper in the main bedroom. Then he left, and I went out with Johnny and the dog."

"Did he know where you were going?"

Duncan gave Roy a funny look. "Yes, as did Amanda. Keith's family. He's not married to Fiona, not yet anyway," he looked at Fiona, who was following the conversation. Roy sensed a tension here, and he let it go, for now. "Instead of asking all these questions, shouldn't you be out there, searching for the bastard who took my son?" Duncan said, his voice rising. "He's even asked for a ransom!" Duncan stood suddenly, his hands becoming fists, his jaws grinding together. "We haven't done anything wrong," he shouted. "But here you are, asking twenty questions, making us feel like we did something wrong." His fingers clenched and unclenched. "Get me my son back," he shouted. "Just do something."

Oliver and Sarah got to their feet, but Roy raised a hand, stopping them. He remained seated. He knew Duncan would be upset; it wasn't surprising. "We'll do everything we can. But we need your help. You knew Johnny the best," he glanced at Amanda, whose mouth was open, and breathing heavily.

"Anything you tell us, even the tiniest, most insignificant detail, can be incredibly useful. Please bear with us."

Duncan stood there, shaking with an impotent rage, then suddenly he folded like a burst balloon. He slumped back on the sofa.

"When you couldn't find Johnny and you got back to the car, where did you find the note?"

"In an envelope. A white lily was stuck to the envelope with a pin, and the note was inside. It said – Don't look for Johnny because you won't find him. He would contact us for the ransom when the time was right. We couldn't call the police, or Johnny would suffer."

"The letter said suffer?" Roy asked, his breath catching.

"Yes."

"No prints on the envelope. Nothing on the flower, or the windscreen wiper." Oliver added.

Roy's mind was swimming as he recalled the Lily Man's words. His father had the envelope in hand, and later, Roy saw it. The words were the same as in Duncan's note.

He nodded. "We'll be in touch. Sorry for bothering you so late." He looked at Amanda and inclined his head. "Thank you."

She sniffed and dabbed her nose again. The three of them rose. Roy caught Fiona's eyes again. She had a hard glint in them, and the thrust in the angle of her jaw wasn't exactly friendly. She turned away and he heard her stomping up the stairs.

Roy walked out first, and the others followed. He yawned, covering his mouth. It was getting past 11 pm. They stopped outside the car.

"Right. See you at the nick at 6 am sharp. Early, I know, but we don't have much time. Now, does anyone know where I'm staying tonight?"

CHAPTER 10

South Yorkshire Police were being generous. Instead of the staff quarters, Roy had a room at the Premier Inn. Sarah and the others dropped him off at the car park, and he drove himself to the hotel at the city centre.

His room was clean, the bed comfortable, and there was a mini bar. He showered, then went downstairs to the restaurant to have dinner. The bar at the restaurant was open, but the kitchen was shut. The barman directed him to a fish and chip shop, and he trudged there. He ate there too, and, by the time he got back to the room, it was getting close to one in the morning.

He took his jacket off and felt the photo in his inside pocket. He put it on the nice, shiny table. Robin's eyes looked at the camera, out of the frame, and into his mind. Roy turned away and got ready for bed. He closed his eyes, he was exhausted. But sleep didn't come easy. Neither did peace, or any sense of rest.

The voices, images, cries jumped around in his restive mind like flashes of lightning. Memories he kept buried so deep down they had become a part of him, a part that he hid form everyone, even himself. But when he was alone, there was nowhere to hide.

It was twenty-seven years ago, but that day was still burned into his memory. It was the summer holidays, and Robin and him were out playing in the fields. Roy was fourteen and the older brother, so his parents let him take Robin out, but Roy still had to ask permission. It was fun playing with Robin. That day, he wanted to play hide and seek in the woods.

"Don't go too far," Roy had said, trying to be serious. He remembered the playful, alive look on Robin's face, and suddenly it was like a knife plunged into his guts, and he croaked in pain, then curled up his knees. Robin's laugh came next, beautiful, innocent, like the rays of sunshine cascading over the trees that day. Roy saw his brother one last time before he turned, and that image too, played on his mind like a never-ending cinema, Robin running away, sunlight on his back, his black hair flopping as he ran. His gold chain, winking in the sun.

The knife plunged deeper, and the pain came, that eviscerating, harsh stab that almost separated his heart from his chest. He buried his head in the pillow and roared, then slammed a fist into the bed again and again, till he rose up and started punching the headboard, then the wall, then the bedside table, then the wall again, till he was hitting himself, fists punching his own face, chest, belly… and then he was on a heap in the floor, useless tears corroding his cheeks.

He got up, chest heaving, a tremor in his spine that didn't bode well. He was coming loose, the rusty screws that held his poisonous soul together had gone flying into the night. He knew this mood only too well. He wanted to hit out or hurt himself. His fists clenched. He avoided looking at himself in the mirror. He couldn't stay in the room; he'd end up breaking something.

He got dressed quickly. He flung open the mini bar fridge and polished off the two small bottles of whisky. The whisky burnt as it went down, making him grimace. In the past, on nights like these, he had drunk a hell of a lot more, till he passed out. The alcohol numbed his mind, and it became a dangerous habit. He had kicked the habit, and he knew the danger signs.

He hated himself. The guilt was like a coat of sharp nettles, itching his skin, infecting his blood. He shrugged into his coat and stalked out of the room. Outside, the fresh night air was cool on his face. He opened his mouth, dragging in lungfuls. Then he walked, unaware of where he was going, only needing space and distance.

Even the main roads were now devoid of traffic, which helped. There was a canal, with stairs leading down to a towpath. A couple of canal boats were moored. He went down the steps and walked down the path. His boots echoed as he went under a bridge. His pace was rapid, as if he was a thief, running away from a scene of crime. He shook his head, trying to dispel the visions. His parents' lives also fell apart. His father took to the bottle, and his mother sunk into a profound depression. Somehow, they kept it together. Roy was glad they were still alive. He wanted to bring them news of Robin one day. Some news, any news. Anything was better than this not knowing, this aching, gaping hole of non-closure.

After all, that's why he became a policeman.

His mind came back to the current case. Had Johnny Reid been taken by the Lily Man, or was it a copycat? After the bodies of the two boys – Mathew Ripley and Jack Peters, were discovered, it was expected that the killer would be caught. But the Lily Man had been painstaking in getting rid of evidence. Not a single strand of DNA was discovered on the boys. The derelict farmhouse was searched and excavated till there was nothing left to use. A bunch of white lily flowers were discovered, dry and wilting.

At that time, the police thought he had left the area. His white van never showed up on CCTV, and chances were he repainted it, then changed the number plates. Maybe even burnt it after he escaped. Escaped with Robin – or did he bury Robin somewhere else? The ground around the farmhouse was searched, to no avail. Digging everywhere was not feasible. In the 2000s when ultrasound technology became available, the sensors were used in the farmhouse, to search for buried skeletons. Nothing was found, which laid credence to the view Lily Man had taken Robin with him when he escaped.

The Lily Man's e-fit, and police artist images were plastered all over the media, and posters were put at every major transport hub up and down the country. Even Interpol was alerted, and the cross European missing person's team hunted him. As no one reported a sighting in UK, it was possible he had escaped to the continent, but that would be difficult with an eight-year-old. If the Lily Man had left the country, it was likely Robin was dead.

All possibilities were open, until yesterday. Until Johnny vanished, and the ransom note appeared.

When the Lily Man was caught on CCTV, he wore a hoodie, and dark glasses. He had a ring on his right-hand index finger. He was young, in his mid-twenties to mid-thirties. Roy had looked at the CCTV footage so many times he had lost count. CCTV images were not great in the pre-digital age, but they had been scrubbed and cleaned by the forensic AV (audio visual) team in Scotland Yard. He knew the man's posture and gait by heart. But he was careful to cover his face well. Those dark glasses were wraparound, and the hoodie came down low. No one had a good view of his face.

Roy stopped as the towpath came to an end in another staircase that went up to the street level. He was tired. There was a bench, and he collapsed on it.

The Lily Man would be in his late fifties or early to mid-sixties now. Would he really risk everything to do this again? And why, after all these years?

Some detectives thought he was dead. The cold case had slowly faded from people's memories, apart from Roy and his parents. Roy never stopped searching. He never would, even when there was no hope. While breath still fluttered in his chest, he would look for Robin, alive or dead.

Could Johnny's kidnapper know what happened? Or was he just a copycat?

A sixth sense told Roy this wasn't a copycat. True, the Lily Man had gained notoriety, and his name was known. But a true copycat would have worked in the same location of greater London, close to the Surrey borders. That would be the copycat's sick way of paying homage.

And yet... the Lily Man had stayed fit and healthy for all these years, to emerge again?

Roy had to believe that. He had to get answers. Most importantly, he had to get Johnny Reid back to his parents. He stood and started the long walk back to the hotel.

CHAPTER 11

Twenty-seven years ago

Robin Roy was shaking. A cold wind whistled through the cracks of the window, and a storm howled and raged outside. The temperature outside had dropped, and it wasn't much better indoors. The bare floorboards were half rotten. The windows were shut, and, in most of them, curtains were missing. The only light in the room was a battery-operated white thing on the floor, and the glare hurt his eyes. The man came closer to him, and he shrank back.

He looked around wildly. The room was big, and the corners were shrouded in dark shadows. He could just about make out the door, but he knew it was locked. It was the second time the man had brought him up here from the basement.

He wanted to run, but there was nowhere to go. Fear paralysed him. He sank down to his knees, shivering.

"Look at me," the man commanded. He leaned forward, and Robin hunched lower, his shoulders quaking. "I said, look at me."

Robin had covered his face with his hands, and he removed them. The man was standing still, watching him.

Then Robin gasped as light glinted on the knife the man held in his right hand. He didn't raise it.

"Don't be scared."

Robin looked at the knife again, and fear blossomed in his heart. Tears rolled down his cheeks. He had lost track of time. He knew it was night, but he couldn't remember what day it was any more. He was in the basement with two other boys. Most of the time they had their hands and legs tied. The man bought them food and untied them one at a time. Today, when he came to get Robin, Robin noticed one of the boys was missing. He wondered what happened to him. His name was Mathew.

"Stand up," the man said. When Robin didn't obey, he grabbed him by the collar and lifted him to his feet.

The man dragged Robin towards one of the shadowy corners. Robin resisted, but it was no use. As he got closer, his eyes got used to the darkness. He saw a chair, and the shape of someone sitting on it. He heard someone breathing heavily, and it came from the chair.

"Stay here," the man commanded. Robin didn't have any other option. Fear rooted him to the spot. He stared at the chair. He could now make out that the person on it was either tied up or restrained somehow. He was moving, and making muffled sounds, like he was gagging.

The man picked up the light and got it closer. As the illumination grew, Robin gasped. It was Mathew. He was tied to the chair. A rope went around his head and mouth as well. His hands were tied behind his back. Mathew's eyes were wild, bulging with fear. He made frantic sounds, trying to speak to Robin, but the gag in his mouth prevented any words from making sense.

Nausea curdled in Robin's guts. He vomited on the floor. His stomach was empty, and nothing but mucus trailed out of his mouth. He retched, then fell to his knees.

"Stand up," the man said, his voice now harsher. When Robin took his time, the man straightened him by the collar and slapped him. The pain rocked inside his head, and he stumbled backwards. The man held out his knife, handle first.

"Take it," he said.

Robin looked at the knife fearfully, then his eyes met the man's, whose face was lit up from below. His eyes were large, and dark. Shadows covered his face, and he was a monster, a horrible creature from his worst nightmares.

"Take it," the man repeated, holding the knife. "Take it or I'll slap you again." He raised his hand, and Robin cowered. The slap didn't come, but the knife was thrust in his face.

Uncertainly, Robin took the knife. The handle was warm in his hand.

"Now," the man said. He pointed to Mathew, who was watching and wriggling on the chair. "Stab him."

Robin looked at the man uncomprehendingly. "Go on," the man encouraged. "Stab him. Anywhere. Do it," his voice dropped to a menacing whisper, "or you're next."

Robin's mouth opened in shock. He stared at the knife, then at the Mathew. He shook his head. The knife fell from his hands, and he stepped back. The man shouted a curse and snarled as he picked up the knife. Then he grabbed Robin by the neck and pulled him forward. "How dare you disobey me?" the man bit out through clenched teeth. He tightened his hold on Robin's neck till he was gagging, spluttering for breath. "This is the throne, do you understand? The throne where it happens. When I give you an order by the throne, you obey. Got that?"

Robin had no idea what the man was saying, but he nodded in terrified silence.

"This is what you have to do," the man whispered. Then he plunged the knife into Mathew's chest. The boy lurched forward, shock and pain written in every line of his face, His mouth opened in a silent scream, but the sound was lost in violence and pain. The man pulled the knife out and stabbed Mathew in the abdomen. He continued to stab him in a frenzy till the blood splattered into his face, and he was panting. He turned to look at Robin, a ghoulish image with flecks of blood on his face, lips bent in hate. Robin was catatonic with shock, his mouth dry, unable to utter a sound. Mathew was now slumped on the chair, but still twitching.

The man reached for Robin, and he fainted.

73

CHAPTER 12

Roy was up at the crack of dawn. He set his alarm for five, but he was up by half four. In truth, he barely slept. His headache seemed worse this morning, and, as he stared at the two miniature bottles on the table, he wondered if he had drunk more, and his mind was playing tricks. He hadn't, or he would be feeling a lot worse now, and probably would've slept through the alarm. He dragged his tired body into the shower, then shaved and got ready.

He was at the Sheffield South and West Station by half five. The waiting room was empty. The same duty sergeant was at the desk. His plump cheeks were sagging, and his eyelids dropped as he sat with one hand cradling his face. Roy knocked on the desk with his knuckles softly. The sergeant opened his eyes and yawned. He frowned at first, then the confusion cleared from his eyes. "You're the DCI from down south, eh?"

"That would be me. Mr DCI from down south. Catchy name, don't you think?"

The sergeant's name badge said Tom Moody, and he blinked at Roy twice before his eyebrows lifted.

"It's too early mate, don't worry," Roy said. "Time for you to go home? Been a long night I see."

Moody grimaced. "Couple of drunks, couple of fights in the town bars. Nothing out of the ordinary."

He reached under the counter and buzzed Roy in. "Take care," Roy nodded at Moody, who stifled a yawn and waved back.

Roy went in the opposite direction to yesterday, following signs for the canteen. He got himself a coffee, bacon and eggs, and sat down to eat. There was no one else in the canteen. He was surprised the canteen staff were here this early, they were happy to serve him. The bacon tasted fresher than the rubbery slices he got at the canteen in London, and so did the eggs. He had barely eaten last night's dinner and he wolfed the food down.

He walked into the office, coffee cup in hand. It was deserted, as expected. The duty detectives were probably at home, having handed over to the day team remotely. Roy stopped in front of the map of Sheffield and the surrounding area. Doncaster, where he'd spent his early years, was just a stone's throw away, next to Rotherham. Manchester, the next big city, and bigger than Sheffield, was not far either. It was strange how many memories swarmed at the periphery of his mind when he looked at the map. He could even see the suburb of Doncaster called Bessacarr, where he used to live.

He traced a finger from south Sheffield to the left, and eastwards, into the Dales. Someone had put a red top pin on Wyming Brooks Reserve already. There was a shelf below the map, with an assortment of marker pens on it. Roy picked up a red marker and circled the area around the Reserve.

He pulled out his phone and checked the distance. It was twenty-four miles. About half an hour's drive from the Reid's home. Seemed like a normal jolly to go on with your son and the dog. From the reserve, the vast peaks of the Dales really began, stretching out to Manchester slightly northwest, and Wales to the south. It was a large, mountainous terrain, and searching it wouldn't be easy. He zoomed into Wyming Brook. The place had four reservoirs, and they were big, natural bodies of water.

He was engrossed in watching the map on his phone and didn't catch the person who moved into the office till they were closer. He was a medium height man in his forties, dressed in jeans and a dark jacket. He wore black, square frame glasses that gave him a scholarly look. He stared at Roy for a while, then nodded.

"Hi. I'm Justin Dobson. I'm the head of scene of crime. Don't think we've met."

"Rohan," Roy said, accepting the extended hand. "I'm the DCI in charge of the Johnny Reid case."

Dobson adjusted his glasses. "Yes, I heard you're coming." He looked around him. "Where are the others?"

"On their way, I think. You have a lab on site here, unless I'm mistaken. Anything to report from the crime scene?"

"Actually, that's why I came down here. I thought I might catch one of you. DS Sarah said you wanted to have an early morning meeting."

Roy hadn't asked Sarah to do that, and he made a mental note to thank her. She had her head screwed on, that one.

They walked over to Sarah's desk and sat down. "What did you find?" Roy asked.

"Boot prints on the dirt track. We got the father and son's marks, but these are different. Adult male size ten, I'd say. They were further down the track that skirts around the woodlands. That path ends in the rocks that leads further up into the hills. It also branches off and leads down to the reservoirs."

"You found the adult boot prints with Johnny's?"

"According to Mr Reid, there was no other child there, nor adult. Just him and Johnny. And these boot prints don't match his. So, yes, it's significant."

"Good," Roy's eyes lit up. "How far do the prints go?"

"That's the thing," Dobson grimaced. "They vanish after a few metres. My guess is he took Johnny and went into the woods."

"There's a path out through the woods? I haven't been to the place yet."

"Yes, there is. Harder to get through, but you can. Must've been harder if the man was carrying Johnny."

Roy sat back, frowning. "Johnny would've put up a fight. Unless he knew the man, of course. His father was behind him, but Johnny went round the curve, so his father didn't see this guy."

He looked at Dobson, who shrugged. "You tell me."

"I am. Mr Reid was way behind, otherwise he'd have seen this man. The prints are fresh, and next to Johnny's?"

"They seem fresh, yes, and they were close to the boy's. And I'm assuming they went into the woods, because there was nowhere else to go."

Roy's mind was buzzing. The man could've knocked Johnny unconscious, then carried him through the woods. He had to know the area well. That meant he was local. He had probably followed Mr Reid out to the Wyming Reserve. The operation had been meticulously planned. No CCTV cameras there to keep watch on him.

"Anything on the forensic boot print database?"

Dobson shook his head. "Nope. I'm still waiting for the gait analyst to get back to me. Don't think I'll get much, but it's worth a try."

Sarah walked in, followed by Rizwan. They nodded at Roy and Dobson, then sat down.

"We found boot prints," Dobson said, and explained the findings to them. "Going back there today to take sample near the reservoirs."

"We need to search the waters," Roy said. "Do we have a boat service?"

Sarah nodded. "Yes. I can call them."

"They need to do it today." He turned to Dobson, "If we assume this man took Johnny into the woods, what was his way out? He had to get to a car somehow. No point in staying there till police are swarming all over the place, right?" Roy glanced at Rizwan. "Can you open up a large screen map of the Wyming Reserve? I want to see exactly where Johnny was last seen."

Rizwan did as asked, and they hunched over his laptop. "They were here, near the Rivelin Dams," Rizwan pointed. "The A57 is just on the other side."

"Mr Reid said he didn't park on the usual parking site but drove up closer to where they walked."

"He went off road," Rizwan confirmed. "It's a big area, and he used this trail over here. I know that place. My football club is not far, in the Redmires Playing Fields." Rizwan scrolled down and to the left to show them. He zoomed back on the trail that Reid had used to drive up to near the Rivelin Dam. "The path goes high up into the woods, and you get a good view from there as well." Rizwan pointed as he tracked the path to the summit.

"I can see why he drove up there," Roy said. "He couldn't walk all the way up with Johnny."

DC Oliver arrived, putting his coat up on the hook. His hair was gelled back, and the tips of his shoes gleamed. "Did I miss anything?"

"A look in the mirror," Roy said. "You missed a bit while shaving." He pointed to his left lower jaw, and concern spread across Oliver's face. He touched his left cheek.

"Really? Where?"

Roy shook his head and went back to the laptop. "I want to head down there now. Let's get there before anyone else does."

Rizwan and Sarah were grinning, and Oliver looked a little sheepish. "I didn't miss anything, did I?" he pointed to his left jaw.

Roy stood and clapped him on the shoulder. "We'll make a detective out of you, yet. Can someone check with the Reid family? I know it's early, but I want an update. They'll be up, trust me."

Oliver reached for the phone and a group of people entered the office, including the stocky figure of Michael Nugent. He was speaking to a man with a receding hairline, and when he saw Roy, he walked over.

"This is Stephen Burns, the forensic psychologist," Nugent said, and Roy shook hands with the man who was close to six feet and looked to be in his fifties.

Stephen was wiry but strong, and exuded a charisma in his lean, fit frame. His cheekbones were prominent, perhaps accentuated by cheeks that had caved in. The tip of his sharp nose was red. A pair of intelligent, dark brown eyes stared at Roy without blinking. "You solved the Mason case. I read about it in the papers."

"Thank you, but it was the team that did it, not me. How's the Reid family doing?"

"They're in pieces. I'm heading down there now. Only spoke to them briefly yesterday. Not really my remit. I deal with the offenders mostly, not the families. But in this case, I was told to get a measure of the family." He glanced at Nugent, a wary look in his eyes. Nugent puffed out his chest and raised his chin in the air like a peacock. Roy watched the interaction with interest.

"Before DCI Roy arrived, I was the SIO in charge," Nugent said. "As you know, in cases of child abduction we need to screen the family first. Hence, I asked Stephen to get their measure."

Spoken like a man who has little experience of leading on such cases, Roy thought, and wisely kept his words to himself. Nugent had a point, as many child offences the family was the first suspect, but there wasn't really much point in getting a forensic psychologist involved this early. Routine policework would uncover most of the problems.

"What did you think of the parents?" Roy asked Burns.

"Distressed, clearly. The father was shaken up more than the mother, due to guilt. He doesn't have a criminal record, and I couldn't see any signs of him lying. The mother was at home alone when this happened. She has no alibi. But I doubt she would have the ability to abduct her own son."

Burns was the only person he'd met in Sheffield so far who didn't have a Yorkshire accent, Roy thought. Definitely a southern man. Regarding the family, he seemed to know what he was talking about.

"I got that impression as well. Have you been involved in other cases of child abduction?"

Burns hesitated a fraction. "The Bristow boy, who vanished from Rotherham last year. He was taken by–"

"Charlie Allerton," Roy finished for him. "He was known to the force, right? He took a young girl out on her paper run. She was twelve years old and managed to escape. She gave a good description, and he was caught, but took the Bristow boy when he was released from prison."

Burns smiled. "I can see I'm preaching to the converted here. Your role in the London Met has become specialised now, right? You're in charge of the children's cases."

"Kind of, yes." Roy didn't elaborate, but he was glad to know someone who had experience of these matters. "Did you deal with Charlie Allerton, then?"

"Yes, I did. Did his profiling initially when he took the girl, and later, after he was caught with the Bristow boy."

"Shame about the boy," Roy said, watching Burns' face change. Eddie Bristow's remains were found in a shallow grave in the woods, a mile from where Charlie

Allerton lived. "Let's make sure we get Johnny back to his parents," Roy concluded, and Burns agreed.

"Gary Hutchins took the Mason girls, didn't they?" Burns asked. "You did well to get them back. He'd dug their graves already, literally."

Roy cocked his head at him, intrigued. "You read the case files?" It wasn't unusual, as the confidential memos were sent to all forces in UK. Gary Hutchins would never be a free man again.

"Yes," Burns smiled. "It's my job to stay update on these cases. And you caught Antony Smith, the Brentford killer. Shame about the two boys he took."

Roy's face clouded, grim memories rising to the surface. "It was," he said shortly. "No excuses. We should've got there before Smith did it." The two boys were found dead a week after they were abducted.

"Can't save them all, but you did your best," Burns shook his head, a sympathetic look on his face.

A woman approached their small group, and Sarah introduced her. "This is Sarah Percival, the FLO. She was with the family yesterday."

Percival was short, sprightly, but with a calm, watchful expression on her face. Her ginger hair was pulled back into a ponytail. She was attractive, with vivid blue eyes, and seemed to be in her early to mid-thirties. She shook hands with Roy, her eyes lingering on his for longer than necessary. Roy inclined his head in greeting. "Nice to meet you. How are things in the Reid household?"

83

"Pretty awful as you can imagine," Percival made a face, then shrugged. "They don't talk much, but when they do it's behind closed doors."

Roy flipped open his notebook. "Keith Burgess. Partner of Fiona, Duncan Reid's sister. Did you meet him?"

Percival frowned, then shook his head. "No, can't say I did. Met Fiona. She was there from yesterday. She seems alright. She went out for a walk with Amanda yesterday. Amanda didn't want to go, but it was good that she got some fresh air. Fiona is also messaging all the school parents, and people in the community from Amanda's phone. Amanda is not quite right, as you can imagine."

Roy nodded. "I got that impression as well. What did you think of Duncan and Amanda? Do they seem close?"

The FLO was always closer to the family, and an FLO who kept an ear to the ground was invaluable, Roy had learnt. They often found out family secrets from a careless whisper that the detectives would never catch.

Percival hesitated, then pulled at his shirt collar. "I've only been there a day. Hard to tell. But I did hear some raised voices from upstairs. I was going up to give Amanda a cup of tea. From their bedroom, I heard Amanda shouting. Then Duncan came out. He went down the stairs, brushing past me on the landing. He didn't say a word. I heard the front door slam, and then the car started, I presumed he drove out."

"Interesting. What did Amanda say?"

Percival pressed both lips, and her face creased in concentration.

"I caught the toe end of their argument. She was saying something like, Just leave then. Just go. I didn't hear after that as it was muffled, but then she shouted, You're useless. He said something too, then he barged out."

Roy held Percival's eyes. "Good work. I thought there was something weird when I met them last night, but shock can do strange things to people. This argument they had might still be just that. But maybe we should dig deeper into their relationship. I'll count on your intelligence reports, if that's ok."

Percival smiled. "No problem."

Roy checked his watch. It was getting close to 7.30AM He glanced at Sarah, Rizwan, and Oliver. "Let's go to the crime scene."

CHAPTER 13

Roy was in the front as Sarah drove. As the road climbed, more of the Peak District hills appeared. They were gentle undulations at first, then the black rock, craggy cliff faces appeared, stern and grim faced in the cloudy day. Behind them, Sheffield was neatly ensconced in the valley, like a city of make believe, nestled in a giant's palm.

On either side of the narrow road that went up to Wyming Brook Reserve, fields opened up, bordered, and divided by grey stone walls. Clumps of woolly white lambs roamed the fields. He could see the sky, leaden grey and foreboding it was, but he could still see it. In London, he was too busy avoiding getting trampled by cars, buses, or pedestrians to look up.

Sarah went into a car park that bore the sign of Wyming Brook, and also mentioned this place was the home of animals who needed protection.

Sarah turned to him. Her blonde hair was pulled tight in a ponytail. She had light red lipstick on, and her makeup was minimal, but the sea green of her eyes was accentuated by the mascara she wore. "It's a fifteen-to-twenty-minute walk from here, guv. Do you want to drive up there?"

"Nope. We'll walk."

They got out and Roy stretched, feeling the fresh, cool breeze on his face. It smelt different here. The diesel and exhaust fumes had gone, and it was nice to take a deep breath in. He followed the others as they made their way to the walking path that curled around the hills towards the Riven Dam and the Reservoir.

The steppingstones were glistening black rock, and overhead a dense canopy of foliage made the forest floor dark. A brook gurgled down from the hills, and in the distance, Roy heard the sound of rushing water, falling over the black rocks like the brook that tumbled over the pebbles in its bed. As they walked, shafts of sunlight pierced the clouds, and slanted in through the leaves above. They picked their way through it, then crossed a small bridge over the brook.

They came out into a clearing, and the road they had taken, and a vista of the city was visible far below. Rizwan led the group, as he knew the area best. Roy was enjoying the walk. His vision of a dreary northern city hadn't quite materialised, in fact, he had completely forgotten how close Sheffield was to the Peak District. He didn't know how long he'd be here, but he was glad he had packed his running gear. This would be an amazing spot to come for a run, if he got any time.

The road sloped down, flattened, then rose up again. Soon, the squad car and two white vans came into view, as did the blue and white tape fluttering in the breeze. Sarah introduced Roy to the uniformed Inspector who was on duty, a man called Jonty Adams.

"Do you have men searching in the woods?" Roy asked.

"We did it yesterday with five teams, and there's two up there right now. Nothing to report as yet."

"Have they checked around the A57? There's a path that exits on the backroads, is that right?" Roy glanced at Rizwan, who nodded.

"Yes," Adams said. "There are tyre tracks there, but not sure how fresh they are."

Roy indicated the white forensic van. "Have you told them?"

"Yes, guv. Dobson's aware, but we saw them this morning, not sure if he's had a look yet."

"He's on his way," Roy said. "Thanks."

He headed up the path, and was about to duck under the tape, when he heard Adams swear. He stopped and looked behind. A group of reporters were headed their way. They were in three large groups, each group holding boom mics and portable cameras. A couple of the women were smartly dressed and done up for work, walking quickly in their flat shoes.

"Had to happen sooner or later," Adams said. Even as he said the words, more of them appeared, descending in a line down the slope that Roy and the others had just taken. A van also appeared, off roading, wobbling on its wheels, the satellite dish on its roof almost falling off.

"Ridiculous," Roy muttered. The van overtook everyone else, and the reporters on their feet made a dash for it, trying to get there before the van did, or at least at the same time. Roy watched the whole fiasco the way a general watches an invading army.

He stepped forward as the van got closer. It was moving fast, lurching sideways dangerously on the open field. The van screeched to a halt, and a man jumped out from passenger seat. He hurried towards Roy, fishing out a Dictaphone recorder as he half ran, half walked. From his right, the remaining horde descended, Roy acting as a nucleus of their attention.

"You're in plain clothes so you must be one of the detectives. Are you in charge?"

Roy knew it was critical to create boundaries with the press, as early as possible. If they knew he was in charge, they would leave the others alone. Besides, there was a press conference later this afternoon, and he would almost certainly be sitting next to Nugent when it happened. Might as well face the cavalry now.

"Yes, I am. The most important thing for you to do is to not enter the crime scene. You have already trampled on potential evidence, so please go back to your desks. We will inform you of any developments. Our Media Liaison Office will be in touch."

Several Dictaphones, microphones, and the shaggy domes of boom mics were thrust into his face. Multiple voices spoke at once, drowning each other out.

"Have you found a body?"

"Is Johnny still alive? Is he up there?"

"Do you suspect anyone in the school or family?"

Roy raised both hands calmly. "Like I said, when we have something, we will let you know. Right now, this is a fast-moving investigation, and I have no other comment. Please let us do our job."

He turned to leave, and the entire horde followed, literally pressing on his back. He turned back savagely, thrusting his arms out in front. The media vultures scattered back like cockroaches swept under a broom.

Roy's face was like one of the mountain cliffs looming around them. His voice boomed out. "Which part of letting us do our job did you not understand?"

The reporters started shouting in unison again. "Where's Johnny?"

"Has any other child been taken?"

"Have you found a body? Have the parents been informed?"

"What about the ransom note? How much money does the kidnapper want?"

Roy wondered how they knew about the ransom note. He shook his head. "No comment. Now, just to repeat, we need to find Johnny. Please let us do our job, and soon we will have some answers for you."

He indicated to Adams, and he hurried over. "Set up a perimeter here," Roy said in a low voice. "Make sure they don't come closer, or they'll be hanging around the tape very soon."

Adams rushed away. Roy stood there for a while. Rizwan and Oliver joined him.

"Skipper's gone up to have a look," Rizwan said. "Shall we stay here with you?"

"No, go with her. I'll see you up there in a bit."

The two DCs trudged off and ducked under the tape. Adams arrived with two uniformed constables. They had foldable plastic barriers with them, the ones that sat on the ground. They put down a few and went back to the van to get more.

Roy turned around, ready to go. A solitary voice rose above the cacophony, and the breeze carried it to his ears.

"This is the Lily Man again, isn't it? The one who was never caught?"

Roy halted. The mob was silent all of a sudden. Then, whispering voices started muttering. Roy clocked an older reporter, hair almost white, sunken cheeked, wiry, thin frame glasses, standing to the left. He didn't have an entourage with him, or at least seemed not to. He stood to one side, not making any effort to come closer.

He looked familiar to Roy. He had come across so many reporters during the Mason case, he didn't know if this man had spoken to him before.

"No comment."

"It's the same MO. He left the white lily with the note, didn't he?"

The older reporter held Roy's eyes for a few seconds. Roy suddenly placed him. He worked for a tabloid, the Daily Mail or the like. He covered missing persons and cold cases. Roy searched his brain for a name and came up with a blank. This man had stayed in his mind because his research was impeccable, and he asked the most searching questions.

And Roy wondered how he knew about the white lily.

"No comment," he said again. "Look, there's a press conference later this afternoon."

"At 4.30 pm," one of the younger female journalists at the front said. "Are you going to be there?"

"Maybe. We can answer your questions then."

"You're DCI Rohan Roy, aren't you?" the white-haired man said. There was a hush, and all eyes turned towards him, then to Rohan.

"Who wants to know?" Roy asked, a discomfort prickling in his spine.

"James Eastwood, of the Daily Trident. I met you three years ago for the Mason case."

"Lucky you, Mr Eastwood. Now, if you'll please excuse me. Hopefully, I shall see you lovely people later in the day."

Three uniformed constables moved forward to the spot that Roy vacated, behind the newly set up barricade.

The reports kept firing questions, but Roy ignored them. As expected, they now kept using his name. The presence of Eastwood didn't bother Roy that much. He was a journalist for a national tabloid, it was expected that he would be here. He had undoubtedly been to the Reid family home and had managed to speak to someone. If not an actual family member, any of the neighbours would be fair game.

He signed his name on the clipboard that one of the constables held out and thanked the man. Normally, at a crime scene, he would don a mask, gloves, and shoe covers. Shoe covers would get cut to pieces on the stones here, and there wasn't any point in wearing a mask in the great outdoors. He paused to think about that. He couldn't remember the last time he'd been out of the great smokestack called London.

Roy trudged up the hill, following the dirt track that had a thin sliver of grass verge running down the middle. Cars could easily travel up here, and this path was perhaps designed for that purpose. He walked on the grass, keeping an eye on the track. Tell-tale depressions from tyres were visible, but he didn't see anything else. To his left, the woodlands opened up, dense and foreboding. If he had the choice, he wondered if he'd come here to walk the dog. Maybe, maybe not. Maybe this was one of Johnny's favourite places and he insisted they come. They had picnics here in the summer.

Roy saw the uniform and cap of a constable come out of the woods. The man waved at him. Rizwan emerged from behind, and the two crossed over to the other side of the track. Roy's phone beeped, and he answered. It was an unknown number. A male voice spoke, thin and anxious.

"It's Stephen, the FLO. You gave me your number."

"I did indeed. Are you at the Reid house?"

"Yes. You need to come down here. There's been another ransom letter, this time asking for money, or Johnny dies."

CHAPTER 14

Roy called Sarah on the radio, and she arrived a few minutes later, her cheeks flushed. She wore a dark blue trouser suit, one that hugged her figure. Her eyes lingered on Roy's. She waved a hand towards the general crime scene.

"It's too big, guv. We're searching, but to be honest, there's been precious little since yesterday."

"Apart from the boot prints next to Johnny's. These woods descend to the fields that border the A57, and there's a back path too, right?"

Sarah nodded. Roy said, "That's where we focus our attention. Anyway, leave it for now. There's been a new ransom note. We need to head out to the Reid's house. I've told the others already. They stay here."

Sarah nodded, and they trudged down the path together. Sheffield was visible in the distance, suspended in a mild haze. The reporters were fewer, but the ones remaining turned vocal as soon as they saw Roy.

"What did you find?"

"Is there a body?"

"Is the Lily Man back?"

That last question shook Roy up. He could see the glaring headlines already.

Child Killer returns.

He escaped once. Will he again?

Uniformed constables restrained the reporters from approaching Roy and Sarah. The van had gone, as had the majority of the reporters, which was one good news. That left the intriguing question of where they had decamped to. Roy had the horrible feeling he knew the answer.

The police couldn't stop the reporters in this open countryside, and a couple of them ran after Roy and Sarah, firing questions.

"Why is the Lily Man in Sheffield? He was last active in London and Surrey."

"Why are you up here, DCI Roy? What do you know about the Lily Man?"

Roy bit his lower lip. Against his better judgement, he stopped and turned. The four reporters who were trailing after them stopped. He strode towards them. The one closest was a young man with bumfluff on his upper lip and an over excited look in his eyes, like a puppy dog with a Dictaphone. Roy reached out a long arm and plucked the phone out of the man's hand. He gaped at Roy.

"South Yorkshire Police have the right to take out an injunction and restraining order against journalists who hamper a critical investigation. As mentioned before, no comment until the press conference."

Roy stopped the Dictaphone recording and handed it back to the young reporter. The other three had gone silent.

"I meant what I said," Roy spoke slowly. "Please let us find the missing boy."

"You can't take out a restraining order against the press. That's illegal," a woman said.

"Not letting us do our job when a boy's life is in danger, that's immoral. And should be illegal. Don't you think?"

Silence again. Roy spun on his heels and walked faster, Sarah keeping pace with him. He appreciated her silence. They got to the car park, and it was like a circus had arrived in town. A green and blue bus stood with its doors open. People were out, stretching, and chatting to themselves.

"Are these tourists?" Roy asked Sarah in a low voice.

"There are better places in the Dales for tourism," Sarah answered. "This place is mostly popular with locals, and I've never heard of this many."

Then Roy saw the T shirt with Johnny's face on it. A group came down from the bus, all of them wearing the same T shirt. He couldn't fault their desire to help. But if they walked all over the crime scene... he knew they wouldn't when the police stopped them. But there could always be a straggler who was overzealous and did some serious damage to the crime scene. He felt a little helpless, watching the crowd move out of the car park, down to the path that led to the Rivelin Reservoir.

"Shall we have a word, guv?" Sarah asked. Roy shook his head.

"Adams and his men will stop them. Let's go, we don't have much time."

He closed his eyes as Sarah drove. His headache was back, and he desperately wished he could sleep. But his mind was churning like a washing machine. And the soiled laundry it was washing never got clean.

Sarah didn't say a word. He watched the open countryside flash by, then the city began, and within minutes they were snarled in traffic. Sarah hit the siren on the unmarked Ford Titanium, and traffic parted reluctantly. Roy had a premonition of what awaited them at Endcliffe Park, and, as they got closer, his hunch proved correct. He counted five media vans, all with satellite dishes perched precariously on top, and a scrum of reporters in front of the Reid residence. The uniformed squads had put up barriers and were manning them. Sarah cut the siren long before she entered the neighbourhood, and she didn't need to be told to do that, which Roy appreciated.

The volley of questions hit them as they walked towards the front door. Sarah pressed on the buzzer, and Roy let the shouts behind him slide off like water on a duck's back. Emily opened the door for them, then led them to the kitchen area at the back. Fiona and Amanda were sitting on barstools at the counter, and Duncan was pacing the floor. He stopped when he saw Roy.

Emily pointed to an envelope that lay inside an evidence bag, on the kitchen counter. Sarah put her gloves on. A white lily was stuck to the envelope with a pin, and she removed it carefully. There was no name on the envelope, or stamp. She took out the paper inside. Roy came closer to look.

The note was handwritten in block capitals.

I want one hundred thousand pounds. Then Johnny will be returned. I will confirm time and place. Get the money ready, in cash. Tell the police, and Johnny dies.

A cold slab of ice coated Roy's heart and squeezed hard. This is exactly what the Lily Man had done twenty-seven years ago. A week after the abduction, he sent ransom notes to the family homes of the three boys, Roy's family included. They were bogus, intended to throw the cops off his scent. He didn't do this for money. He did it to satisfy his depraved, evil mind.

"Take it for forensics," Roy whispered. Sarah nodded and put it in her pocket.

"Well?" Duncan demanded. "This bastard now wants money. We don't have a hundred grand lying around. What do you suggest we do?"

"We don't negotiate," Roy said. "It seems like the hardest thing to do, but we have to call his bluff. If his past actions are anything to go by, this is a diversion, and time-wasting tactic."

Duncan was going to say something but then he stopped. Roy looked at his watch. It was close to nine AM. He glanced at Sarah, and she was staring at him.

"We will have updates for you later today. Please stay at home, and if you have any questions, ask Emily."

Duncan came forward. His face was as white as a sheet. His lips were cracked, and a tremor coursed through his body.

"Please bring him back, Detective. Please."

Roy observed him for a few seconds, then looked behind him at the two women. Amanda sniffed, but her eyes were on the floor. Fiona was watching them. Roy dragged his attention back to Duncan.

"We're doing our best, I can assure you. Be strong. Your wife needs you now."

Roy followed Sarah out the door. He turned on the porch to have a word with Sarah. "Any more arguments?" he asked in a low voice, keeping an eye on the kitchen's closed door.

"I heard some more words last night. But I couldn't tell who was talking. It was one of the upstairs bedrooms and the door was shut."

"Thank you. Keep an ear out, it's very helpful."

Roy nodded and left. He actually had to brush away a few microphones that were thrust into his face. He got into the car quickly and Sarah put the siren on, scattering the assembled crowd of onlookers and journalists.

When they got to the office, the wide, squat figure of Nugent was speaking to another detective with his back to them. Nugent spun around when the detective pointed. His face was mottled, and there was an upward curl in his lips. It didn't bode well, Roy thought.

"In my office, now," Nugent grated, then stormed off.

Sarah shut the door behind them. A bunch of newspapers were strewn across Nugent's desk. He picked one up and threw it on the floor. Roy could see the headlines, and he shook his head and sighed.

Child Killer Strikes Again.

The Killer That Got Away.

Sheffield Under Lockdown.

"Who?" Nugent thundered, so loud that the prefabricated walls of his office shook. "Who the hell leaked the news before we even get a chance?"

"It's not too difficult," Roy said. "The family have started spreading the news on social media, and it's gone viral. Caught some journalist's attention on Twitter, and they start digging. No wonder they're all camped outside."

"It's not a leak from us, sir, in case you're wondering," Sarah said.

"Damn it," Nugent fumed, collapsing on his chair. He got up and flung the window open. He leaned out the window and lit a cigarette. He took a few quick drags then chucked it, and slammed the window shut. He cleared his throat, and it sounded like a bulldog being strangled to death. He took out a tissue from his pocket and hacked phlegm into it. Roy glanced at Sarah, who had a terrified expression on her face. He couldn't help smiling.

Nugent wheezed for a few seconds, his face still red. "I got a call from the Chief Constable this morning. We need to get our arses into gear. If I don't, he'll have my guts for garters."

An old northern expression Roy hadn't heard in absolutely yonks. "We're on it. I've got a lead that I want to close in on this morning." He could feel Sarah's eyes on him as he said the words.

"You do?" Nugent looked relieved. "Ok. Get cracking then."

"What lead?" Sarah asked, as they walked back to her desk.

"Keith Burgess. Might be nothing, but he's the only person who had contact with Johnny, and Johnny would go with him of his own free will. Keith knew where Johnny would be, and he was the only person who had that knowledge, apart from his parents."

Sarah sat down at her desk and pulled up her laptop. "I've got his details from the lads."

"You check HOLMES. I'll call him," Roy said, fishing out his phone.

CHAPTER 15

Keith Burgess's phone rang out and Roy left a message. He looked up his address on the map. He lived in a place called Attercliffe. It was close to the giant shopping centre of Meadowhall, another place Roy remembered from decades ago. Meadowhall was the main mall in South Yorkshire, and he had memories of traipsing around after his mother, whining for an ice cream.

Roy pulled up a satellite image of where Keith lived. It looked like a council house, at the end of a cul-de-sac. The whole area of Attercliffe, in fact, looked like it was funded by the council.

"You need to see this," Sarah called from her desk. Roy hurried over. Sarah's laptop screen showed a mugshot of a man with a light stubble, hard jaw, receding hairline, in his late forties or fifties. A quick glance at the date of birth in the PCN confirmed his age. Keith Burgess was fifty-two.

"He's been done twice for burglary and spent three years inside for armed robbery. Got arrested multiple times for GBH. But this is the real news," Sarah scrolled to the bottom of the page, where Burgess's name was on the sex offender's list, in big red letters.

"He picked up his neighbour's son from school. He made friends with the boy earlier. He kept the boy overnight, then pretended to find him in some field and brought him back. And that was only because the parents suspected him. Other parents saw him picking the boy up from school. He abused the boy. The father broke down Burgess's door the next morning. He said he found the boy in the early hours of the morning and was about to return him."

Sarah shook her head and clicked on the confidential report. "This is really disgusting. He made the boy do all of this?" She turned away from her seat, and Roy took it.

He had seen men like Burgess before. Violent and disturbed, pure evil when it came to contact with children. Many of them were abused as children themselves. He looked at the man's photo. A chill ran down his spine, and hair stood up on the back his neck.

Burgess was the right age to be The Lily Man. Twenty-seven years ago he would've been twenty-five years old. That fit with the witness description, and CCTV images. And, like the Lily Man did with one of his victims, he had picked up this boy from his school.

Roy's hand shook as he reached for the cursor and scrolled up and down till he found Burgess's history. He went by a couple of aliases – Kevin Donald and Kirk Bellamy. Neither of them rang a bell. He was from Rotherham, which wasn't far away. He had lived and worked in this area most of his life, it seemed. Had he ever gone down south? Did he kidnap those boys, Robin included, do his evil work, then come back here?

Is that why he was never caught?

Most paedophiles lived near to their victims, Roy knew. And many of them knew the children's families. Many paedophiles acted like normal members of society; they hid in broad daylight. It was hard to catch them unless a parent complained, because their innocent victims were often shamed into silence. A far as location was concerned, Burgess broke that mould. He travelled far to find his victims. All the behaviour analysts and the psychological profilers had insisted The Lily Man would be someone local. All three of his victims were taken from within a three-mile radius. He knew the area well. He lived within a five-mile radius, they said. They were wrong. By the time the search radius was expanded, The Lily Man had bolted.

Although he did his nefarious work almost three decades ago, he remained on England's worst known serial killers list, someone whom the police had never truly forgotten.

And now he was back.

Roy looked at Burgess's photo again, and the drumbeat of his heart built to a raging wave. He wasn't aware that Sarah was standing next to him till she spoke.

"Guv?"

He turned to her slowly because it was almost impossible to wrench his eyes off the screen. Sarah's sea green gaze had a tinge of concern in as she stared at him.

"You alright? Looks like you seen a ghost."

Roy blinked, then passed a hand over his face. He stood. "We need to get him. Do you know the way to Attercliffe?"

"Yes, shall I call for backup?"

"Yes, do. But let's be on our way and wait for them catch us."

*****

Sarah put the siren on as they sliced through the traffic of central Sheffield, and then she cut it as they got closer.

"Did you get in touch with Burgess?" she asked, her eyes fixed on the road.

Her radio squawked. It was the backup uniform team. Their message came over on the loudspeaker as well.

"Sorry, we got caught up in an RTA and robbery near Nether Edge. Will be with you ASAP or request other units."

"Copy that," Roy said and hung up. "We don't have time to waste. We need to go in now."

Sarah eyed him. "Are you sure? The man's done armed robbery. He could have a gun."

"Or guns," Roy said, a grim set in his jawline. "He would be stupid to try and shoot us. And there's just a chance we might catch him napping. Either way, we have to do this now."

107

The radio squawked again, responding to Sarah's request for backup. None was available currently; all units were busy elsewhere.

Sarah parked at the top of the road where Burgess lived. The street was decrepit, a burnt-out car sitting on bricks, rubbish bins overturned. The houses had seen better days, with plaster falling off the frontages, and boarded up windows.

A woman with a pram was walking towards them. There was an off licence in the corner where they had parked, and a group of youths stood outside, watching their car. The youths couldn't be any more than eighteen, all of them in hoodies, most of them should be in school.

"You stay here," Roy said. He felt for his telescopic steel baton and can of mace. The baton was about eight inches long but with a single downward flick it extended to double the size. It cracked human heads and windows with equal ease, and, in the right hands, it was always a formidable weapon. He didn't have his can of mace on him, but he did have the handcuffs.

"This woman," Sarah indicated outside at the mother with the pram, who had drawn closer, but had stopped to check the baby inside. "I think she lives around here. Burgess is in number thirty-six, in the middle of the road. I want to ask her if she knows him."

"Good idea."

They both got out. Roy hung back as Sarah approached the woman. "Ayup," she said. "You alright luv?" Her native Yorkshire accent seemed stronger on the street.

The woman was looking at them warily, her eyes flicking from Sarah to Roy, standing just behind. Her thin white face was pinched, cheeks sunken. Her eyes were red and tired, like she hadn't slept all night.

"Who're you, like?" Her voice was thin like her face, and cackly.

"I'm DS Sarah, and this is DCI Roy, of South Yorkshire Police. Do you know the man who lives in number thirty-six, goes by the name of Keith Burgess?"

The woman narrowed her eyes slightly, then shook her head. "No, I don't, sorry." She tried to walk past but Sarah blocked her.

"This is important luv, alright? A boy's gone missing, I'm sure you've heard. Keith Burgess was in contact with him, and we need to find Burgess. Do you know if he's there?"

The woman's eyes widened, and her knuckles got tighter on the pram handle. Her eyes moved around, and she shifted on her feet. Roy got the distinct impression she was trying to look behind her. There was now fear in the woman's gaze, and her breathing faster.

Roy sensed movement to his left, and when he looked, he saw the three of the bigger boys had sidled up closer on the opposite pavement. One of them had a phone in his hand.

"I'm going in," Roy whispered to Sarah. "These boys could be messengers."

"And she's too scared to talk," Sarah whispered back. She turned to the woman. "Can I please have your name and contact details?"

"What is this, police harassment?" The woman frowned. "You don't need my details. Now, if you'll excuse me."

"Get back in the car and go round the back. See if you can cut him off," Roy said, and Sarah nodded. The woman wheeled her pram out of the way and walked towards the off licence and the main road.

Roy moved briskly and came to the door marked thirty-six. It was a large terrace, and it was in a sorry state. Green paint flaked off the battered front door. One part of the bay window had cardboard covering it. The curtains were drawn, and all the lights were off, as expected, as it was daytime.

The rusty metal gate was coming off its hinges. It almost collapsed as Roy pushed in. The front garden had waist high weeds, and there was a pungent, foetid smell coming from it. Roy put his ear to the front door and listened. There was no sound from inside. He looked behind him, and the group of three hoodied lads had followed him and were watching on the opposite side of the pavement. He turned back to the door and pushed it. It was locked, as expected.

Roy walked to the front garden and looked at the terraces on either side. The one on the right was just as decrepit as this one, and one whole panel of the bay window was missing, replaced with a piece of timber. As these were terraces, that was another possible entry point. But Burgess's house bay window also had a cardboard over one panel.

He went up to the window and pushed the cardboard. It was fixed to the window frame with nails, but it was moving. He pushed harder, till the old nails splintered, and came off the window frame. He didn't want to make too much noise, but neither did he want to waste time. His radio crackled and he turned the black knob to reduce the sound.

"No path in from the back," Sarah said. "There's two layers of houses, gardens stuck back-to-back. I'll come back to where I was."

"Copy that."

Rohan shoved the cardboard harder, and it gave way. He caught it before it fell inside the room. With some difficulty, he was able to pull the cardboard piece out. He put his hands on the windowsill and pushed up from ground level. If the gap was wide enough to get his shoulders through, he could manage. He got stuck, and then had to wiggle his shoulders, while pushing up with his hands. That left him with little to no help in stopping himself from toppling inside. There was an old sofa, and he tumbled into it. A cloud of dust blinded his vision, tickled his nostrils. He rolled to the floor, coughing as lightly as he could, gagging at the dust that

111

choked his nostrils. He knelt on the floor for a few seconds, wiping his eyes, waiting for the dust to clear.

The door was shut, which was a blessing. The carpet had gaping holes, exposing the floorboards. Apart from the frail old sofa, there was a small coffee table in the middle of the room. A few inches of dust lay on the top. The rest of the room was bare, including the dust-filled shelves on the walls. Roy tested the carpet, then tiptoed his way to the door. He opened it a fraction, stopping when it creaked. He could poke his head out. The corridor was bereft of carpets, only floorboards. Several of them had gaping holes, making walking on them a hazard. Ahead, he could see the open door of a kitchen. It looked derelict, but there was a fridge, and the red light on the wall fuse board meant something was working.

The door next to the kitchen was shut. Roy tiptoed out on the hallway. The front door was shut, as he'd seen from outside. He stepped gingerly towards the room next to the kitchen. One of the problems with his height was his size eleven shoes that made a horrendous noise everywhere he stepped. He winced at every creak of the floorboard. As the kitchen was open, he decided to check it first. A wave of rancid, rotten odour hit him like a punch in the face. He screwed up his nose, and then put a hand over his mouth to prevent himself from gagging.

The smell was stronger, like a palpable presence he had to wade through as he opened the kitchen cupboards. They were mostly bare, but there was some evidence of life – a packet of crips, a roll of bread that wasn't mouldy, and a couple of eggs. There was also a frying pan on the hob. The sink contained a plate, cutlery, and a cup – all unwashed.

The garden door was locked. The garden was in a worse state than at the front, shrubs and weeds had overgrown to the point it looked like a jungle. Roy couldn't even see the back fence, but he could make out the garden of the opposite house behind it. He gave this a second of his attention, because his danger instinct was going off like a claxon.

Someone was here, or came here, that much was obvious from the kitchen. He moved to the next room, pushing the door open softly. Without going in, he stepped back as quickly as he could, flattening himself against the wall. No one came crashing out. There was no sound. He slipped the baton into his hand, and with a flick, extended it to its full length.

He crouched, then moved into the other room. This was like a dining area, but it was stone cold and utterly bare. Even the carpet was missing, and parts of the floorboard had caved in. The rotten smell carried on here from the kitchen, and, keeping a hand over his mouth, Roy checked the door that opened into a patio, that looked out to the garden that probably contained near extinct species of life.

A sudden creak. Distinct, and loud, over his head. Roy froze, listening hard. It came once again, softer this time. There was someone upstairs. He made sure the knob on the radio was turned down to silent. Then he went to the staircase and moved upstairs.

CHAPTER 16

He stopped at the landing. It was a typical terraced house, with a bathroom to his right, followed by another three doors, probably all bedrooms. All the doors were shut. His eyes were drawn to the left, at the last bedroom. The sound came from there, he was sure. He tightened his grip on the baton. There was another door on his left, and he pushed it open. It was a small study or nursery room. Like the rest of the house, it was completely bare. The smell had followed him upstairs, but thankfully it was a few degrees less potent than in the kitchen.

He got to the last bedroom and nudged the door. It fell open. It was completely dark inside. He couldn't make out a thing, not even the shape of any furniture. The blackness lay there like a congealed mass, waiting to swirl around him. Roy could feel his heartbeat pulse loud against his eardrums. Knees bent, arm raised, he moved closer to the door. He groped the wall for a light switch and found one. He flicked it, but nothing happened. No bulb.

Breathing faster, every nerve on fire, he stepped inside the jaws of the darkness. His feet scratched on bare wood. The darkness was so complete he couldn't even see his own hand when he moved the baton in front. Was there no window here?

He was groping around like a blind man. He couldn't feel any furniture. The rotten smell was still present, but diminished, and it was replaced by another odour he couldn't place, like a computer printer, or stacks of paper. He stepped further inside, his muscles taut, gripping the baton. He sensed the sound before he heard it. It was the creak, and it came from behind him, by the door.

He turned swiftly, but he was too late. A giant shape bulged out from the darkness like a silent scream. Something hit him in the chest, a square, heavy force that hurled him backwards. He slammed on the floor, breath exploding from his lungs. He lost his grip on the baton. He heard a grunt, and then a hard fist landed on his face, thrusting his head to the left. Pain mushroomed like a red fireball in his brain, nausea rocked in his guts as he saw stars. He blinked, trying to get up, because he was dead meat as long as he on the floor. But the man above him had other ideas. Two large hands gripped his neck and started to squeeze. He heard the man grind his teeth, increasing the force on his neck.

Roy grabbed the man's wrists, but they were like iron prongs. His eyes bulged and he gagged as the pressure increased. He couldn't breathe, and the last remaining air in his lungs was fluttering to a fast death. He choked, then hit the man on the sides with his arms. It was no use. He reached upward and found his face. His nails scratched the nose, then he managed to dig one hand into an eye socket, and he pushed his finger in for all he was worth.

The man howled in pain, and the pressure on Roy's throat lessened. Roy bucked with his waist and the man lost his balance. His hand came off the man's face and he rolled over to the side. He was about to stand when he sensed the man coming at him again, arms flailing. Roy ducked, and he heard the distinct swish of something long and metallic over his head.

His baton.

Roy cursed, and rolled on his shoulder, getting to his feet swiftly. His eyes were used to the dark now, and, while he couldn't see properly, he could now make out the man's shape as he moved around.

The man rushed him again, coming from the right. Roy curled himself into a ball shape and rolled himself like a ten-pin bowl at the man's feet. He grabbed the man's legs just as the blow came down, hitting him in the upper back. Roy grunted with pain but didn't let go of the man's feet. The guy was obviously big, and he toppled over, crashing to the floor, making it shake. Roy twisted quickly, grabbing the man's waist, and slamming him down. He was trying to get hold of the hand that held the baton, and the man knew that. He rained down blows, and Roy heard the movement and tried to jerk his head away at the last second. He was only partially successful. The steel made contact with his skull with a harsh clang, and before he could move, it came down again. This time it landed with savage force on his forehead, and Roy felt nothing all of a sudden, only a blinding numbness as the world slipped on its axis.

And as he collapsed on the floorboards, Keith Burgess's face flashed before his eyes, yellow teeth, and crooked smile. He was mouthing something, and he heard it as his vision faded to black – I'm The Lily Man. You'll never catch me.

Even as the universe faded to black and blue, he felt rough hands grab his hair, and raise his head for the killer blow.

NO, a voice roared inside him, rising up from the pits of his consciousness like a tidal wave. His brother's face swam before his eyes, melting and changing, a little seven-year-old reaching out his frail hands over the anguish of decades, begging for help.

"NO!" Roy didn't know if the words came from his mouth, but he screamed out the sudden adrenaline that spiked in his blood, propelling himself forward. He didn't even know what he was hitting, but his big hands were bunched into fists of steel, punching, kicking, spitting, and kicking.

A force flooded his veins from nowhere, and, if he was going to die, he would go down fighting. The sudden turn took his attacker by surprise. Roy heard an angry curse, and then a muffled cry as his punches hit something soft. He heard something metallic clang on the floor, which he hoped was his baton. Roy didn't care, his arms were now around the man in a rugby tackle grip, and he used his legs to hurl himself forward. The man responded by slamming his fists, then his elbows on Roy's head and shoulders, punches that bounced off his head like bricks collapsing on them.

But the man couldn't stop Roy from pushing him backwards. They fell against something that cracked and splintered like glass, and then suddenly light exploded around them like a giant flashbulb.

Roy opened his eyes to find himself flying in the air, his arms still around the beasts' waist. Then he was falling, and both of them landed on a wet, hard surface with a blow that turned his spine into jelly. His eyes rocked, and he could see the grey cloud scudding the sky, trees waving in the breeze, and above him, the now demolished window they had just crashed through. He raised his head, and the world turned upside down, the sky inverting to the ground, and the black earth rising up to meet his face. His face hit something flat and wet, and then he didn't remember anything anymore.

CHAPTER 17

Voices. Incoherent and barely audible, but human voices. They grew louder, rushing past him like a train emerging from a tunnel. Roy winced, the black shroud over his senses contracting, then dilating, finally shrinking from the periphery. Where it shrank, shards of light emerged, pinpoint pustules of incandescence, and they grew brighter, like the voices that came and went. He heard his name being called, and sensed movement, like his head was rolling from side to side. He forced an eyelid opened, and the muscles obeyed. As soon as they opened, he screwed his eyes tightly shut, the light hurt.

"He's back," a male voice said. "Doesn't like the pen torch though."

"Why..." Roy croaked, "Why..." He couldn't say anything more, and shook his head, feeling lances of anguish burn through his skull. Okay, that was a bad idea. As little movement as possible, then. He opened his eyes fully. He was half upright on a bed, and the road in front of him was a mess of flashing blue lights and figures in police uniform. A hand rested on his shoulder, and he looked to his left to find Sarah's concerned eyes gazing at him.

"You alright, guv?"

"Me?" He croaked, then licked his dry lips. His throat felt like he'd run a marathon, then been deprived of water.

"Hang on." Sarah left his side, then returned swiftly. She had a plastic cup of water and held it to his lips, then helped him sit up straighter.

He drained the cup, and she got him another. He almost choked on the water but managed to keep it all down. A ginger haired female paramedic came over.

"You took quite a fall there," she said. "Lucky you didn't hit your head on the way down. You've got three stitches on the hairline anyway."

Roy felt his scalp and realised for the first time he had a bandage. He pressed on it and winced.

"I'd leave it alone if I were you," the paramedic said. "You also had a concussion. We're going to take you into hospital for a check-up."

Roy shook his head, and the pain sparked down his spine again. He grimaced, clamping his teeth together. "No way. I've got work to do." He looked around him, and was relieved to see Sarah walking back, Oliver and Rizwan flanking her.

"Where's the guy who tried to kill me?"

Sarah answered. "Keith Burgess? We think it's him anyway. He got away. The two of you must've crashed out through the back bedroom window. We found you on the roof of the kitchen extension, passed out. One of those kids who followed you confirmed Burgess by photo. It was him in there, but he escaped before we got to you. Sorry, guv."

"Look around. He can't be far. Someone had to see him."

"Uniforms are doing a door to door, guv."

Roy cradled his forehead in his hand. "I had him. Right here. Can't believe he escaped."

"You did your best," Sarah said sympathetically.

"Not good enough," Roy growled, but tugged at the corner of his lips as he glanced at Sarah. He swung his legs down, and then stood, putting his arms out to steady his balance. He didn't fall down, that was a start. He sensed Rizwan and Sarah move to support him, but he waved them away.

"I wouldn't advise that," the paramedic said.

"Neither would I, if I was you," Roy said. "But I'm me, and that's the problem. I'll be alright," He flashed her a grin, feeling as far from alright as he ever had in his life.

The paramedic was having none of it. She was young, but she also knew her job. She stood in front of him. "Sir, I'm afraid I must insist. You took quite a fall there. If you get vomiting or excess drowsiness-

"Then I probably have a subdural hematoma and I need a Burr hole craniotomy to release the blood clot. Yes, I know. I'll come around then, ok?"

The paramedic's mouth was open, and she forgot to shut it. Roy shrugged. "I used to be a medic in the Army. Done some stitching in my life, too."

He walked past her, put his hands on his waist, and stared at the street. The morning air was fresh on his cheeks, and it was good to be alive. It was touch and go there, and he should've done better. He cursed himself for going in without back up. For not sending a unit into the garden. That's where he escaped through.

Burgess had to be a tough nut to fall like that and still make an escape. He looked at the house, which now had a ring of policemen around the front door. A white forensic van had arrived, and he saw a white coated Michelin man go inside. At least forensics, or scene of crime, would get some evidence. Roy couldn't wait to see what Burgess had been up to these last few years.

He started walking towards the house in slow, unsteady steps. Sarah fell in line next to him. He could feel her eyes on him. "You took a fair battering in there. Sure you're ok?"

"You should see the other guy," he smirked, and felt the cut on his lip. He caught the look in her eyes. Concern, mixed with something else he couldn't place.

"It's just the way you went in there. Not my place to tell you to be careful but–"

"I appreciate it." He raised his eyebrows in what he hoped was a meaningful expression and smiled. He also needed to change the subject.

"Now then, as they say around here. Have you been inside?"

Sarah squared her dainty shoulders. Her eyes flashed and her lips thinned in a look of disgust. "Yes. Not worth seeing again, but I'll come with you."

He nodded, then crossed the flimsy iron gate and walked up to the battered door. The uniformed constable on duty touched his cap and moved to one side. Markers were laid on the floorboards where they could step. A couple of forensic officers were taking samples from the kitchen. Roy went upstairs, wincing as his knees flexed. His entire body seemed to have been through an assault course from his basic training days.

Another forensic officer was shuffling around in the bathroom. Roy stopped on the landing and called out to him.

"Any toothbrush or shaving gear?"

The woman lowered her mask. She was tall, and with her white Tyvek hooded coat, he'd mistaken her for a bloke.

"Yes. Got them both. He definitely lived here. No women's stuff around though. He lived alone."

Roy nodded. Sarah spoke behind him. "But he wasn't alone though, was he? Duncan Reid's sister's his girlfriend."

"Allegedly. We don't know what state their relationship is in."

"Can't be that bad if he's visiting her brother's house. She's introduced him to her family."

"True."

He walked past the other two bedrooms and stopped in front of the last one. The door was open and two bright halogen lamps lit up the room. One of the two windows at the rear was broken. Broken glass was removed from the corner, and the flimsy panels were removed. Light poured in through the opening. This was the hole he'd fallen through. Roy moved up to it and looked below. The flat kitchen roof wasn't that far down. Shards of glass and bits of wood littered the roof.

He stepped back and looked at the windows again. How had he not seen even a glimmer of light when he walked in here? He turned, and the answer lay huddled in one corner.

A black drape, large enough to cover an entire room. A blackout drape, like the ones used in film studios. One forensic guy was kneeling by the opposite wall. Roy's breath caught in his chest as he saw the two camera tripods in one corner, and the white screen that was now on the floor, torn down.

This was a studio. Burgess took photos here…. and he shuddered to think of what, or whom. Underage children, like the neighbour's son he had picked up from school?

Nausea curdled in Roy's guts. He exhaled, then forced himself to look around the rest of the room. More lights on stands, standard studio equipment littered the corners of the room.

Something about the place gave Roy the creeps. Despite the morning air filtering into the room, there was an odour of stale sweat, musty and old, clinging to the walls. He went out into the landing, and into the next bedroom. There was a mattress on the floor, and a sleeping bag over it. The carpet was thin with gaping holes in it. There was a wardrobe in one corner, and Sarah opened it. Some clothes were folded, surprisingly neatly in one corner, and a couple of shoes were also present.

"Those will be good for DNA and boot prints." Sarah said, as she squatted, and lifted one shoe with a gloved hand. "I wonder if it will match the boot print from the crime scene."

"HOLMES showed nothing, and the forensic boot print database also returned zip," Roy said. "But bag it all. We might've missed something."

He snapped his gloves on, then lifted a corner of the sleeping bag. A half empty pizza box lay under it. He removed it and lifted the bag further, crinkling his nose at the dense smell under it. Then his eyes lit up. A laptop. It was slim and silver coloured, and he wasted no time in grabbing it.

"Bingo," he showed it to Sarah. She took out a larger specimen bag from her pocket and Roy inserted the laptop in it carefully. Sarah took it next door to the forensic guys. Roy entered the first, and last bedroom, next to the bathroom. It was completely barren, only dust and cobwebs gathering on the corners. Wallpaper peeled off, and his boots raised small puffs of dust.

"I think we're done here," he said, and checked his watch. It was half past ten. It had been an eventful morning, but the clock was ticking. He needed to grab Burgess before he got far.

"Let's head back to base. I want the whole neighbourhood under lockdown. Stop and search every car, every person in and out of this street, and two on either side. We engage as many uniformed units as needed. I'll call in help from Sheffield south and central."

Roy knew Attercliffe was in Sheffield north and east, a different zone, but still under the same South Yorkshire Police.

"I'll start making calls on the way back," he said, marching to the stairs, Sarah following.

CHAPTER 18

Roy spoke on the phone while Sarah drove. He was speaking to Oliver, who was at the Reid residence.

"Yes, bring them both in. Duncan Reid and his sister, Fiona. Leave Amanda at home, as long as she's not alone. Percival's there with her?"

"Yes," Oliver replied.

"And get an interview room ready, and ask them if they want a lawyer, in which case inform the duty solicitor. I don't want any delays."

Roy hung up, then called switchboard. Sarah took a corner fast and his head banged against the windowpane. He winced in pain, just as the operator answered.

"Sorry," Sarah said.

Roy nodded and spoke to the operator. "DCI Roy speaking. I want an All-Points Bulletin for a Keith Burgess." He read the date of birth, address from the piece of paper on his lap, which was a printout from the office laptop.

"Are you authorising?" the operator asked.

"Yes, and so will the chief constable, so please put the APB out. Further details to follow."

Sarah was pulling into the car park when Roy got through to the Media Liaison Team. He spoke on the phone as he hurried after Sarah.

"I want posters of Burgess everywhere during the press conference. Alert the media please. Give them what they want about him. Inform Crimestoppers, call the news editors, pull the stops out. Got it?"

The MLO chatted to Roy for a while, while he marched down the green lino floored corridor, and followed Sarah into the canteen. She ordered a coffee and a yogurt fruit concoction that looked far too healthy for him. He didn't have an appetite but accepted the coffee with a murmur of thanks.

Rizwan was sitting at his desk, absorbed in his laptop. He looked up as Sarah and Roy approached.

"I'm digging into Burgess's assets with the financial team," he said, then licked his lips. He stared at Roy with a somewhat reverential look in his eyes. "You okay, guv?"

"Never felt better, but we need to catch this fucker before he gets any further. What have you found so far?"

"He's got the house that you visited, but he also owns two garages in Hillsborough, which isn't far. A uniform team have broken into the garages. It's full of old junk, nothing too exciting so far, but they're still going through it."

"Good work. Get hold of the prison warden's report when he was discharged from HMP Strickland. I want to know who visited him when he was an inmate, and what he got up to."

Sarah was on the phone, and she hung up as Roy sat down wearily at what had become his desk, an empty table with a phone and desktop computer, next to Sarah's.

"Oliver just gave an update. He's coming in with Fiona. Duncan's at work, a squad car's been dispatched to collect. He's the manager of a builder's warehouse in town."

Roy rang switchboard and asked for the number of the Traffic department. "DCI Roy speaking. Can I please have the CCTV footage from Burgess address in Attercliffe." Rizwan handed him a file with all the details, including the reg number of Burgess's car. "I want that car traced, over the last two weeks. I want to see where it went, what it did. There's an APB out on him already, so see if you can trace him now."

"His car is not on his street," the man on the other end replied. Roy knew he was probably checking the tv screens arranged along the wall in front of him. "We noted the APB already. We're trying to see if we can get hold of the car with ANPR."

Roy thanked the man on the line and hung up.

"He drove off then," Roy told Sarah and Rizwan. "That's funny. How did he have time to come round the front, risk discovery, and drive off in his car? I think he ditched his car before. He was expecting the heat."

Sarah said, "He was, but you still managed to surprise him. I don't think he was ready. Hence the studio gear was still there, as well as his laptop. He was still living there."

"CCTV should tell us what he did with his car," Rizwan said. "I'll check up with traffic."

Sarah raised the evidence bag and took out the laptop. She handled it carefully, with gloved hands. Before opening it, she glanced at Roy. He knew what was on her mind.

"Let's get prints and swabs done first," he said. "Then we can have a look inside."

Sarah slid the laptop back inside the evidence bag. Rizwan stood. "I'll take it, Skip."

"Good lad." Sarah handed the pack to Rizwan. Roy watched him walk with purpose towards the corridor. Forensics was two doors down.

"Nice to hear you lot call a sergeant Skipper. Same down south."

"Not much difference, you'll find," Sarah said with a straight face. "Sheffield might be smaller, but believe me, we have our fair share of nutters up here."

Roy leaned back in his chair. "I believe you. Any news from the uniforms doing door to door in Attercliffe?"

Sarah checked her radio and phone. "Last update was ten minutes ago. Nothing as yet."

"Where could he have gone? Someone might be hiding him. They know we don't exactly have the manpower to search every house, and even if we could it might well cause a riot."

"Especially in Attercliffe. There have been riots there before."

Roy closed his eyes. It helped his headache. "Did Fiona know about Burgess? I'm assuming she didn't, because who wants to go out with armed robber and child molester?"

"Takes all sorts, don' it?" Sarah made a face. "But I get your point."

Roy's phone beeped and he glanced at it and his face brightened. "Fiona's arrived. Duty solicitor's been briefed. Shall we head down?"

CHAPTER 19

Twenty-seven years ago

Robin Roy woke up, shivering cold as usual. A thin noose of light slanted in through the basement window. The noose curled around the darkness, lifting it to show a sorry sight, the two boys, huddled together on a single bed. The basement was always cold, and the duvet the man gave them wasn't fit for winter.

Robin and Jack had become friends. They didn't know how long their nightmare would last, or if they would ever see their families again. When they asked the man, he slapped them.

Jack was still asleep. He was a year younger than Robin's eight years, and smaller. Robin stiffened as he heard the basement door creak open. Then he heard the man come down the stairs. He curled himself up into a tighter ball, terrified. He could sense the man was now standing by the bed.

"Have you been to the toilet?" he asked. The toilet was a hole in the ground in one corner of the basement. It was covered with a wooden slab, and there was a tap next to it. The smell was awful most days, and Robin tried to keep as far from it as possible.

He nodded in silence. The man looked at Jack who didn't wake up. Then he put the bowl he was carrying, on the ground. It looked like porridge, with a spoon in it.

"Eat," he said. Robin was too scared to move. The man came around the side, and Robin shrank away. He had touched Robin already, and it was awful, disgusting. Robin didn't know what to do, apart from obeying. This time, the man didn't reach for Robin, but put his hand over Jack's head. Then he shook Jack till he woke up. Jack screamed when he saw the man and shrank back against Robin. The boys held each other, shaking with fear.

"Come with me," the man told Jack. The boy gaped at him, his skeleton shoulders and ribs heaving with fast, jerky breaths. He shook his head, eyes like saucers. Robin had an arm around him, holding him close.

"Come on," the man beckoned, one hand resting on the bed. When Jack didn't move, the man reached out. Jack screamed and twisted, and Robin held on to him, but the man was too strong. He wrestled Jack off the bed, then put him on the ground. He slapped the boy around the head twice.

"Stop it, or you'll get hit even worse," the man bellowed. Jack seemed to understand, and went limp on the floor, but still bundled up into a tight ball. The man carried him upstairs. Robin heard the door shut, and only then did he let out his pent-up breath. Tears spilled out of his eyes. How long would he have to live like this? Why couldn't his parents and brother, Rohan, find him?

He got up and forced himself to eat the porridge. The man often forgot to give them lunch. Robin thought he went to work in the day and came back in the evening. He got up and paced around the room, then went back to bed. He had nothing to do, so he went up the stairs slowly. He braced himself for the man to appear any minute. Heart thudding against his chest, he got to the top step, then put his ear against the door. He could hear some sounds, but they were faint. Then he heard it again, and it was Jack, crying out. Robin sat down on the step and held his head. He wanted to help Jack, but there was no way.

He put his eye to the keyhole. He could see a hallway, its wall made of rotting wood, with gaping holes. The floor was bare boards. Wind whistled above his head, finding its way through the gaps in the woodwork. Jack shivered. He tried the handle, but the door was firmly locked. He pulled at it, but the door was heavy, and it wouldn't budge.

He tiptoed downstairs and curled up on the bed. His hands and toes were like icicles. He pulled the duvet around him, and useless tears spilled out from his eyes.

*****

Robin didn't know how long he had slept for. He woke with a start, disturbed by the noise from upstairs. There was a clanging sound, followed by heavy footsteps, and then doors opening, and slamming shut. It was evening, and the light had gone from the skylight. Robin felt for Jack and found nothing. He was alone in the bed. He got up and felt along the wall near the staircase till he found the light switch. The single yellow bulb showed the bare bed, and nothing else.

Then Robin heard the door open. He ran back to the bed, terrified. He wanted to hide underneath it, but the ground was ice cold. The man came down the stairs slowly. Robin cowered under the sheets. He could feel the man as he stood next to the bed.

"Get up."

Robin knew better than to lay there. He obeyed. He stood and put his shoes on. The man pushed him towards the stairs. Robin climbed, head bent. He wanted to ask where Jack was, but he knew better. A horrible dread was curdling in his guts, and he felt sick. For once, the lights were on in the corridor. The man pushed him towards the room where he had stabbed Mathew. Robin stopped, fear paralysing his feet, chest heaving. He shook his head when the man pushed him again.

He expected to be hit, but the man stepped past him and opened the door. Through it, Robin saw a ghoulish sight. Two floor uplighters were focused on Jack. He was tied to the chair, which was on a platform, and the whole ensemble made it look like the boy was on a throne. Jack was gagged so he couldn't scream. His head hung over his chest. The rest of the room lay in darkness, and Robin heard the whirring of the generator.

The man reached out a long arm and pulled Robin inside. Robin shook with fear, and struggled against the man, but it was useless. The room was cold, the howl of the wind loud in his ears.

He shivered as the man made him stand in front of Jack. The boy lifted his head, and his eyes widened when he saw Robin. He wriggled and tried to speak, but only muffled squeaks emerged from his throat. The man held out a knife.

"Take it," he said to Robin. Robin shook his head, stepping backwards. That earned him a stinging slap across the cheeks, and he cried out. "I said take it," the man shouted. "Or you're next."

Death was a better option than going through this again. Robin wept and sank to his knees. The man grabbed him by the collar and lifted him clean off the ground.

"Jack didn't want to play with me," the man whispered. He got something out of his pocket. He held it in front of Robin's face. Robin startled and moved away, but then he saw it was a flower. A white lily. He knew these flowers. His mother grew them in the summer.

The man rubbed the lily against Robin's face. It was strange, the sweet smell of the lily mingling with the stench of urine and blood.

"There you go. I knew you'd like it. You're pretty, just like the lily." The man made Robin hold the flower. "But he," the man screamed suddenly. "He wouldn't play. He doesn't like the lilies." He pointed at Jack, his face bulging with blood, eyes firing up red like a demon's. He went up to the chair and slapped Jack. The boy's head slammed to the right.

"Bad boy," the man screamed. Robin cowered in terror. The man leaned over him. He held out the knife. "Get rid of him. Then you can go free." He whispered, coming forward. "You like lilies, don't you? Kill the boy, and I'll let you go."

The words hit home. He didn't know what to do, but he knew he wanted to get out of here. Gulping, he grabbed hold of the knife. He stood, shaking like a leaf. Jack's head was lolling over his chest again. Robin held the knife over him, then brought it down on the boy's arm. Jack jerked upright, his eyes bulging with pain. Robin stared in shock at the blood spilling from the arm. He dropped the knife and stumbled, then fell on the floor.

"Get up," the man bellowed. "Pick up the knife."

Robin's face was a mess of tears and mucus from his nose. He was numb with terror, unable to draw a single breath into his lungs. He turned and tried to run, but the man grabbed him. He hit Robin a few times, till Robin collapsed on the floor. Then Robin heard the sickening sound of the knife stabbing Jack again and again.

When he finally looked up, he saw blood pouring out of Jack's neck and chest, flooding the chair. The man stood next to chair, the knife in his hand, dripping with blood. Robin screamed in fear and anguish, and hugged his knees, burying his face between them.

CHAPTER 20

Fiona Reid was looking decidedly pale. Her sallow cheeks seemed thinner, and she looked up with sightless, vacant eyes when Roy and Sarah walked in. The duty solicitor seemed fresh out of law school, with a thin line of bumfluff moustache on his upper lip, and a wide eyed, rabbit in the headlight stare. Roy almost felt sorry for him.

Sarah spoke for the machine, identifying everyone. Roy made himself comfortable, as much as he could with his head throbbing and body aching, on a stiff wooden chair whose legs were screwed to the floor. The steel top table reflected the recessed spotlights from the ceiling. Sarah got up and went to the water cooler in the corner and put two plastic cups of water on the table. Roy drank from one and thanked her. He smiled at Fiona, who looked like she was awaiting a death sentence.

"This morning, Keith Burgess assaulted a police officer and then escaped. He has a criminal record for armed robbery, and for kidnapping and sexually molesting a child. Did you know about that?"

Fiona had gone from pale to grey, and she swallowed with a grimace, like she was feeling nauseous. She placed a hand on her chest and closed her eyes for a few seconds. "No, I did not. He never…" Her words trailed off. "My god. I can't believe it." She clutched her forehead.

"So, you've never been to his house?"

Fiona looked confused. "Yes, I have. The one near Nether Edge, you mean? That's where he lives."

Roy and Sarah exchanged a glance. "Do you have the address?"

"Yes, I do. I drove there a few times." She provided the address, and Sarah wrote it down, then excused herself so she could send it to Rizwan and Oliver upstairs. Roy wanted to go, but it would have to be a search the two DCs upstairs to handle. He spoke on the machine, noting Sarah's absence.

"How long have you been seeing Mr Burgess?" Roy asked.

"Almost a year. I live in Sheffield as well, in Brightside, not far from Meadowhall. I met Keith at a bar there. He's a mechanic with his own garage. I've seen where he works. Well, he owns the business. That's why I can't believe any of this. Are you sure you've got the right person?"

Roy pointed at the stitches on his forehead, and the blue-black bruises down the left side of his face. "Well, these seem to suggest we did. It's possible the Keith Burgess," Roy raised both hands to make quote marks, "you knew, is very different to the real Keith Burgess. Can you please describe him to me? I want to know his height, girth, hair colour, eye colour and any visible distinguishing marks."

Roy had the description in front of him, he knew it by heart. Fiona said, "He's a big bloke. About your height, I'd say, if not a touch taller. He's not fat, but he's big boned. His hair is blonde, and he's got blue grey eyes." She thought for a while. "He's not got any moles or such on his face. He does have some lines on his cheeks, but most men his age do."

That was almost exactly the description on Burgess's online file. Roy let go of the pent-up breath that was building on his chest. The slim chance that the man who assaulted him was not Burgess was now almost impossible. His attacked in that house was as big as him, easily. No wonder they both crashed through that window.

He nodded, keeping his face impassive. "When did you last see Burgess?"

"Last night. We met up for dinner. He had an early morning, so had to get to bed early. We don't live with each other as yet. He drove me back to my place."

"What car did he drive?"

"A Vauxhall Corsa. Black coloured. I can only remember part of the reg number. It's new, from 2022."

Roy nodded. All of this was coming together. That was the car they were looking for.

"What about the day before? Did you see him that day? That was when Johnny disappeared."

Fiona frowned, thinking. Then she stared at Roy, suddenly realising the portent of his question. "I… I didn't see him in the morning. I heard that he had gone round to give Duncan a hand with painting the rooms, like. I was working till about six pm, got home around six thirty. I called and texted him, and he called me back later in the evening. Said he was tired and going to bed." Her hand went to her mouth as her eyes widened. "Oh god, you don't think… he took Johnny?"

"It's a strong possibility. He knew Johnny, and Duncan told him where he was going for a walk."

Sarah came back into the room. Roy stopped the recording and started again, informing the machine that Sarah had returned.

"We need to piece together Burgess's movements the day Johnny vanished. In the morning, he was at the family home. He met Johnny as well, and, from what his parents said, he was friends with the boy. Used to play football with him in the garden."

Fiona was now turning a shade of lime green and looked like she might vomit any time. "He told me he likes children." She held her forehead and her neck bent forward. "I feel sick."

Sarah whispered in Roy's ears. "Rizwan and Oliver have gone to the address in Nether Edge. No uniformed units are free, so they went on their own. I told them not to take any risks."

Roy nodded. He was glad the two DCs were together. But a knot of worry tightened in his mind. He didn't want them to come to any harm, and he should be there with them.

However, Fiona knew Burgess the best of anyone currently, and he needed to get more out of her. He gave her a few minutes to compose herself.

"Did you ever meet his folks? Or his friends?"

"His folks are up in Scotland, or that's what he told me. I've met a couple of his friends, down at the pub. I've been round for dinner with them at his house. He wasn't a loner, if that's what you mean."

Roy nodded. He was getting a picture of Burgess. Like many child abductors, he was normal and easy going, with friends in the community. He tried to control the shiver that coursed through his spine and failed. The real monsters hid in daylight, they slid between the raindrops, smiling and waving at you. That's why it was so hard to catch the bastards.

"We need the details of these friends, if you have them. Or at least their names, and description."

Fiona nodded. Sarah took over placing her elbows on the desk and grabbing Fiona's attention. "How well did Duncan Reid, your brother, know Burgess?"

"We met for a family dinner at Duncan's house, and they became friends after that. Keith fixed Duncan's car and helped him with some housework."

Worming his way into the family, his eyes on little Johnny. A bolt of white-hot rage seared through Roy's soul. His jaws clamped tight.

"As far as you know, did Keith always live around here? Has he ever worked, or lived, down south?"

Fiona shrugged. "He didn't really talk much about his past life. Yes, he's from around here, Rotherham to be precise. He told me he was born there. His family moved to Edinburgh when he was eighteen or something, but he stayed here."

Roy mulled it all over. Burgess didn't have an alibi for the day or evening when Johnny went missing. That was critical.

"We need the phone number you have for him. Please don't leave the city. We need you to be at home in case we need to speak to you again."

CHAPTER 21

"Duncan Reid?" the man with a double chin wiped the tendril of ketchup sliding down his mouth. A chunky bap of bacon rested on the wrapper in his hand. His abdominal girth suggested he enjoyed his food, and he didn't look happy about being disturbed.

"Yes," Rizwan said patiently. "He's the warehouse manager and you're his foreman, right?"

"I am, yes." The man chewed noisily and then swallowed, his Adam's apple barely visible in the rolls of neck fat.

"Listen mate," Rizwan leaned in, bringing his face closer to the man, whose name badge said Tony Biggins, in keeping with his bulky frame. "Duncan's little boy's gone missing, and we need to get him back. So how about you make an effort to find him, right?"

Tony took a swig of water and glared at Rizwan. Then he got to his feet slowly. "It's his lunchtime, and he's probably in his office. Follow me."

Rizwan glanced at his watch. It was getting close to half eleven. Precious minutes were slipping by. Oliver was on his way back to the nick, both of them having checked Burgess's house in Nether Edge. They found little of interest, not even a laptop. Burgess had clothes and suitcases there, and he clearly lived there, which meant he treated the place in Attercliffe as his evil lair.

They had also found the house in Nether Edge was rented under a false name, which is why it had not shown up as one of Burgess's assets.

Rizwan went up a steel staircase, following Biggins' ponderous bulk as it barely fit in the narrow rise up to the first-floor perimeter that wrapped around the warehouse. Biggins huffed and puffed and waddled his way to a glass fronted office that had a 360-degree view of the floor downstairs, but whose curtains were now drawn, not allowing easy visibility inside.

Biggins tried the door handle and it opened. Rizwan peeked in sideways. The office had a table in the middle, overflowing with files. There was a steel cabinet next to it, and some shelves. But no human being. Duncan's name was attached to the front door, so it definitely was his office.

"Like I said," grumbled Biggins, his face red and sweaty, "he's on his lunch break."

"Where would he be, if not in his office?"

"You could try the café outside."

Rizwan had called Duncan to make sure he was in his office, which Duncan had assured was the case. A little worry unfurled in Rizwan's mind. He went down the stairs and went outside. He had seen the café on his way in, it was outside the iron fence that ringed the warehouse complex. This was an industrial estate, and many of the workers used this solitary café, so it was quite packed.

Rizwan walked around, drawing a few curious looks from the punters, who were all workers. He went to the counter and gave Reid's description to the girl at reception. She shrugged and denied knowledge, then indicated the busy dining room. Rizwan thanked her.

He strode out and called Duncan again. He didn't answer. On a hunch, Rizwan walked round the cark park. He knew Duncan drove a green Ford Focus. He went around the corner, to the back where there was on overflow car park. His eyes were drawn to a figure taking something out of his car. It was Duncan. Rizwan ran towards him.

Duncan heard him and turned. He saw Rizwan and his face turned ashen. He held a pair of boots in his hand.

"I was looking for you. My name is DC Rizwan." He showed Duncan his warrant card. "I called you."

Duncan nodded. Before replying, he shoved the boots back in the car's trunk and locked the car. "Shall we go back to my office?"

Rizwan stared at him, not sure why a sense of unease lay over his skin like nettles. Duncan was fidgeting. His hands went inside his pockets, then came out and he rubbed them on his thighs. He tried a smile, but it was wiped off when he saw the look on Rizwan's face.

"Actually, we haven't taken samples from your car. The abductor obviously left the note on your car's windscreen wiper. Do you mind if I take a look around?"

Duncan looked at the car, then at Rizwan. He shrugged. "Sure. Why not?"

Rizwan glanced inside the Ford Focus. He out on his gloves and took out the swabs and evidence bags. There wasn't much to do, as fingerprints had already been taken from the wiper and come back negative. Rizwan's curiosity was piqued by Duncan's attitude. Why was Duncan here, when he had promised Rizwan, he would be in the office?

Rizwan made a show of taking swabs from the windscreen. He broke off the cap of the swab stick and inserted it into its sterile holder, then placed the stick inside the evidence bag.

"Are the doors open?"

"Yes," Duncan said, watching him closely.

"Was Johnny sat in the back?"

"Yes. On the passenger side."

Rizwan opened the rear doors, while Duncan stood opposite on the driver's side. The seats were clean, and a few crumbs of food lay on the floor. Rizwan knelt and looked under front seats.

"Can I have a look at the boot?" He asked when done.

"There's nothing in the boot, really," Duncan shrugged. "Johnny never went in there." He smiled sadly.

"I know," Rizwan nodded. "Just for the sake of completion."

Somewhat reluctantly, Duncan opened the boot. There was a golf bag in there, stuffed at the back. An anorak lay over it. Rizwan's eyes were drawn to the pair of shoes in the right corner. Duncan was holding them just now. They were large, size eleven, if he had to guess. Larger than Duncan's feet size, Rizwan guessed. Duncan was under six feet. Rizwan was five ten, and Duncan was the same height as him.

"Those your shoes?" Rizwan pointed.

Duncan nodded. "Yes. I use them for fell walking, with roll up, double layer socks, hence they're a size bigger."

"I see." Rizwan couldn't help thinking about the boot prints at the crime scene, next to Johnny's. These shoes looked the right size.

"Do you mind if I take a look at them?"

"Sure, go ahead."

Rizwan picked up the boots in his gloved hand and turned them over. They were mountain walking boots, he knew because his girlfriends' parents were ramblers, and he had been on a couple of treks with the family.

The boots in his hands were made by a well-known brand and had barely been worn. On the sole, he found small stones and rubble. Duncan had walked in these, but not much. Rizwan knew he was being obsessive, but he couldn't shake the discomfort niggling in his mind.

"Can I take these shoes, if you don't mind? I just want to exclude everything you see. Helps us to focus the investigation on the right track."

Duncan's face was a blank as a wall. "Sure, go ahead."

Rizwan smiled. "Thank you." He put each shoe in a separate evidence bag. "Now, shall we head back to your office?"

Duncan nodded and locked the car. They walked next to each other, Rizwan carrying the evidence bag. He stopped by his Honda Civic to put the bags in. Then he followed Duncan inside the warehouse. Tony Biggins was still sat outside, and still eating what seemed to be a new sandwich. He waved at them, and Rizwan waved back.

Once they were in the office, Rizwan pulled up a chair opposite Duncan, sat at his desk.

"You know about what happened this morning at Keith Burgess house in Attercliffe?"

Duncan swallowed, looking aghast. "Yes, Amanda told me. I'm so shocked. Are you sure this was Keith?"

"He was living in that house, according to the neighbours. Yes, it was him. We are going through CCTV evidence now to see if we can monitor his whereabouts over the last couple of days. Did you know that Keith was on the child sex offenders list?"

Duncan's head lowered, and he remained like that for a while. "Yes, I just heard. I can't believe it."

"It's not your fault. You didn't know who you were letting into your house. He tricked your sister, Fiona as well, it seems. The house she's been to was one he was renting under a false name. Men like Burgess often have double identities."

Duncan shook his head, then blew out his cheeks. Rizwan said, "Burgess was at your house the morning of the abduction, day before yesterday. He was helping you to decorate one of the bedrooms upstairs. Is that correct?"

"Yes. He also played football with Johnny and me in the garden, when we took a break."

"Can you remember any occasion when Burgess was alone with Johnny?"

"Oh god." Duncan placed his forehead in his right-hand palm and leaned forward. "I can't remember specifically. Unlikely, I'd say, as Johnny was either at school, or with Amanda at home."

Rizwan recalled what Emily Percival, the FLO had mentioned about the arguments.

"So, as far as you know, every time Johnny saw Burgess, there was another adult present?"

"Us, yes. I mean my wife and me."

"Good. If you don't mind me asking, how are things between you and your wife?"

Duncan frowned. "What do you mean?"

Rizwan leaned forward slightly and spread his hands. "Every relationship has its ups and downs. This is just a general question, and it doesn't have anything to do with the case." He waited, looking at Duncan with purpose.

Duncan took a deep breath. "It's all fine. My wife and I are very happy together."

Rizwan nodded, although he was far from convinced. "How well did you know Mr Burgess?"

"Clearly, not very well. Makes me sick, to be honest. I hope you catch him soon."

"Did you ever visit his home in Nether Edge?"

"No. He came to ours though, and we met him in the pub with Fiona, a couple of times. By we I mean Amanda and myself. We were friends. He seemed like a good sort. Ran his own car mechanic business."

"Did you ever see him on your own? I mean, you two were friends, obviously."

"He was more of a family friend as opposed to my mate, if you know what I mean. He was Fi's boyfriend, and that's all we knew him as."

"Do you have any idea where he might be now?"

"Sorry, no."

CHAPTER 22

Sarah and Roy were on their way to the garage that Burgess owned. The dashboard radio squawked; Sarah's channel was linked to it.

"Units one and two on their way. Do you copy?"

Sarah answered. "Copy that. ETA?"

"Five minutes."

"Thank you."

"At least we have backup this time." She glanced meaningfully at Roy, who couldn't help but agree. He'd been stupid to go after Burgess on his own, but he had little choice.

She pulled up next to a long garage, with four cars parked in the forecourt. A mechanic in blue overalls watched them, wiping his hands on a dirty rag. Sarah got out and followed Roy as he approached the mechanic.

Inside, three cars were on hydraulic lifts inside, a few mechanics tinkering under the chassis. A number of tyres were stacked in every corner of the interior, and the floor was dark, like it had old blood spilt all over it. That familiar stuffy smell of old car engines and diesel fumes hit Roy's nostrils. He stopped in front of the mechanic who was eyeing them warily. He showed his warrant card.

"DCI Roy from South Yorkshire Police. We need to speak to Keith Burgess?"

The mechanic looked at the warrant card, then behind him. One of the mechanics inside had stopped working and were staring at them. "I don't know where he is."

Roy had taken a closer look inside. There were mechanics working on each of the three cars. He counted four in total.

There was an office in the far corner, lights on but blinds drawn. Would Burgess be stupid enough to be in there? He doubted it. But he did notice the office might open into the back. There was no way of making sure from here.

A siren wailed behind them, getting louder, then suddenly cutting out. A squad car pulled up, and Sarah went to meet them. All the mechanics had now stopped working. Roy didn't look behind; his eyes were focused on the garage. A couple of the mechanics stepped out into the sunshine, blinking. But one man stayed in the shadows behind the hulk of a stripped-out car and ran into the office.

"Hey, you," Roy shouted, and ran after him. The office had a small, prefabricated façade. Roy clutched the doorknob and turned. The door was locked. He rattled the handle and shouted for entry. There was no response. He leant against the door with his left shoulder, and the door bent, but it didn't give way. He leaned harder, and felt the corners start to buckle and splinter. He took two steps back and gave it a firm kick, and the lock disintegrated, flinging the door open.

The room was a mess. Papers were strewn all over the floor, and the desk drawers were open. The window next to the desk was open, and through it, Roy glimpsed a man running, the same man he'd seen going into the office. He wore dark blue mechanic's overalls. Roy didn't waste time. He slid over the desktop, scattering more paperwork to the floor, and put his hands on the window ledge. He jumped out, not aware there was a slight drop to ground level. He landed awkwardly, rolling his ankle, and fell. He got up, pain lancing up his foot. The mechanic was several yards ahead now. Roy ran after him, but his left ankle was giving him trouble. Two uniform officers streaked out from a side street, just ahead of the mechanic. He skidded to a stop and turned around to see Roy.

"Stop now," Roy shouted. "There's no escape."

The man didn't listen. They were in an alley, and the wall to their right was shoulder height. Over it lay the side entrance of a semi-detached house. The man jumped on the brick wall, his hands scrambling for the top. Roy got there before the uniforms did. He grabbed the man's waist, and the man kicked back, trying to get his knee into Roy's face. The uniforms caught up with them, and they pulled the man down. Once the mechanic was on his front, face down, one of the uniforms handcuffed him.

Roy put his gloves on and frisked the man's pockets. The large overall pockets were bulging. He pulled out two large plastic bags, each with what looked like white bricks in them. Roy whistled. He tore into one of the bags with the Swiss army knife he kept attached to his waist.

He tasted the white powder on the tip of the knife blade. Then he grimaced.

"These are one kilo bricks of cocaine. You got a wholesale supplier, right?" He put his face close to the man, who was still lying face down. "Or does your boss, Mr Burgess, get them for you?"

The man said nothing. The uniforms sat him against the wall. Sarah joined them, speaking into her radio. Roy crouched on the ground next to the man.

"We want Burgess, not you," he said softly. The mechanic was young, no more than his mid-twenties. He was chunky at the shoulders, with thick biceps. Tattoos covered his arms. He had a ring on his left wedding finger. He glanced at Roy. "You got mouths to feed. A spell inside won't be good for you. You need to make this deal, don't you?" Roy pointed at the four bags. The man followed his gaze. "Burgess is wanted for taking a little boy. He's done it before. We will find him, and put him in. You know what happens to kiddy fiddlers in prison?"

The man swallowed, his eyes wide. He stared at Roy, who held his gaze.

"Didn't know that about Burgess, did you? Well, he's a dirty bastard. And he's going in for a long time. Now," Roy leaned forward. "I don't know you well, but I don't think you want to end up like him. Inmates will know you're his man. Once they know, what do you think will happen?"

The man licked his lips, sweat pouring down his face. He looked at his shoes.

"What's your name?"

"Simon Jenkins."

"Well, Simon, you're going in for a while, I'm afraid. And inside, they'll know you're best mates with a kiddy fiddler like Burgess. They'll come after you." Simon breathed fast and heavy, eyes wide as he stared straight ahead. Roy whispered in his ears. "Tell us where Burgess is, Simon. You'll go down for this crap, I can't help that. But I can put in a good word for you and believe me, that's going to make big difference. You get a lighter sentence and get out early with parole. Get back to your family. You help us, we help you. Or you take the fall for Burgess, and we grab him sooner or later anyway, then you meet up with him inside. Friends with the child molester. Both of you get shanked in the showers."

Roy leaned back, giving Simon space. The uniforms were too far to hear their conversation, but he could tell Sarah was listening. He stood and wiped the sweat off his forehead. His shirt was sticking to his back. When he glanced down at Simon, the man was still staring at his shoes.

"Alright then," Roy said to the two uniformed constables. "Take him in. Simon Jenkins, I'm arresting you on two charges. First is for possession and intention to distribute. The secondary charge is assisting a child abduction. You have the right to remain–"

"Hang on," Simon spluttered, his cheeks glowing crimson. The two constables had to restrain as he tried to get closer to Roy, who was walking away. "Hey, stop," Simon shouted.

Roy turned and raised an eyebrow. Simon huffed in silence for a few breaths. "Alright. I'll talk. Do we have a deal?"

"Yes," Roy walked back to him, trying to hide the limp in his left ankle. "Start talking. Where's Burgess?"

CHAPTER 23

Eight-year-old Eddie was fast on his bike. He eyed it now, looking through the widow of the kitchenette. He had just finished a bowl of cereal that his fourteen-year-old sister, Lucy prepared for him. Their mother was fast asleep, and he was glad that she was alone in her bed. He didn't like any of the men she brought home with her. They smoked and snored, and smelt funny in the morning.

Eddie really wanted to get on the bike. It was padlocked to the side of the caravan, next to Lucy's bigger bike. It was half nine, and, for some reason, both him and Lucy were up early. Lucy could sleep till midday sometimes during holidays, his mother said because she'd become a teenager. Eddie knew it wasn't, Lucy could laze around in bed for many years before she became thirteen. And what was this thing called a teenager anyway? Lucy was different now. She was quieter, but sometimes she became loud and had arguments with their mother.

The loo flushed and Lucy came out. She eyed the empty cereal bowl. "Do you want more?"

Eddie shook his head. "I want to go out on the bike. Come on."

Lucy was a head taller than Eddie. Her black curls framed her face, then fell past her shoulders. Lucy's last argument with mum was about cutting her hair short, like a boy's. Mum didn't like it, but Lucy did. Lucy liked a lot of new things, like the ring on her nose, which Eddie didn't like, and neither did mum. It made her look weird, and sometimes Eddie thought Lucy only did these things to look different. She had black nail polish and wore black clothes as well, which was just strange. But she was still his older sister, and she loved him, which was a relief. Eddie couldn't wait for Lucy to get past this "phase", as mum called it.

Lucy made a face. "It's too early. I can't be bothered."

"Can I go on my own then? Please?"

"No," Lucy said firmly.

"I won't go far. Promise."

Lucy's phone dinged, and she reached inside her pocket and pulled it out. A smile crept upon her lips, and her cheeks became redder as she read the message.

"Is that your boyfriend?" Eddie said, coming closer to have a look.

"Shut up," Lucy snatched her phone away, turning her back to Eddie. Her fingers moved as she sent a message back.

"Come on," Eddie whined. "I'll just go around the campsite. Please."

Lucy looked up from the screen, frowning. "I said no. Now go and play on your Nintendo or something."

"I want to go out."

Lucy didn't reply. She sat down and remained focused on her phone. Eddie went to the window of the sitting room and looked out. Some of the caravan doors had opened, but most were still shut. Woods ringed the Fox Hagg campsite, their tall green and brown branches stretching out to the horizon. There was a path down the side, that went out into the open greenery of Fox Hagg Nature Reserve.

Eddie saw a man standing at the edge of path, near the exit of the campsite. The man was medium height and dressed in dark jacket and jeans. He had seen that man before, at the same place. He had smiled at Eddie as he ran past. Now, Eddie thought the man was looking at their caravan. He didn't think much about it. He looked back at his sister, who was engrossed in her phone.

"I'm going to call mummy."

Lucy's head shot up. "No. Let her rest. She was back late last night."

Eddie screwed up his face. "Was not."

"Yes, she was. How do you know? You were in bed."

Lucy's eyes lost their glimmer, and she looked away. Eddie knew she didn't like their mum's boyfriends either.

"I know she's sleeping alone. She won't mind if I wake her up." Eddie went for the bedroom, but Lucy moved quickly and stood in front of him.

She bit her lower lip, and her nostril flared. "Why do you have to be so annoying?" She shoved the phone in her pocket. "Alright, come on. But not for long, ok? We have to come back when I say so."

"Yes!" Eddie had unlocked the door and he was down the steps as fast as he could. He waited impatiently for Lucy to come down with the padlock keys. She also had helmets, and fastened one on Eddie's head, scolding him to remain still as he fidgeted.

Eddie was on his bike soon after that, pedalling fast, ignoring the shouts of his sister. He slowed down and looked behind him before he left the exit. Lucy was catching up fast. As Eddie went out the gates of the camp site, he didn't see the man who had been standing there.

A dirt track led to the car park, and through it, another path led to the massive sprawl of the Nature Reserve. Eddie went up one of the main paths that sloped up gently. He heard Lucy call for him, and he stopped. Lucy wasn't that great at going up slopes, and he waited for her to catch up. Her face was red, and her forehead sweaty by the time she got to him.

"Go slow, okay?" She panted. "And stay in sight."

"Okay," Eddie said, and whirled off. The path went deeper into the woods. The trees were denser, standing close together like silent sentinels with bushy hair, watching Eddie as he cycled down the path. A breeze filtered through the branches overhead, and it sounded like a chorus of voices, whispering secrets.

The canopy overhead became thicker, obstructing the light. The path levelled out at the top, and the view from here was stunning. In the distance, Eddie could see the reservoir, with the stone path that circled it. He loved cycling there, watching the still waters below. There was also a big white house, nestled in the breast of the emerald woods. He wanted to explore that house, see what was inside, but mum and Lucy wouldn't let him.

Lucy was still coming up the slope, head bent over the bike handles, her face red. She saw him and shouted something, and he didn't hear it well, but knew he wanted her to stay there.

Fat chance. It was downhill from here, and Lucy would catch up easily. "Race ya," he called out to his sister. Then he raced ahead, eventually slowing as the path wound down a shallow slope. The woods flashed past him, the trees closer to the path now, the still air within their dark breast watching Eddie.

As he came to the ground level, Eddie saw a deer on the road ahead. He halted and watched the animal. It was a female deer, it didn't have antlers. The white spots on its tawny skin were like splotches of snow, and it's dark, shapely eyes were mesmerising. Eddie had never seen a deer this up close. His mouth opened as he drank in the view.

The deer turned its head to look at Eddie, then bolted down a path that led into the woods. Eddie didn't waste time. He took a hard left, following the animal. He knew deer wouldn't hurt anyone. They got scared if anything.

The brambles and thorns caught on his legs. He was wearing jeans, but it was still hard to pedal his bike. He gave up after a while and went forward on foot. Thick bushes and plants towered all over him. There was a hush here, not just the absence of sound, but something deeper, more primeval. Every footstep he made sounded like an intrusion into the kingdom of a green, earthly, silent kingdom. He heard a flickering in the undergrowth and flinched backward. An animal scurried through, and he couldn't see what it was.

Eddie stopped, his heart beating like a piston, his breath harsh in his ears. Suddenly, he was scared. He looked behind, but all he saw was the bushes, and the tall trees.

"Lucy?" he called out. Silence. "Lucy!" This time he shouted, but there was still no sound. He looked around, and the trees seemed to look down on him, and he was their prisoner now. Panic flared in his heart. He wanted to get back. He started to walk the way he had come.

But before could take a step, a hand reached out, and clasped over his face. It was a big, heavy hand, and it smelt like diesel fumes and sweat. Eddie cried out, but only muffles emerged from his throat. He kicked and fought, but a wet cloth wrapped around his face, and within seconds, he was feeling sleepy, his eyelids shutting out the blue sky and the shaking trees, the branches moving like fingers that said – told you so.

CHAPTER 24

"Attention all units," Roy said on the radio broadcast. Sarah had the siren on, but the windows were up, and his words being transmitted to every single police patrol car in the South Yorkshire Force.

"Divert to 60 Langsett Road, Hillsborough." He repeated the address, talking as fast as he could. "Suspect is armed and dangerous. Approach with extreme caution." He repeated his message twice, then hung up.

Their Ford Titanium was screaming down the A61 dual carriageway, where roadblocks were being set up to close down a lane on the northbound exit route, that led further out of Sheffield, towards Huddersfield. A gridlock of cars was already starting, and Roy regretted the roadblocks, but catching Burgess was critical. He had set up the blocks with traffic, and not discussed them with Nugent, and he knew he would catch some flak for that, but so be it.

Sarah took the exit for Hillsborough centre, a low-income suburb northwest of Sheffield. She cut her siren but kept the lights flashing. Roy watched the betting and pawn shops, the boarded up high street windows, and the grey, morose parade of flats above the shop fronts. Single mothers pushed prams, and clusters of young men with hoodies stood on street corners. The view was familiar to him from the mean streets of southwest London. The scenery didn't change no matter where he went in England.

People ran across the road as Sarah jumped a red light. She slowed down but left the alarm alone.

"Five minutes to ETA," Roy said, his eyes on the dashboard satnav.

"Ten minutes away, guv," Oliver's voice came on the radio. "Units are in place already, but not on the road as you requested."

"Copy that and thank you."

Sarah cut the blues and twos, and the unmarked black car took a left turn into Langsett Road. She parked at the top of the road, and number 50, according to the map, was at the other end. After that, there was a road with a fence, and a canal ran alongside the fence. Simon Jenkins had told them Burgess owned number 60, but he also had a canal boat.

"Units in place, back and front, 60 Langsett Road" his radio crackled. He glanced at Sarah, who was starting at him. The uniforms were dressed in black and had done well to conceal themselves.

"Breach," Roy gave the one-word command. Four men streaked out from nowhere at the top of the road, crossing to number 60. The lead man had a portable battering ram. The others were AFO, and their SO15 assault rifles were slung from shoulder straps. The battering ram made short work of the door, and the men went inside.

Sarah floored the accelerator, and the car shrieked forward, then came to a stop outside the house. The entire street was deathly quiet, only curtains fluttered at windows. Roy jumped out and ran inside. Another team had moved in through the garden.

"No one here," came the shout from upstairs. "All rooms checked."

"The loft?" Roy shouted back, going up the stairs. One of the AFOs had a stick in his hand, and he unhooked the trap door, then pulled down the ladder. Roy went up the steps. His left ankle throbbed, and so did his head. He stopped before the opening and felt around the edges till he found a switch. The yellow light that filled the small loft space revealed woodwork, old furniture and rolled up carpets. He scrambled upstairs, brushing cobwebs from his face.

Another uniform followed after him. It didn't take them long. The loft was empty apart from the old junk. Roy twirled the black knob on his radio.

"Units in place on the canal? The boat is Edelweiss. Black canal boat with dark green top, and yellow windows."

Oliver's voice came on the line. "Units in place. Eyes on the boat. No sign of activity. Awaiting orders."

"Wait till we get there."

Burgess used the canal boat to shift the drugs, according to Simon. One of his many attributes, Roy thought. He caught up with Sarah on the street, and with the uniforms and AFOs, they went to the main road, then helped each other over the fence. They landed on a grass verge with trees on it. The verge sloped down to the towpath, where boats were moored on the still, dark oily waters of the canal.

The men were huddled low in the bushes, it wasn't easy to spot them. Roy went down the middle, and Oliver, wearing a black jacket, turned to see. Next to him, spreadeagled on the ground, was Rizwan, watching with binoculars. Ahead, there was a row of black jacketed uniform officers, all hiding behind vegetation. A woman walked down the tow path with her dog, oblivious that a few feet away, scores of policemen had gathered for a raid.

Roy and Sarah slid down next to Oliver. "No one's been in or out," Oliver whispered. "The engine's off, and no sign of the boiler working." If it was, there would be steam let out from the top of the boat. Roy watched the boat carefully. It was a standard longboat, with curtains drawn across all its windows. A bicycle was locked on the deck, and steps led down to the entrances at either end. Flat rows of plants were potted on the rooftop. The boats could be deceptively spacious.

Questions burned in Roy's mind. Had Burgess already fled Sheffield? Even if he was on the boat, why hadn't it sailed by now? And the last, but most important thing – was Johnny on the Edelweiss?

Movement caught his eyes. The edges of the boat began to quiver. A soft hum, rising above the traffic on the road behind them, floated to their ears. The water by the boat started to churn. Steam appeared from the short, black chimney on the roof.

"Shit," Sarah said. "We need to move." She looked at Roy, who shook his head.

"No. He might just be checking out the engine. At least we know he's there. Just wait."

He watched with a sinking heart as the boat began to quiver more. Water at the rear churned faster, and the boat started to move. It went back, and the nose began to turn, facing the broad of the canal.

It was Roy's turn to swear. He wiped sweat with a wet jacket sleeve. "Alright, damn it. Get ready to board."

He spoke on the radio, passing the message on. He wanted to be the first on the boat. If Burgess was the Lily Man, if he had taken his brother, then Roy wanted to be the first to confront him. And, with any luck, alter his facial geography.

Roy bent low at the waist, and scurried down the slope, past the assembled officers. The Edelweiss was clearly ready to sail. It was leaving the towpath, pushing further into the canal. Roy jumped on the deck and went swiftly down the stairs. More feet thumped aboard, both behind him, and on the fore deck.

The blue door that led to the cabin was locked. A few good kicks didn't do the job. The boat had picked up speed now, and when it straightened, Roy almost went over the side. He had to grab the officer with the battering ram, the bloke was following the heavy weight into the canal. Cursing, he steadied himself. The officer lifted the battering ram and smashed it into the door. Running steps could be heard inside. A window opened and then shut. Another gusty blow, and the door splintered apart.

Roy pushed ahead of the officer and came across a surprisingly well-kept kitchen and lounge area. The red seats on varnished wood looked deep and comfortable. The kitchen was clean, and there was a plate on the table, with half eaten eggs and bacon. Roy ran across, into the cabin next to it, and found the door locked. This time, his kicks were enough to break it down, and he lumbered through. He caught a glimpse of the man charging through the cabin, his broad back and height suggested it was the same man who had accosted him earlier.

Burgess.

The man went through another door and locked it again. The boat swerved suddenly, and Roy, and the officers now behind him, went crashing into the beds on either side. The boat had no control. The engine was on, and it was moving at speed, slicing sideways across the canal. Roy looked outside the window. He saw another boat, its window so close he could reach out and touch it. He braced himself for impact, but somehow, the other boat slid past the Edelweiss. Its rear end must've bumped the edelweiss, because a grazing, cutting sound screeched above the engine, and the whole boat shuddered. But it kept moving.

The officer with the ram broke down the other door, and they piled into the next cabin. Shouts and commotion could be heard on the deck, with pounding footsteps. Roy's radio screeched.

"The bank guv!" Sarah's voice was high pitched and panicked. "We're going to hit the opposite bank."

Roy got to the end of the cabin, and hauled himself up the stairs, and into the deck. The boat swerved again, he lost his footing and fell down the stairs. Cursing loudly, he hauled himself back up. Someone screamed. He arrived on the deck to see four men grappling with Burgess, one hugging his waist, another grabbing his legs. Sarah was to the side, and she got her can of mace spray and buzzed it in Burgess's face. He howled, and Roy recalled with satisfaction he had almost gouged the bastard's eyes out. But the problem wasn't Burgess anymore.

It was the opposite end of the canal that was now rushing up to meet them. Trees leaned over the canal, and the cement jetty was only a few meters away. A few people stood on the tow path, staring at them with stricken looks. Burgess seemed to sense it and renewed his struggle to be free.

Roy got a hand to Burgess's collar, but an overhead branch crunched into his skull, right where had the stitches. Then the bone shuddering collision happened, shaking the deck like it was a pack of cards. The side of the boat slammed against the concrete pier, and men dropped off the boat like confetti. Roy was seeing stars, and his vision was impaired. A warm bead of blood was coursing down his forehead again. But he had an elbow hooked around Burgess's neck, and he pinned the man down to the deck.

He spoke through gnashed teeth. "You didn't say hello last time, dickhead. Where's your manners?"

CHAPTER 25

Rizwan and Oliver helped fish out the uniform officers who had landed in the water. They needed help, as, with chest rigs and heavy boots, swimming was practically impossible. The two DCs threw fishing lines, ropes, anything they could get their hands on.

Roy handcuffed Burgess, but it was Sarah who went downstairs into the engine room and switched off the ignition. Then she came up and dropped anchor. By the time she was back on the deck, her blonde locks astray, cheeks crimson, Roy had snapped a pair of ties on Burgess's feet, much to the bastard's indignation.

"Keep an eye on him. He might have a weapon," Roy told Sarah, then he helped the DCs, who were on the bank now, helping the sodden uniformed officers get to dry land. They were bruised, battered and dripping, but at least they were alive, and one part of the mission was achieved. Burgess was in custody. Roy went back on deck, where Sarah was patting Burgess down. She found a pocketknife in his left sock and put it in an evidence bag.

"Thanks," Roy said. He knelt on one knee, the throbbing pain in his head now like a steady drone. His eyes felt weirdly defocused and he had to blink to bring Burgess's red, sullen face into sharper view.

"Where's Johnny?"

Burgess said nothing. Roy took a fistful of his collar and pulled the man towards him. "Asking you nicely. Last chance."

"I'm a victim of police brutality," Burgess spat, one corner of his lips trailing a black line of blood. "I'm innocent and I know my rights."

"Innocent of the children's photo evidence we found on your laptop? Innocent of knocking my head in?"

"The laptop is old news. You can't prove it was me who hit you." His blue eyes flashed, and his jaws hardened.

"A DNA swab should do it. But we're wasting time. Where's Johnny?"

"I have no idea. Why the hell are you after me? I was minding my own business."

"If minding your own business means taking those photos then I have to come after you." Roy relaxed his grip a little, Burgess was starting to choke. "Johnny. Where is he?"

And where's my brother?

"I don't know!" Burgess shouted. "Just leave me alone."

"Mathew Ripley. Jack Peters. Robin Roy." Roy said the names slowly, and watched Burgess's face slacken, and his eyes widen a fraction. He licked his lips, and there was a change in him now, a realisation that he was trapped. "Those names mean anything to you?"

174

Burgess averted his eyes. Roy gripped his chin and turned it towards him. Burgess resisted, but he was in handcuffs.

"It was you," Roy said, his breath suddenly faster, and an invisible hand closing around his throat. He had trouble speaking. He raised himself above the weight that suffused him, pulling him down like a lead balloon, desperately trying to get the words out.

"You're the Lily Man," he whispered.

A sickening grin spread across Burgess's face. "You're so stupid. You can't see what's right in front of your face."

A line snapped in Roy's soul, like a high-tension rope stretched taut between two mountain peaks. He plummeted with it, a red curtain descending over his eyes, like the blood coursing down his forehead.

He was barely aware of his own actions: a snarl that was more of a sob, fingers bunching into a fist, elbow cocking back, then punching Burgess in the face. In slow motion, he saw Burgess's head snap back, and the man went limp.

Roy roared, a scream of anguish ripping out of his throat. He scrambled back and stood, almost collapsing against the side of the deck door. His head hung low; hands were claws as they came up to cover his face. He wanted to rake his nails over his face, scar his burning eyes, let the blood flow. He fell to his knees, and closed his eyes, taking deep lungfuls of air.

"Guv?" Sarah was kneeling in front of him, and she had a hand on his shoulder. "You okay?"

Roy looked skywards and blinked. It was such a nice, sunny day. He felt like plucking the bloody sun out of the sky, smashing it. "Yes," he rubbed his eyes. "I'm fine."

Behind Sarah, Burgess was stirring. His eyes opened and he looked around, then found Roy. The man's lips moved without speaking. Roy shook his head.

"Can you please help me search the place?" He asked Sarah.

She nodded and stood. Burgess was fidgeting and cursing on the deck. He tried to kick Sarah as she walked past. She narrowly avoided getting tripped up. Roy lost no time in giving him a good kick back, right in the ribs. Burgess howled in agony, and let forth a stream of invective, directed at Roy. "Try that again, and you'll get a lot more of those," Roy said, then followed Sarah.

They went through the cabins, turning the beds, wardrobes, desks inside out. After an hour, they were sweating and panting, but there was no sign of Johnny. Roy was looking for a hidden trapdoor on the floor. He spent a long time on his hands and knees, painstakingly knocking the wood to see if the sound changed. As time dragged on, he grew increasingly desperate.

The uniforms took Burgess to the nick, but Rizwan and Oliver joined them. After almost two hours, Roy knew it was a thankless task. Johnny wasn't here.

176

Roy stood, holding a hand to his bleeding scalp. He wiped it with his sleeve, smearing the white shirt crimson.

"Right, you two get back to the nick. Please get Burgess lawyered up and ready," he told Oliver and Rizwan. "Sergeant and I will finish up here."

The two DCs murmured their goodbyes and left.

He wanted to get above deck, but Sarah stopped him. She took out a pad of tissues and held it to his forehead. Roy winced, and tried to move away, but Sarah gripped his arm.

"Wait, guv. The stitches have come undone. Hold it here and let me get some Sellotape."

"There might be some downstairs," Roy grumbled. He felt like a right pillock, standing there holding the white tissue to his forehead. When he removed the tissue, it came away blood red, and he could feel the slow bead descending down his forehead again.

She was in the kitchen with his back to her, rummaging around in a drawer. She had taken her jacket off, and he tried not to notice her pert buttocks, bent over the counter. She turned with a roll of Sellotape in her hand. She pulled at it, then ripped off a piece with her teeth.

"Sit down," she indicated the seats. Roy did as told. There was something strangely alien but comforting in her soft touch as she leaned over him, applying the makeshift plaster to his wound. A little calm in the middle of total chaos. He got up when she finished, because they needed to find Johnny, and also because he felt a tad dizzy. He needed to finish up here and be back in time to question Burgess formally before the press conference.

"Thanks for that," he said. "Want to take a photo now, so we can admire your handiwork later?"

"Not my best handiwork. But we can take a photo because you look so fetching. Nicest mugshot you ever had." She laughed, and he rolled his eyes. "We should put your mugshot in the most wanted board in the nick. You'll fit right in there," Sarah said.

"I'm most wanted by many people, as you'll find out," he said mysteriously, and Sarah raised her eyebrows.

"Really guv?"

"I rarely joke Sergeant, another thing you need to learn about me."

"I'm a fast learner, guv," She grinned.

"Good, because this curve's a steep one." He raised a hand like it was going up a slope. He didn't know what to make of the sudden twinkle in her eyes, and he didn't want to acknowledge to himself it was easy to look at.

He became serious. "Right. Let's head back and face the music."

CHAPTER 26

It was carnage outside the police station. Hordes of reporters had descended on the gates, waving their arms and microphones. Three bored looking uniformed constables stood behind the gates, watching them with arms crossed over their chests. The shaggy tops of two boom mics were thrust through the grilles of the gate.

Roy's headache was worse just looking at the chaos. The uniforms saw them approaching and opened the gates to let them through. In unison, the media mob turned upon the black Ford Titanium. Flashbulbs popped as reporters thrust their cameras and faces close to the window.

"Inspector Roy have you caught the killer?"

"Is Johnny dead or alive?"

Sarah wheeled the car into the car park, and the barrier rose behind them. At the gates the screaming continued, getting louder as Roy got out of the car. His name was almost being chanted by the baying hordes. Grimacing, he slowly unplucked the dressing from his forehead. He walked to the gates, despite Sarah's protestations.

"If I give them something now, they'll leave us alone till the press conference," Roy growled, heading past the barrier. The screaming rose to a crescendo as he approached. He raised his hands, and the hordes were quieter.

"We have made significant progress in the case. There will be important updates at the press conference in two hours' time. Please attend. Until then, please let us do our jobs."

The crowd erupted. They wanted to know where Johnny was. That makes two of us, Roy thought bitterly as he walked back.

Sarah was waiting for him at the entrance, speaking to Oliver. They both looked up as he got closer. He knew something was wrong instantly. Sarah looked like she'd been slapped, and Oliver had shed his normal suaveness for bug eyes and shallow breaths.

"Another child abducted today. An eight-year-old boy called Eddie Hearn, from a campsite in northeast Sheffield," Oliver said.

"And the location isn't far from Wyoming Reserve," Sarah said.

Roy swore and touched his forehead. "What time?"

"The boy went out biking with his older sister around 10 am. He was reported missing after the mother couldn't find him, and she raised the alarm. Other people at the caravan site searched before the police arrived. The call came to switchboard at 11 am."

"Enough time for Burgess to grab the boy, store him somewhere, and get back to the boat," Roy uttered the thought circulating in all their minds. "Right?"

Sarah said, "It would be tight, but he could do it. If he kept the boy somehow around the campsite, it would be easier for him to get back to Hillsborough. Say he grabbed the boy just after 10 am. Locked him up somewhere by 11 am. That gives him more than an hour to get back."

"And we nabbed him around one in the afternoon?" Roy asked.

Oliver nodded. "Yes, about that. He's downstairs. Asked for a lawyer, and even told me he wants to press charges against you."

"I'll press a hammer to his head," Roy growled. They started walking down the green lino corridor. The uniformed inspector, Adams, was going out and he gave Roy a wave.

"You got him then, eh?"

"We did. But we don't have the boy as yet."

Adams grimaced. "Bloody crap that. The lads out there will keep looking. And the ladies," He added, looking at Sarah.

They said goodbye and moved on. The detectives' office was buzzing. Several heads looked up from their desks. Roy went to his place between Sarah and Rizwan and collapsed.

"You need to get that looked at."

Roy shifted on his seat to find Stephen Burns, the forensic psychologist. Burns pointed at Roy's head

"Was that stitched up?"

"Yes. But I have a habit of getting myself into more trouble than I can handle. One consequence of which is that I don't have time to get to the hospital."

"The FMPs downstairs, in the custody cell. He's administering to Burgess, who's claiming a concussion from your punch. I want to interrogate him, but I can't till the doctor's done. Neither can you."

The FMP or forensic medical practitioner, sounded like a great idea. He couldn't really keep dabbing his forehead every five seconds for much longer, and definitely not at the press conference. "Good idea, Stephen," Roy said. He stood wearily, every cell in his body wracked with pain. His joints were stiff as rusty nails, and the headache was getting worse. Rizwan was sat next to him, engrossed in his laptop.

"Have you got any Nurofen?"

It was Stephen who answered. "Here – I get migraines, so I keep some handy."

Roy thanked him and took the packet. He popped a couple, and gratefully accepted the coffee that Sarah came back with.

Rizwan said, "This is the CCTV from Burgess' garage. This is him, right?"

The team gathered around Rizwan's desk. Roy saw the unmistakable hulk of Burges as he walked in and out of the office, and then out of the forecourt. He glanced at the time and date stamp. It was yesterday morning.

"What about the day before? When Johnny was abducted?"

"Haven't got that far yet. Will keep looking."

Roy nodded and stretched his back. He wished he hadn't immediately, because a bout of dizziness overcame him. He had his back to the wall, and just leaned against it.

"I'm heading down to get my head fixed," he said, clutching a new piece of tissue to his damned scalp. "Please get all the info about Eddie Hearn. Can someone go to see the parents?" He looked at Sarah, who was sat, sipping her coffee. "I know it's been a long day but looks like it just got longer."

"No worries," Sarah said. "We'll get it sorted while you're doing the media circus."

"Thanks. Let me get the stitches done, then you and I can have a little chit chat with Mr Burgess."

Roy lumbered down the corridor, his shoes making a slapping sound on the floor. He looked askance at Nugent's office. The door remained shut, but the light was on inside. He couldn't stand facing Nugent now. Luckily the door was still shut by the time he got to the staircase. He held on to the rail as he slid downstairs.

The custody sergeant held out a clipboard where he put his name and rank, then he sat down in the holding area. The FMP emerged from one of the cells, and he recognised her by the plainclothes. She wore a mask, which she lowered as she got closer. She was brown haired, in her forties, with a kind face.

"You don't look very well," she put her bag down and sat beside him.

"Best introduction I've ever heard. I'm DCI Rohan Roy by the way. Been bashed about a little today, hence I'm looking so good. Not so pretty normally." He held out his hand, and she shook it.

"Dr Kate Forsyth," she smiled. She snapped her gloves on and had a look at the wound. "I think we can manage this here. The local anaesthetic will sting, but then you shouldn't feel anything."

"A few pints might have the same effect."

"Can't work after that, can you?" Dr Forsyth said, leaning over her bag, taking out syringes and vials.

"That's true. But you're making the cardinal mistake of assuming I want to work."

She pushed a needle into the rubber top of the vial and loaded the syringe. "I heard about you. You're the new detective to help with the Johnny Reid abduction case."

"Help would be a stretch, although we managed to catch our main suspect. He left his mark of respect, as you can see."

"And the boy?" She stood, with the syringe raised. She lowered her hand when she saw the look on his face.

"Yeah, that," Roy shook his head, becoming downcast. "I need to get back on it. Don't have much time left, we need to find him. The longer it goes, the worse it gets."

"Good luck. Everyone wants Johnny back."

And now Eddie, Roy thought bitterly, flexing his jaws. The nightmare of his teenage years was back to haunt him. There would be no rest till the boys were found.

Dr Forsyth dabbed the wound with stinging sterile wipes. "Just sit back and try not to move."

"At least you didn't say this is going to hurt."

"This is going to hurt." She suppressed a smile as Roy rolled his eyes. Roy leaned his head against the seat, and she put a hand to his left forehead, and injected with the syringe in her right hand. Roy gritted his teeth as the needle invaded the raw nerves, spread through the blood. Then Dr Forsyth stepped back.

"Are you a local GP as well?" Roy asked. He knew most FMPs were doctors in the area who moonlighted in the police stations.

"Yes, I am. I'm a partner at the Endcliffe Park Practice, not far from here."

Roy's brain clicked into gear. "Would you happen to know the Reid family? Duncan and Amanda, parents of Johnny."

"As a matter of fact, I do. Seen Amanda a few times over this year. Seen Johnny as well, when he was a baby. Not seen Duncan however."

"What do you think of Amanda?"

Dr Forsyth raised her eyebrows. "Confidential information, Inspector Roy."

"I understand. Anything you say remains confidential and could help us find Johnny. Besides, doctors have to disclose information if it's for the public good, right?"

She nodded and sat down beside him. She spoke in a low voice. "Amanda and Duncan have a troubled relationship. He was unfaithful to her, and she never really forgave him. For Johnny's sake, she stayed on. But she's having difficulties trusting him. He stays out late for work. Other women sent messages to his phone. He said they were work colleagues, but Amanda doubts that."

Roy's mind was whirring. Maybe it wasn't just the shock factor that made Amanda look so distant from her husband.

"Amanda also didn't like Duncan's friendship with Fiona's boyfriend, Keith Burgess. He came around often apparently, and they sat drinking beer. Duncan also went to see him, and returned home late, drunk. She thought that man was a bad influence on Duncan."

Roy stared at Dr Forsyth. "Did Amanda mention anything specific about Keith Burgess?"

"Amanda just didn't like him. It was all coming to a head before Johnny disappeared. She was planning on leaving him. They had discussions about separating as well."

Dr Forsyth stood. "Now then. Let's see if you can feel this." She tapped his wound with a needle, but he was so absorbed in his thoughts he forgot to respond.

"By the way, there's another thing." Dr Forsyth leaned back. "The Reids also had financial issues. Duncan was about to lose his job. Amanda's father supported them with money. That was also a factor."

Roy stared at her, then he brushed her hand away and stood.

"One minute, doc, I'll be back." He marched towards the custody sergeant's desk. He asked to use the phone and he slid it across the table.

Sarah picked up on the third ring. "It's me," Roy spoke quickly. "Bring Duncan in for questioning. Arrest him if you have to. He's closer to Burgess than we realised. In fact, I have a really bad feeling about Duncan. Get him here, and don't let him go."

"Arrest him? Really?"

"Keep it quiet, but if he wants to leave, arrest him. I need to see him, ASAP."

Roy hung up and marched back to the benches against the wall where Dr Forsyth was waiting with a bemused expression.

"Something I said?"

"You've helped more than you realise." Roy sat down with a sigh.

"Be still now," the doctor said. She worked away, and Roy closed his eyes. He felt the needle pushing and stretching his skin, but he felt no pain. His mind was a different matter. He felt sick inside, a sea of vitriol lurching in his guts.

Duncan told Burgess where he was going.

Duncan found the Lily Man's note. He had the ransom letter, asking for the hundred thousand pounds.

Would Amanda's father pay that? And would that money end up with Duncan's mate, Burgess?

Could Duncan have kidnapped his own son?

CHAPTER 27

Roy shook hands with Dr Forsyth when she finished. "Anything more you can remember about the Reid's, please get in touch." He cursed himself now for not contacting the doctor sooner. GPs were family physicians, and they often knew secrets about a family no one else did.

"You take care. Get those stitches removed in seven days' time."

Roy felt the dressing. It was a small, thin strip this time, not the bulbous padding that DS Sarah, bless her, had done earlier.

"Thank you," Roy said, and meant it. Once Dr Forsyth had gone, he sat down and faced the corridor. The grey doors of the custody cells stretched out in front, on either side of the equally grey lino covered floor. He knew what he had to do. He got up and asked the cell number from the custody sergeant, who took him there. The sergeant slid back the eye slot and Roy also had a peek. Burgess was dressed the same, in a t shirt that was torn at the front, and black jeans. He lay on the hard bunk bed, arms clasped under his head, staring at the ceiling.

The sergeant opened the door, and Roy stepped in. The door remained open, and the sergeant came back with a chair, which Roy accepted with a murmur of thanks. He shut the door after the sergeant left.

Burgess glanced at him, then resumed his upward stare. Roy glanced at his watch. It was getting close to 3 pm. He wanted to see Duncan before the press conference at four thirty. But in many ways, this was what he waited for. Over the last twenty-seven years, his nightmares were filled with a man who was a shadow, a monster with no face who had stolen his brother, broken his parents, destroyed his peace.

Now, was he finally face to face with that monster?

He watched Burgess for a while. The lax cheeks, the stubble on them, his vivid blue eyes, fixed on the ceiling. The utterly bored look in his face.

"I know you don't have to speak to me without a solicitor present," Roy began. "But you'll be doing yourself a big favour."

Burgess said nothing. His eyes shut, and the rest of his body remained still, like he was asleep.

"Mathew Ripley. Jack Peters. We found their bodies. What happened to Robin Roy?"

Burgess's feet moved a fraction, then his lips twitched. His eyes remained closed. But there was no hiding the faint mirth on his face. The bastard was enjoying this. Roy clenched his teeth and shut his eyes briefly. He had to stay in control.

"You ran away from Surrey. Came back up here. That's why we never found you. Well, the game's over, Keith.

Tell me where Johnny is, and you won't end up on the general ward of the prison. You know what happens to your sort there."

He paused. Burgess remained silent. Roy whispered again. "Tell us where Johnny is, and what happened to Robin Roy, the boy you took all those years ago?"

More silence. "Is Robin dead, like Mathew and Jack?"

Burgess sighed and said nothing. Roy wanted to get up and shake him, slap him around the face. On the boat… Burgess told him something on the boat, and he tried to remember. In the heat of the moment, he had ignored it, but now they came back to him with a sudden clarity.

You're so stupid you can't see what's right in front of your face.

Was that Burgess just playing games? Or did he mean something else?

"You're going away for life, Keith. In prison, no secure unit for you. Hope you're ready. On the boat, you said I can't see what's right in front of my face. Did you mean Duncan?"

Burgess stiffened ever so slightly, and that was enough answer. His eyes remained shut, and his lips went flat. His nostrils flared, and his Adams apple bobbed up and down.

Roy's mind was in turmoil, and a nausea was churning in his guts. "Duncan's going to talk. You put him up to this."

You evil, sick, bastard, he thought to himself, but there was no point in saying them out loud.

"One last chance. Where's Johnny? And what happened to Robin?"

Burgess's eyes opened. His head moved, till he focused on Roy. "Wouldn't you like to know?"

Roy gritted his teeth together, his legs quaking with the tension of keeping them still. "Just tell me."

"Like I said," Burgess's voice was so soft Roy had to strain his ears. "I don't know what you're talking about. You're stupid. Now leave me alone."

Roy wasn't letting go that easily. "Eddie Hearn. You got him this morning, from the Fox Hagg camp site. Where is he?"

That drew a response. "You're having a laugh. I have no idea who that is." Then Burgess shut his eyes again.

CHAPTER 23

Roy had quit smoking years ago, but he needed one now. He stormed out of the custody unit and went out to the rear car park. He found a spot by the wall, with only rows of cars for company. He kicked the wall, then banged his fist against it. He was about to headbutt the wall as well, but common sense prevailed. He roared against the wall; fists clenched against it. A ball of frustration exploded inside him, radiating against the walls.

It was Burgess. He knew it. He could see it in the man's eyes. But he had no evidence to link Johnny's abduction to Burgess. The fact that he knew where his father was taking him was not enough, and any lawyer would make mincemeat of their argument. They had even less to link Burgess to Eddie, but Roy felt it in his bones. Burgess had taken him. He even had a sly smile on his face as he denied all knowledge.

Robin's face flashed before his eyes, unbidden. An over excited, thin shouldered, little boy, his smile bigger than his face could fit. Then he was gone, running away into the woods, the sunlight glimmering on his gold chain. That heaviness came back to claim him, settling like a black glacier in his heart, dragging him to the ground. He slumped to his knees, and stayed like that for a while, as if in supplication to an evil deity who held him in a remorseless grip.

He shook his head and held on to the wall as he stood. Thoughts of Robin came with the waves of guilt, and that brought up on useless rage. No, that wouldn't do.

He needed to keep his mind clear and functioning. He strode back inside, waving at the two uniform constables going past him.

He picked up a coffee and a few muffins and sandwiches, then went up to the detectives' office. His team weren't there, so he put the food on his desk, and started munching on his BLT. He hadn't realised how hungry he was. Sarah appeared, her cheeks flushed, and lips pressed together.

"What happened?"

"We can't find Duncan Reid. He's not at work, where Rizwan left him. His wife says he's not at home."

Roy nodded. He pointed at the sandwiches. "Have one if you're hungry. Got some veggie ones as well."

"I don't eat bread, but thanks. Trying to keep as close to zero carbs as possible."

Roy grunted, and bit into his sarnie. Rizwan and Oliver appeared with cups of coffee.

"I'm done with the CCTV," Rizwan said, picking up an egg and cress sandwich at Roy's invitation. He sat down at his laptop and pulled up the images.

Oliver said, "Burns wants to see Burgess. Shall I tell him you're done with him?"

"I'm just getting started with him," Roy growled. "Long way to go. We need to charge him to make sure he doesn't get out of here. But yes, tell Burns to go ahead, and tell him I want his report when he's done."

Oliver looked at the sandwiches with a hungry glint in his eye. Roy said, "Get fed and watered first."

Oliver grinned and pounced on some food. Rizwan called from his desk, and they went over.

The CCTV was playing in the Burgess' garage. The man himself was visible, tinkering by the side of a car, then speaking to one of the mechanics. Roy saw the time and date stamp and his heart sank. 3 pm, two days ago. At that time, Johnny and Duncan were walking the dog in Wyming Nature Reserve.

"Speed it up till 5 pm. That's when Duncan called, right?"

"Just before five." Rizwan did as told. Burgess was on screen again, walking around the garage. He was locking up in fact, and was the last one to leave the premises. Rizwan scrubbed back to three thirty, then 4.30 pm. At every point, Burgess was seen.

"I've been through this twice now, guv," Rizwan said. "Burgess was there between three and 5 pm the day Johnny was abducted."

Roy staggered back to his chair, and rested his elbows on the desk, then gripped his forehead.

How was it possible? It had to be Burgess... but he couldn't be in two places at the same time. Roy went back to Rizwan's laptop.

"Play it again. And this time, freeze it when Burgess shows his face to the camera."

Rizwan did as told, Sarah and Oliver helping as they munched on their sandwiches. Burgess' face appeared in close up as he looked in the direction of one of the two cameras. He made no effort to hide his face. If anything, Roy thought with a sense of disquiet, he had that sickening grin on his face, that same nauseating, lopsided, evil smile that was a half snarl.

Rizwan repeated the process at various stages of the footage. Burgess spent time in his office, then walked around the floor. The cameras at the rear of the garage didn't show him right till the end, at 5 pm, when he got into his brown Honda and drove off.

"He was there, guv. No doubt."

"If he was there, then who took Johnny?" Sarah asked the question in everyone's mind.

The answer was so horrific no one could speak for a while. Roy raced to his desk and picked up the phone.

"DCI Roy. Please put out an all-units alert for Duncan Reid. Yes, the missing boy's father." He spoke to the traffic switchboard for a while, then hung up.

Sarah and the two DCs were huddled over the laptop, ignoring him. "That's him," Sarah said, pointing at the screen.

196

Roy walked over. The screen showed a black and white film of a man getting out of his car and walking down a road. He looked up and down the street, then went inside a house. The street looked familiar to Roy, as did the man. Rizwan's fingers flew over the keyboard, and they saw the man from the opposite angle. Rizwan zoomed in, and Roy knew instantly.

"It's Duncan."

Oliver said, "And that's Burgess' house in Attercliffe."

They watched as Duncan went inside. Roy checked the date and time stamp. Two days before Johnny disappeared, around 9 pm.

"Go back to the week before," Roy asked. "Check the same location, same time."

He went to his desk and sipped the coffee while Rizwan and Oliver scrubbed through the films. Sarah walked past him and out into the corridor. She returned presently with a large evidence bag that contained a black laptop.

She took it out and put it on her desk, and Roy eyed it. "That's the laptop from Burgess's house?"

CHAPTER 28

"Yes. His prints were on it, and IDENT-1 shows a match. Cybercrime used their encryption stuff to decode his passcode."

Sarah shuffled her chair back and Roy dragged his to her table. Sarah opened up the laptop. The desktop screen was full of photo files.

"Dare we look at these?" Sarah glanced at Roy. "Dilly at cybercrime said they're all photos of children and she couldn't bear to see them."

"If they've been looked at already, then best we ignore them. My only interest would be in old photos. If Burgess is the Lily Man, then there might be some material from his early years."

Sarah nodded and checked through the folders. "Dilly told me she arranged all the files in date order." Her admittedly shapely fingers, Roy noted, were bereft of any rings today. He had noticed that earlier too, he was a detective, after all. But yesterday, she had worn a grey ring on her right-hand little finger. That was missing today.

Sarah's eyes scanned the folders, as did Roy's. Sarah bent her lips downward. "Nothing past 2018. Maybe that's when he bought this laptop. He could have other stuff saved on a cloud folder somewhere."

Roy grunted in frustration. "Can I have a look please?"

Sarah looked at him questioningly, and the question was bleeding obvious. He said, "Sorry, I trust you, but I've got this habit of double checking."

Sarah shrugged, but he was aware of the look in her eyes. He took the laptop to his desk and banged on the keyboards till he was satisfied. He felt like hurling the damn thing at the wall.

He couldn't look at the photos. He'd seen their type before, and he didn't want to bring up his breakfast. If Robin's photo was hidden somewhere in these files... no, he couldn't miss that. But neither could he bring himself to open up the individual images and look at them. No sane person could do that without revulsion corroding their skin like acid.

He turned to Sarah. "Where's Dilly's office?"

"Third floor, in cybercrime." Sarah watched as Roy picked up the laptop and stood. "Shall I come with you?"

"No, that's fine. I'll be back in a minute."

He went up the staircase, taking three at a time. His leg muscles screeched in agony, and the dizziness returned. He had to stop on the third-floor landing to catch his breath, then he opened the door and walked into the corridor. The office space was open plan, with several technicians' desktops laid out in a row. Their name and ranks were on desk badges. A brown-haired woman in her mid to late thirties turned around as Roy arrived.

"Dilly Russell?"

"Yes, who's asking?"

Roy introduced himself and pulled up a chair. He took out his wallet, and then Robin's photos, which always stayed with him. He had three of them, taken from different angles. They were re sized and cut to a smaller shape.

"Years ago, this boy vanished. He was taken by the Lily Man, who we think the owner of this laptop is. You've been through the files, yes."

Dilly's eyes were troubled. She swallowed once. "To be honest, I couldn't look at most of them. But I found everything and arranged them in order."

Roy tapped Robin's photos. "This boy never returned. We've looked for him ever since he took the three boys, all them years ago. Can you run an image recognition for this face on all the folders in this laptop?"

Dilly's face brightened. "Oh yes, we can do that. Do you have digital copies of these photos?"

"I have more on my phone, in fact. Shall I send them to you?"

Dilly nodded and gave Roy her email. "This won't take long. You can get a coffee if you want."

Believe me, I've waited for this moment all my life. I don't care how long it takes.

Aloud he said. "No, I'm fine here."

200

Dilly nodded and turned to her screen. Roy watched as she downloaded the photos he sent her, and then uploaded them to her image recognition software. Then she ran the software on the laptop. Roy watched the green tube on the screen slowly running from left to right. He tried not to hold his breath. Tried not to breathe like he'd just run a mile. Tried to make his heart not twist and bend like it was getting stuffed inside a tiny box full of thorns.

None of it worked. He could only watch the screen as the green line came to the right end of the screen, and then it dinged. Dilly clicked once on her keyboard, and a line with text appeared. Roy leaned forward like he was catching a rainbow.

No matches found. Perform another search?

The white letters blinked on the black box. He stared at it like he'd forgotten how to read. It took a few seconds to register.

Dilly turned to him. "Shall I do another search?"

He looked at her like he'd just seen her. He had to clear his throat before the words came out.

"Is there any point?"

"Not for those photos. That face, I mean. The software picks up on every aspect of that face. If you have any of another person, I can try that."

Roy looked back at the screen. "That's fine, thank you."

He rose slowly, like Atlas standing with a couple of globes on his shoulder. Every joint screamed in pain as he walked back to the staircase. The ache in his body dwarfed the anguish inside, it felt like a storm of knives was battering his soul. Sharp, prickly points that drew bright cherry red blood. Another dead end. How many more?

He went slowly down the stairs, each step a heavy weight. Finally, he sat down on a step, and lowered his head to his knees. The storm raged within, a pain that would never find utterance, a hurt that would never heal.

After a while, he stood, and carried on. Back at his desk, the team looked up as he entered. He avoided Sarah's eyes, they bored into him. He had long felt women had a sixth sense about emotional torpor that men either ignored, or just didn't get. And right now, he didn't want to face it.

Rizwan said, "He's there again, last week on Sunday, same time. 9 pm." He pointed at his screen and Roy leaned over Oliver to have a look. The figures moved, and Roy was looking at Duncan coming out of Burgess's house.

Oliver said, "His wife never mentioned he saw Burgess this many times. Fiona didn't seem to know either."

Roy put his hands on his waist. "Time to bring Duncan in."

Rizwan made the call to the Reid household. He spoke to Amanda, then hung up. "He's gone for a work meeting tonight, and will be back late, he said. I'll try his mobile." He called Duncan, and left a message.

Oliver yawned, and covered his mouth. Roy said, "It's been a long time. All of you, get some rest. Tomorrow's going to be a busy day."

CHAPTER 29

Twenty-seven years ago

Robin pulled the oversized coat around his body and shivered. He was standing outside, and it was still dark out here. He was in a courtyard that was uneven, with large potholes in the ground. Rainwater filled the holes, black and colourless. He could see the house for the first time. It was derelict, with wooden beams that were rotten everywhere, windows cracked, shutters missing or hanging half open. It was big, its triangular roof like a strange conical hat whose top was blunted with rain and decay.

It was the morning after Jack's death. The man had dragged him out of bed at the crack of dawn. He ordered Robin to get ready and then stood and watched as he went to the toilet and got dressed. Then he marched Robin outside and told him to stand there. Robin wanted to run away, but the courtyard was ringed by a high fence. Despite the building being so dilapidated, the fence looked stout, as did the gate. A car stood inside the gate.

Robin watched as the man emerged. He had two long black bags on either shoulder. He put them down on the ground.

"Come here," he called to Robin. He did as told, and, as he got closer to the black bags, he realised what they were. A shudder of revulsion swept over him, and he forgot to take another step. The bags contained Jack and Mathew.

"I said come here," the man called out again, louder. Robin hurried past the body bags, acidity rising up his throat. As he got closer to the steps where the man stood, he turned and vomited. The man swore and moved away. Robin stood, wiping mucus with his shirt sleeve, nausea still racking his guts. The man told him to follow, and he did so. Inside the hallways, the man opened a door and took out two shovels. One was smaller, and he handed that to Robin. He took it without question.

"Come with me. Don't even think of running. No one's going to hear you if you shout. Try anything and you know what happens." The man pointed to the two body bags. Robin's head sank over his chest, then he nodded. The man lifted the two body bags on his shoulders and walked down the courtyard. Robin followed. There was an overgrown garden that ringed the courtyard, with tall trees, and weeds that reached up to Robin's head. The man waded into the undergrowth, and he seemed to know where he was going. They came up on a path that went deeper into the garden, which seemed to widen out into a general woodland. They came upon a small pond, and the ground around it was muddier, softer.

The man put the bags on the ground. He tapped the shovel on the ground a few times in different places, then chose a spot and started to dig. He looked at Robin.

"Don't just stand there. Come here and help me. That's why you've got the other shovel."

Robin hefted the shovel in his hand. It was heavy and he had difficulty carrying it this far. He had no idea how he would dig. On the other hand, for the first time, he had a weapon in his hand. Could he hit the man with this? But the man was far stronger, and his arms already felt heavy. He doubted he could deliver anything near a killer blow to the man. The man watched him as he got closer with the shovel.

"Go on then," he commanded. "Start."

Robin wiped the snot from his nose and started to dig. It was hard work, and soon he could barely lift the shovel. He dropped it and sat down at the edge of the hole. The man picked up Robin's shovel and put it behind him. Then he carried on digging. After what seemed like a long time, the hole was big enough. Without ceremony, the man dragged the two body bags into the hole.

"You've had your rest," he growled at Robin. "Now do the easy bit."

Robin took the smaller shovel and started to put the freshly dug earth over the body bags. As he did so, a whimper came from his chest, and tears sprouted in his eyes. He knew there was no point in stopping to dry his eyes. He wiped his tears and carried on covering the grave.

The man helped him near the end. Then he picked up leaves, branches and covered the new graves to hide them. He pushed Robin ahead of him, and they went back out into the courtyard. He popped open the boot of his car.

"Get in," the man indicated the open boot. Robin could see a pillow and a folded-up duvet inside. It was a makeshift bed, of sorts. He looked at the man. His experience had made him dumb, but he had no desire to get inside

"I said get in," the man said. He looked at his watch and got agitated. "Five already. Come on, we have to leave." He moved forward to grab Robin. The boy knew what was coming next. He put his hands on the car, and the man helped him climb aboard. When he lay down inside, the man slammed the boot door down.

It was pitch black inside, and the smell of gasoline was strong. Robin hated small spaces. He closed his eyes. The car started, then moved slowly, gradually picking up pace. Robin kept his eyes shut, and soon, the rhythmic movement closed his eyes.

He didn't know how long had passed, but when he woke up, the car had stopped. He heard sounds, and then the boot door yawned open. Robin screwed his eyes shut at the sudden light. He could see the man's now familiar shape, blocking out the sunlight. The sky was too bright behind him. Robin shielded his eyes.

"Get out," the man said. He helped Robin scramble up and out on the ground, then he kept a hand on his collar. Wind whipped his hair, and he shivered in the sudden chill.

He was on a hilltop. He could see the gravel road the car had come up, and, far below, lay a city he'd never seen. It was daylight, and he could see tiny cars move on the road, smoke rise from a tall chimney in a factory. He didn't have long to admire the scenery. The man pulled on his collar and turned him around. They walked up the gravel path, and a house came into view. It was made of grey stone slabs and had a thatched roof. It looked like an old farmhouse. A stone fence surrounded it. The man opened the iron gate, and they walked up to the door. The man had a key, and he opened it. Inside, it was surprisingly nice. There was a rug on the floor, and an empty fireplace. Through a hallway, they came across a large kitchen area with table and chairs.

"Now listen, boy," the man said. Robin shrank away from him, but the man pulled him closer. "There's nowhere for you to run. And if you try, you know what happens."

He marched Robin down the kitchen, with its low wooden beamed ceiling. They came into a hallway with stairs going up to a dark upper floor. The man half pulled half walked Robin up to the first floor. There was a landing, and four doors ahead of them. He shoved Robin inside a door. There was a bed and a desk. The window was shuttered and closed.

"Stay here," the man said. Robin heard the keys lock the door after it shut.

CHAPTER 30

Oliver pressed the buzzer at the front door of the semi-detached house. He straightened his tie and brushed off an imaginary fleck of dust from his shoulder. Then he patted down his gelled hair. Rizwan cast an eye at him.

"Stop preening. You're not a peacock."

"True. But you are an ugly duckling." He laughed.

"I'm a black swan mate," Rizwan retorted.

The door opened and Fiona Reid appeared. Both Oliver and Rizwan showed their warrant cards.

"Thank you for agreeing to see us. I spoke to you on the phone," Oliver said.

"Yes. Please come in." Fiona walked away, and the two DCs followed. It was a small but comfortable family home, decorated nicely with photos on the wall, flowers on the stand below the hallway mirror and soft carpets.

Fiona walked into the open plan kitchen at the back. She pointed to the sofa sets in front of the TV, and the tall chairs at the kitchen island. She poured herself coffee from the maker.

"Can I offer you anything?"

The men shook their heads. Fiona sat down at the counter with her steaming mug and wrapped her hands around it. Her face looked drawn and tired. She didn't have any make up on, and it was late afternoon. She was dressed in jeans and a tee shirt. An attractive woman in her forties, Oliver thought, but she was worried. Fiona kept her eyes on the mug, like she was afraid of the questions coming her way.

"Did you see Keith Burgess this morning?" Oliver asked.

"No. I haven't seen him since the day… since Johnny disappeared. I saw him the night before, like I told your Inspector."

"He's not tried to call, or get in touch?"

Fiona sighed. "No, and I don't want him to either. He had this whole double personality. I can't believe it. He took me for a fool, and I feel sick when I think about him. You can be sure I'll contact you if he gets in touch."

"Thank you," Oliver tried a smile that normally women liked, but Fiona only looked away. "Do you know if he had a house in north Sheffield? Like, around the Fox Hagg Nature Reserve, or the Totnes Golf Course?"

Fiona thought for a while. "He never mentioned anything. The house in Nether Edge wasn't his, was it?"

"No ma'am. He was renting it under a false name."

"I'm sorry to ask you again. Just want to be double sure. You didn't see, or you don't know where Keith Burgess was this morning?"

A ripple of irritation spread across Fiona's face. "I already told you. Look, I love my little nephew. Why would I lie to you? And have you found him? His parents are in pieces. Shouldn't you be out there instead of asking me stupid questions?"

Rizwan spoke. "Ma'am we're sorry. It's just that another boy was abducted this morning. An eight-year-old called Eddie Hearn. He was out camping with his mum and sister in the Fox Hagg camping site."

Fiona's mouth opened, then she raised a hand to it. Realisation dawned in her eyes. "Sorry, I didn't know. That's why you're asking... oh god. No, I haven't seen him. He's out of my life, believe me, for good."

She took a few seconds to compose herself. She sipped on her coffee. Oliver asked, "Have you heard from the Reid's recently?"

"Yes, I spoke to Amanda yesterday. She's received another ransom note. For that hundred-thousand-pounds." She looked at Oliver expectantly, and he slid his eyes to Rizwan.

"She told you about another ransom note?"

"Yes," Fiona's shapely eyebrows lowered. "She told me Duncan informed the police."

Oliver's jaws tightened, as did a knot of tension in his guts. "Have you heard from Duncan recently?"

"Not since… yesterday actually. He's not been in touch today."

"We can't find him either. He's not at work or home. Can I please ask, were Amanda and Duncan in a happy marriage?"

A guarded look emerged on Fiona's face. She blinked twice, then took a long sip from her coffee. She looked at the bi folding doors that led out into the garden. "They had their troubles. Last year, Amanda accused Duncan of cheating on her. He denied it. I didn't speak to him, but Amanda told me. It's not the kind of thing I can talk to him about." She looked back at Oliver and shrugged. He nodded.

"Sure. Did Amanda talk to you more recently? Did she say anything about leaving him?"

Fiona clutched her forehead and her eyes closed. She stayed like that for a while. When she spoke, her hand remained over her eyes. "I told her to reconsider. I didn't want her to leave my brother. Daniel's not a bad sort, he gets a little carried away sometimes. I told her to think about Johnny." Fiona removed her hand from her face. She stood and leaned against the counter.

"Daniel was about to lose his job. Did Amanda tell you?"

"Yes. Amanda's father's a rich property developer. He's been helping them out over the last few months. Duncan's pay was cut as the business wasn't doing well. He's looking for other jobs but they're not easy to find."

212

Rizwan asked, "When did Amanda tell you about the second ransom note?"

"This morning." Her eyes narrowed. "Why do you keep asking me about that? Duncan already informed you, right?"

Oliver glanced at Rizwan, who nodded slightly. "No ma'am. This is the first we're hearing of it. If you hear from Duncan, can you please find out where he is, and notify us immediately."

CHAPTER 31

Duncan stared at his phone in confusion. He wasn't carrying his normal phone. This was a pre-paid burner phone that didn't have any GPS – a Nokia brick. Even then, he knew the calls and messages would ping across the masts and might give his location away – but no one knew it was him. Apart from Amanda, whose text he was now looking at.

"Why didn't you tell the police?"

He frowned, then decided to call her. She answered on the first ring.

"I spoke to Fiona. The police went around to her house. They didn't know about the second ransom note."

"Because we need to keep it from them. You read what the note said. We won't see Johnny if we get the police involved."

There was a pause. "Have you picked up the money?"

"Not yet. I'm on my way." Duncan felt the guilt settling in his heart like a cold slab of ice. His hands shook, and with an effort, he kept his voice steady. "Brian's going to meet me there, right?" Brian was Amanda's father.

"Yes, he will." He could hear the struggle in her voice. "Are you sure this is a good idea?"

"The police haven't done anything yet, have they?"

"They got Keith. It makes me sick, Duncan. You bought him into our house. He's scum of the earth." Her voice was like a whiplash.

"Hang on. Fiona bought him to us. I didn't." He hated the defensive note he sounded. He hated everything about himself, and about Keith. He wished he'd never seen that bastard's face. He blamed Fiona.

"You know what I mean," Amanda persisted. "He's scum and you should never have given the time of day."

"Not my fault. Anyway, the police have him. If he had Johnny, we would know by now."

"Would we?" Amanda's voice broke, and he hated her, he hated himself. "Would we really, Duncan? What sort of a man does what he did to that poor boy he picked up from school? And he was in our house, Duncan, in our fucking house."

Amanda sobbed, and Duncan took the phone off his ears. He sat down on the rocky ledge and lowered his head to his palms.

"Look, Mandy, I'm sorry, okay, what do you want me to say? At least I'm trying to make this right. Give me this chance, ok? Keith couldn't have taken Johnny if the kidnapper's still leaving us ransom notes, right?"

Even as he said the words the guilt stabbed in his heart. A festering wound that might not ever heal.

"Duncan, you can't mess this up you hear me? You mess up everything else, but not this. I'm warning you." He heard the rebuke in her tone, and anger bristled inside him.

"Oh really? And nothing's ever your fault, is it? Miss I'm too posh to work full time. All women your age are working mothers. They help the family. And you sit on your backside while I–"

"I've helped you enough! My dad got you the job, or have you forgotten? And then you piss around with your slappers. Shame on you! Do one thing right for once in your life. Bring my son back." She hung up, and she might as well have slapped him across the face. Duncan crunched the phone in his palm, grinding his teeth in anger. Stupid bitch. Who did she think she was?

He started walking fast. Well, he'd show her. She didn't know who she was dealing with. Yes, he had messed up, in a big way. But he was about to make amends. Most importantly, he would get his son back. Then Amanda, Brian, all of them could go fly a kite. Duncan was on a hilltop, not far from Wyming Nature Reserve. He got into his Ford Focus and fired up the engine. Brian was waiting for him in the park with a bag of money.

CHAPTER 32

DS Nugent flung the cigarette out his window, then slammed it shut so hard it made the wall shake.

"What do you mean he was there when the boy was taken?"

Roy had sat down without being asked to.

"We saw the CCTV from his garage. He was at work. He even looked up at the camera." Roy stopped, the gaps in his mind coming closer, sliding into one another, forming a whole. There was a pattern here, a shape, but it was vague, like it was behind a layer of smoky glass. Just out of reach.

You're so stupid you can't see what's right in front of your face.

He'd seen Burgess's face. Up close, and on the CCTV.

You can't see what's right in front of your face.

Nugent interrupted his thoughts. "Well, now there's this other kid. Jesus Christ. Two abductions in three days. The chief constable's killing me. Her phone's been ringing non-stop this morning. I said you're on the case." Nugent glared at him. "Tell me you got something."

"We got Burgess. And there's every chance he got Eddie Hearn this morning. We know for certain he wasn't at the garage this morning. I arrived late morning and he wasn't there."

"So, he got Eddie, stashed him somewhere and then got on his boat. He was moving out, right? Wouldn't he want to take the boy with him?"

"Not unless he planned to come back soon. Maybe later tonight. Easier in the dark."

Nugent puffed out his cheeks. "Bloody typical. We get our main suspect and now he's off the bloody hook. And you," he wagged a finger at Roy, "went ahead and punched him."

"I should've blown him a kiss instead. Sorry, sir. Will remember next time."

"Shut up," Nugent ground out. "He wants to press charges. More form filling and money spent on useless lawyers."

"If you remember," Roy pointed to his forehead stitches, "He left me this nice souvenir, then did a runner." Nugent went to speak but Roy stopped him. "And he can't say it wasn't him just because I didn't see his face. His DNA swab will match the skin and hair samples in the room, and on my fingers. My nail clippings are with forensics. We're waiting for a match."

Nugent grumbled. "We need to charge him. His solicitor's kicking up a fuss already."

"So, let's charge him." Roy spread his hands. "We know he took Johnny. And Eddie Hearn." His eyes locked with Nugent. "Unless there's another person." Even thinking about it was disquieting. But all angles needed covering. "Unless it was Duncan Reid who took his own son. He was there. He could've written the note and left the flower. He could also have done the ransom notes."

Nugent tapped a finger on his lips. "Where is he?"

"Duncan? We can't find him, but feelers are out. We'll spot his car sooner or later. He couldn't have gone far. There's an APB out for him."

"The media will go bonkers if that gets out. Make sure it's under wraps. Don't mention it at the press conference."

Roy raised an eyebrow. "I wasn't born yesterday, sir. But we do need to tell the Reid family – like Fiona especially, because it's her boyfriend. I'll charge Burgess formally as soon as Burns is done with him. Then I'll be out to meet the Hearn family. I'll make it back by 16.20."

"You better be," Nugent barked. "The hounds are expecting you."

Roy left the office and bumped into Burns just outside. Burns apologised and Roy asked him to sit at his desk.

Sarah was there, tapping away on her laptop. She saw them and nodded. Burns sat down opposite Roy and patted down the few strands of hair on his balding scalp.

"So, what did you think?" Roy asked, looking at his watch. It was five minutes to three and he needed to leave on the hour to see the Hearn family and have any hope of getting in time for the press conference.

"He doesn't talk about his childhood," Burns started. A film of moisture had formed on his upper lip, and he pulled out a handkerchief and wiped it. He also wiped the thin sheet of sweat on his scalp. "Most people like him were sexually abused as children, and that might be the case with him. Most child sex attack victims are known to the child or family, and in this case, that was true, as long as we're sure Burgess did take Johnny. He certainly took the other boy, hence he's on the register."

"What do you think? Did he take Johnny?"

Burns smiled sadly. "I was going to ask you that, as it's your job. Not an easy answer, I know. He certainly has all the traits of a child sex abuser, and he had the opportunity."

"And he tried to kill me when I stopped him from leaving, so clearly, he's got something to hide. The more I think, the more it seems possible. And yet," Roy sighed. "He wasn't at the Wyming Nature Reserve when Johnny was there. He was in his garage."

Burns opened his mouth to speak, then thought better. His eyebrows met in the middle of his forehead. "What? He was in his garage when Johnny went missing?"

"Unless he has a body double, which I very much doubt, yes, he was. That leaves his father, and he's now

220

avoiding us. There's something funny about that family, to be honest. I felt it from the start. The Reids' marriage is falling apart. They kept that under wraps, and I only found out by accident from their GP."

"Where is the father?"

"We don't know that's the problem." He glanced at Sarah, who shook her head. Her phone rang and she answered. Roy turned back to Burns, who was fidgeting like he needed to get something off his chest.

"Is there a chance Burgess took Johnny? Yes, there is. But like you said, he couldn't be in both places at the same time. And this boy, Eddie Hearn, he couldn't have taken him."

"Why not? He had to leave Hillsborough early in the morning, to be at Fox Hagg on time. He hid the boy somewhere–"

"Where exactly?" Burns interrupted. "It's not that simple to hide an eight-year-old. I also think Burgess gets pleasure out of control. He wants these boys to do his bidding, and that could be an extreme perversion, but not necessarily sexual. That's the thrill he gets – controlling another human being. My opinion is that if he took Eddie, he would do something to the boy first. Not just hide him and then come back."

Roy mulled it over. He had some knowledge of these screwed up, violently damaged human beings like Burgess, and what Burns said made sense. They kidnapped the boys for a reason, and often, they couldn't wait. They needed immediate gratification, like a hungry predator. It made Roy's skin crawl, and his lips stretch in a snarl.

"Maybe," Burns said softly, "He couldn't do what he wanted and had to escape. You got Burgess in the nick of time. Perhaps you foiled his plans."

Roy stared at Burns. He had thought the same, what a coincidence it was that he was there, by the canalside, just as Burgess sailed off. A few minutes later, and the man would've vanished. Roy didn't believe in simple coincidences. Simon Jenkins, the young drug dealer he caught at the garage – did he notify Burgess? Or did one of the other mechanics?

It was possible, and that's why Burgess was escaping. Luckily, they got there first. Roy felt a newfound appreciation for Burns. The man was an experienced forensic psychologist and getting inside a criminal's mind was never an easy task, but those that did it well helped to solve the case.

"Are Johnny and Eddie dead?" Roy asked. He was aware of Sarah's eyes on him, listening closely.

Burns lowered his head. The bright halogen light reflected off his scalp. His grey eyes were darker when he looked at Roy. "I don't know. But we can't give up hope."

CHAPTER 33

Rizwan and Oliver were standing inside Amanda Reid's kitchen. The FLO, Sarah Percival was also there.

"I thought he told you about the second ransom note," Amanda frowned. "Maybe he got busy and didn't have time."

Oliver was watching Amanda closely. Her entire attitude was off. She seemed very composed, like she'd practiced this beforehand. The skipper, Sarah, had taught him a few things about liars. The small muscles of the face don't contract when they lie. Like the crow's feet around the eyes and lips. Liars frown excessively, and the forehead muscles bunch up in big frowns.

On Amanda's face, there was no tension around the eyes or mouth. She was cool as a cucumber.

"You told him to tell us, is that correct?" Oliver asked. "What time today?"

"Sometime in the morning, after we woke up."

Rizwan said, "I've actually seen your husband since then. I went to his office to ask him about Burgess. He didn't mention anything."

"I'm sorry. He should've." Amanda shrugged. Then her face paled. "Any news of Johnny?"

Oliver said, "We're trying everything. As you know, Burgess was on the sex offender's list, and he is our main suspect. He's in custody and DCI Roy's about to interrogate him. Do you know about the press conference today?" Oliver looked at Percival, who nodded and shuffled forward.

Amanda said, "Yes, Fiona told me. I don't want to attend. Johnny's a little boy, he won't hear me," Amanda's haggard drawn face became downcast. The tip of her nose trembled, and tears spilled out of her puffy eyes. Fiona put an arm around her and made her sit on the sofa.

Oliver and Rizwan pulled up chairs. Oliver put his elbows on his knees. "We need to know where your husband is. It's very important."

Amanda dabbed at her eyes and nose and sniffed. Her eyes flicked between the two DC's.

"Why is it so important?"

"We want to ask Mr Reid some more questions about his relationship with Mr Burgess. He's our key suspect, as you know, and we have reason to believe Mr Reid was close to him."

"Close?" Amanda's forehead knotted together. "What do you mean close?"

"Mrs Reid, your husband went to Burgess' house in Attercliffe quite often, and certainly in the days and week prior to Johnny disappearing."

224

Amanda's face went white as a sheet. Her body stiffened then she went statue still. Only her eyelids blinked. She didn't speak.

Oliver dropped his voice. "Did you know about Burgess' house in Attercliffe?"

Amanda's eyes were wider now, like she was suddenly seeing more than before. In silence, she shook her head in denial.

"Did your husband ever tell you that Burgess lived there? In addition to living at his house in Nether Edge, I mean."

Again, only the head moved in negation, the rest of Amanda's body seemed carved out of rock. Rizwan shifted in his seat, and Oliver frowned. Something was wrong, he could feel it. Rizwan touched his forearm, and he looked at his fellow DC.

Rizwan said, "Mrs Reid, are you okay?"

Amanda turned her head to him. "Oh my god. What have I done?"

"Can you please tell us what's going on?"

Tears spilled out of Amanda's eyes as her head lowered onto her chest. Her shoulder shook, and she remained like that for a while. Emily comforted her, then reached to get a box of tissues from the coffee table. Amanda wiped her nose and face.

"Duncan told me about the second ransom letter. He was worried if we don't pay up, then we will lose

Johnny. He didn't trust the police anymore, and I have to be honest, neither did I." She looked at Oliver, then to Rizwan. "I mean, I know you got Burgess. But he doesn't seem to know, does he? And how could Keith send us a ransom note when he's in custody?"

Oliver said, "Your husband said he got the second note this morning, and Burgess was free then. He could've sent it."

Amanda shook her head. "Keith had another life, and it was a bad one. Yes, he could've taken Johnny. But there's a chance it's someone else."

Oliver sense a deep unease unfurling in his limbs. Something was very wrong. "Mrs Reid, we don't have much time. Can you please tell us what's going on?"

"Oh god." Amanda clutched her forehead. "Maybe I got this all wrong. But after the second note, Duncan persuaded me to ask my father for the ransom money. He's gone to get it now from my dad."

"Where?"

"In Meersbrook Park."

CHAPTER 34

The Hearn family were still at the camp site. The entrance was guarded by two uniformed constables, and one of them spoke on the radio as they saw Roy and Sarah approaching in their black Ford Titanium. The message arrived on the car's dashboard.

"Report car approaching gates number–"

"This is DCI Roy and DS Sarah," Roy cut in, turning up the volume on his radio.

"Copy that, sorry."

Sarah said, "They're from Sheffield North station, that's why they didn't recognise our car. I should've put my lights on."

"They recognise it now," Roy said, waving at the two constables. Sarah drove down the narrow road that was just large for a car towing a caravan. A short, stone fence flanked the road on either side, and behind it, rolling green hills undulated to a valley below. A river ran through it, sun sparkling on its waters. It meandered through the valley, then winked one last time as it vanished around the bend of a hill.

"Nice place," Roy said, and he meant it. It was peaceful, apart from the three police cars in the car park. A knot of police officers stood around the pedestrian entrance of the camp site, and some people, who were clearly living in the caravans, were speaking to them. Sarah kept driving, and Roy glanced at her. At some distance from the main entrance, Sarah pulled in on the grass verge.

She turned the engine off and tapped a finger on the steering wheel for a few seconds before speaking.

"You can tell me to mind my own business, and you're the SIO, plus my ranking officer. It's been a long day. Now this," she hooked a thumb at the camp site. Then she looked at him and held his eyes. "Something seems to be bugging you, and I don't mean getting bashed around twice today, and getting stitches on your forehead." She swallowed once. "I just want to know you're okay. I've been in tough cases, and I know it's not easy. But like I said, you can tell me to shut up, and that's fine."

Roy said nothing and looked outside the window.

Sarah said, "I'm a single mother, guv. My boy's got ADHD. I know life can be hard." Roy turned to her, but she was looking down at her hands.

"Does your son go to a normal school?"

"Yes," Sarah's eyes remained downcast. "But he's disruptive. He's been sent home so many times I can't remember. Now he's on tablets, and he seems calmer."

They didn't speak for a while. A breeze picked up outside, bending the branches of the tall oak trees that spread down the hill.

"Sorry to hear that. How old is he?"

228

"Ten now. Right handful." She grinned. "You got children?"

"One girl. Fifteen years old and acts like she's twenty-five. Only calls me when she wants something."

"That's true love, in't it?"

"If you say so," Roy said, then smiled. "Who looks after your son when you're at work?"

"My mum lives close by. She does the school pick up and looks after him till I get back. I drop him off most mornings. Unless I'm really busy, then my mum does it."

"You came in early today. Take your son to school tomorrow and pick him up."

Sarah went to speak but Roy lifted a hand. "Like my little girl, your boy will grow up very quickly. Use this time. I mean that and won't expect you early tomorrow. OK?"

Sarah looked uncertain. "Is that okay, sir?"

"I wouldn't be saying it if it wasn't. Now let's go and find Eddie."

He got out of the car quickly, before Sarah could ask anything else about him.

Adams, the uniformed sergeant who had manned the Wyming crime scene was also here. He came forward when he saw them.

229

"Lighting does strike twice, it seems," he said with a rueful expression. "All my years here, never seen anything like this." He held out the clipboard and they signed their name and rank on it.

Roy looked around the site. A few people at the entrance were still chatting to the sergeant at the gate. The stone and shingle fence around the campsite went on a long way, and Roy couldn't see the end, but to the right, behind the caravans, the fence continued in the distance. The site was big, with many caravans, and Roy couldn't see the other end. Green hills rose behind the caravans, studded with trees and white sheep.

"Where was the boy taken?" he asked. Adams pointed a finger in the opposite direction, towards the wilderness. "That's the Fox Hagg Nature Reserve. The boy and his sister went cycling down there. He saw a deer, the sister thinks. He chased after it, on foot. He didn't come back. She looked for a while, then came back to raise the alarm."

Adam pointed back to the camp site. "Mum's in caravan forty-five, with the sister. Do you want to see them first?"

Roy indicated the woodlands. "Have forensics arrived?"

"Ten minutes ago."

"I'll let them crack on. Let's go and see the mother first."

It wasn't hard to spot number forty-five. It was the only one with a uniform constable standing outside.

Roy saw the sterile boards placed outside the caravan, and the sheets covering the steps. The constable touched his cap, then handed them shoe covers and masks.

"Forensics have already been, right?" Roy asked as he put the purple nitrile gloves on.

"Yes guv."

Sarah went first and knocked on the door. It opened a fraction, by a woman wearing an oversized onesie, a fluffy blue one with a mickey mouse hoodie, and two blue ears. Her cheeks were pale, and eyes sunken, but red rimmed. Sarah showed her warrant card and introduced herself and Roy. The woman stepped to one side.

As soon as Roy walked inside the caravan, he was hit by a wall of cigarette smell. The ashtray on the kitchenette table was full to overflowing. It was even a tad smoky inside. The windows were open, and curtains parted, but that wasn't enough. Roy hesitated. The woman, Eddie's mother clearly, had enough on her plate. Being told to open the door was probably a breach of her privacy right now.

As he stared at her grief-stricken face, her eyes suddenly alive with a forlorn hope when she saw him, he was reminded of another woman from many years ago – his mother. She too had stared at the senior detective that fateful day of Robin's disappearance, with a similar combination of despair and piteous hope. With an effort, Roy wrenched the image from his mind. The effects of that memory lingered, a bitter after taste as usual.

He cleared his throat. "Mrs Hearn?"

"Clara Witney," she said. "Hearn's his dad's name." Her hands twisted on her lap, and her feet tapped on the floor. Her long hair was tousled, and she'd made a quick attempt at brushing it, or someone had done it for her, just not very well. "Have you found anything?" Her voice was impatient.

"I can assure you, we will do everything, and I mean everything, to get Eddie back. First, I need to ask you some questions."

The feet didn't stop tapping. "It's like that other boy, isn't it? Johnny Reid. He was taken a couple of days ago. How can you not know who's doing this?" Her face twisted in reproach, and her eyes suddenly glowed with fury, sending a dagger to Roy's heart.

What could he say? What platitude could he offer? Every word was useless, but he had to do his best.

He raised a hand, his voice firm. "We will get Eddie back. I promise you we will do everything. I need you to be strong. I need you to believe. Got that?" He locked eyes with her. The psychology of hope was the strongest medicine at this moment in time. It might well evaporate as the days went by, but Clara had to believe in something, or she would simply disintegrate.

Her hands stopped twisting. Her spine sagged a little, and she exhaled.

"Now. Tell us what happened, starting with where you were last night."

"I went to my friend Lisa's for a gin and tonic. She's here with her mum and two kids. They're in number thirty-six. My girl Lucy's fourteen, and she looked after Eddie."

"What time did you leave, and when were you back?"

"Around half nine, after I put Eddie to bed. I was back after eleven. I stayed in touch with Lucy all the time. I was only a few yards down the road. This is a safe place. We come here every summer."

"Where's their father?"

"We're separated. He's moved to Edinburgh."

"Does he know Eddie's missing?"

"No."

Roy thought about Duncan Reid. "How close are the children to their father?"

"Not very. He sees them once or twice a year. He's got another family up there."

Roy made a note in his diary, and Sarah did the same. "What happened after you came back?"

"Lucy was in bed next to Eddie, and she was up, watching something on her phone. Eddie was fast asleep. That's…" Her eyes suddenly flared, and a whiplash of anguish tormented her face. "That's the last time I saw him."

A tap gurgled, then a toilet flushed somewhere. A side door opened, and footsteps sounded on the floor. Then a head poked out of a bedroom. It was a teenage girl, almost as tall as Clara, who was about five seven. She had dyed black hair, but the brown bits were becoming more apparent. Her eyes were puffy, and crimson tinged. She glanced at Roy and Sarah, frowned, then looked at Clara.

"Who're they?"

"I'm the senior investigating officer," Roy said in as friendly a voice as he could muster. He said his name and introduced Sarah.

"Have you found Eddie?" The girl demanded, coming out and leaning against the door. She wore black jeans and a black T shirt that said – No Easy Day, with a skull and daggers logo under and above it.

"You must be Lucy," Roy smiled at her. She reminded him of Anna, except the black clothes. Anna was pink and flowery, a girly girl.

Lucy didn't smile back. She sat down next to her mother, shoulders touching. "Shouldn't you be out there, looking for him?" Lucy demanded. "He's not here, is he?"

"You were with him this morning, right?" Roy kept his voice low and gently. "Tell us what happened and start from when you woke up."

Lucy swallowed, and she kept up the bravado for a while, then her lips trembled. Clara clutched her hand, and Lucy held it tight, like it was an anchor.

"I told Eddie to wait, but he wouldn't. He wanted to go for a morning bike ride. I went with him. Once you're out on the hilly bit, the road goes down for a long time, around a bend. I lost him there. I went down as fast as I could, but he was quicker going uphill, so I was always catching up. I told him to stop but he wouldn't listen."

Lucy paused to take a breath. Sarah said, "You're doing good. Carry on."

"When I got to the bottom, I couldn't see him. I did see a couple of deer run across the road and I know he would've stopped to watch them. He does that always."

"Did you actually see Eddie doing that?" Sarah asked.

"No. But I thought I heard his breaks squeak downhill, which meant he stopped." Lucy continued. "Then I came back up the hill when I couldn't find him. The hill ends in a path that goes through a valley. I saw his bike at the edge of the woods on the hill... and I went in, looking for him. I couldn't find him." Lucy's hands tightened on her mother's and the other hand became a claw on her jeans. She started to sob, and Clara put an arm around her shoulder. "I'm sorry..."

"It's not your fault," Sarah said, and the others echoed her sentiment. Roy's radio crackled to life, and, a beat later, so did Sarah's. She went out to answer, and Roy carried on with his question. Before he could utter another word, Sarah was back, calling him outside.

"Duncan Reid made a plan with his wife to pay the ransom to see if they can get Johnny back. He told her not to talk, but she has now, to Oliver. Duncan's on his way to Meersbrook Park to get the money from her dad, Brian.

"You stay here," Roy said. "I'll catch up with them."

CHAPTER 35

Meersbrook was in the south of Sheffield, and Roy was on the opposite pole. He put the location on his satnav, and then hit the sirens. It was late afternoon now, and traffic had thickened around the city centre. He went up on the kerb more than once and overtook an ambulance. A squad car stood by Meersbrook Park with its lights flashing, and he recognised Oliver's BMW from the carpool. He didn't see any uniform officer at the gates, which was a mistake, but they were short of staff, and all of them were inside, searching.

As he ran into the park, he pulled out his phone, studying the park exits. The park was bigger than he had imagined. It was roughly triangular at the top near the main A61 road, where he was now. Roy stopped to get his bearings. His radio crackled again, and it was Rizwan. He told them his position.

"There's a bowling green opposite from where you are. East to west. We got Duncan's burner phone number from his wife and traced it there. Five minutes ETA. See you there."

Rizwan was panting, and Roy broke into a run himself. It was a nice day, the park was crowded, and he had to slow down in case he barged into someone. He stopped after a while and looked at his phone map. He was a pulsing green dot, and he was getting closer to the red pin which was the bowling green. A bout of dizziness overcame him, and he had to put his arms out to balance himself. A woman pushing a pram frowned at him, and he put on his best smile, then realised he was just coming across as creepy.

Roy shook his head as the dizziness worsened, and the ground seemed to tilt up, the path moving, and the green grass on either side moved up and down. Dear god, he needed to get a hold of himself. He slowed his steps, then went into the field, and ran along it. It was less crowded than the path. The fields sloped up and down, and, by the time he got close to the bowling green, his shirt was sticking to his body like a second skin, and his jacket was tightly bunched in his right hand.

He saw a couple of high visibility jackets flash near a group of elderly people by the bowling green. His left ankle was now a throbbing mass of pain, and it seemed to be vying for competition with his blasted head. The stitches were swelling, and would pop soon, he was sure of it – his entire forehead was hot to the touch. People stared as he lumbered down the slope like a great big oaf – arms swinging, panting, and boots smacking on the grass.

As he got closer, he saw Rizwan and Oliver, speaking to a couple of bowlers in their whites. Roy wondered why Duncan would meet Amanda's father here… unless Brian, her father, was here to play bowls. He could see the players pavilion behind the bowling green, and the benches in front of the small, white

238

fenced pavilion. He left the DCs and uniforms to carry on with their search and skirted around the pavilion till he saw the car park.

He was looking for a green Ford Focus, Duncan's car. Rizwan had told him what car he drove. He found it at the end of the car park, under the shade of a tree. He looked up the reg number on his phone, then called Oliver and told him.

"He can't be far. Send one of the uniforms here, and I'll look around."

"Can't find Brian either. He's not playing today, according to a couple of the old timers here," Oliver said. "Brian's 78 years old, he can't go far."

"He must've driven down. See if you can get his car reg number."

Roy went to the entrance gate and looked around. There was a cricket pitch across the path, over a fence. A match was about to start, the players, all in white, were limbering up. It was a good idea to meet up here as no one would notice them. On the other hand, there could be lots of witnesses. The more he thought about it, the more it seemed likely that Duncan would sit in Brian's car, and he would hand the money bag over, or they'd go for a drive. And if Duncan's car was here, he couldn't be far.

He walked towards the cricket pitch, his eyes scanning, mind buzzing. Duncan was presumably still wearing the brown coat that Rizwan had seen him in earlier today, and blue jeans with white trainers. A cluster of trees moved in the wind across the cricket pitch, and a few benches were laid out under the trees. On one bench, deep in the shades, he saw a white-haired old man, with a taller, younger chap next to him. They weren't easily visible, as they were partly-hidden by the hanging branches of a tree.

Roy put his jacket back on. The white shirt was easily visible. He walked casually, but his eyes were focused on the pair, who seemed to be deep in discussion. As he got closer, he stood behind a thick tree trunk and watched them. It was Duncan, there wasn't any doubt. The silver haired man was explaining something to him with a finger raised, and Duncan had his head bent. It didn't look like he was enjoying the conversation.

Roy twirled the black knob of his radio. "Suspect sighted opposite cricket pitch, nine o clock from the bowling club. Approaching now."

"Copy that, guv," Oliver replied. "Moving into position."

Roy sauntered down the path, hands in pockets, almost whistling. His eyes remained on the pair. He increased his pace when Duncan reached under the bench and pulled out a brown leather bag by its straps. He was about a hundred yards away, and still hadn't seen Roy.

Duncan stood, and said a few parting words to the older man, who remained on the bench. Roy was closing the gap fast. Duncan turned and saw him. He froze when their eyes met, then he turned and ran. Roy cursed and went for it, breaking into as fast a sprint as his tired body and sore ankle allowed.

"Suspect escaping. Going up the hill towards the A61 entrance."

"Copy that," came another panting voice he didn't recognise. "Attention all units…"

The radio crackle continued, but Roy reduced the volume. His lungs burned as he pumped his legs up the hill. Duncan was younger, and perhaps fitter, which was really annoying. But Roy was damned if he was getting away. He wheezed and whined like an old engine and dragged in deep breaths. He crested the hill and saw Duncan heading towards the trees on the left, behind which he could see the faint outline of a fence.

"Stop," he screamed. As expected, Duncan didn't listen. He went into the trees and vanished from view. Cursing freely now, Roy barged into the woods, and almost got knocked down by an overhanging branch. It hit him next to where the stitches were, which was the first bit of luck he'd had all day. Holding his head, heaving like an ageing horse, he lumbered between the trees.

Duncan had slung the bag over his shoulders, and he was climbing the fence. A shadow streaked down the side, and it was a uniformed officer. He was joined by another, then Roy saw Oliver behind them. The uniform officer was tall, and he leapt up, and grabbed Duncan's foot. The others joined him, and Duncan lost his balance, crashing down on top of the three men below him.

Roy got to the scene just as Duncan was on his chest, screaming obscenities. Rizwan put a knee on his back and handcuffed him.

CHAPTER 36

The shadows were getting longer as Duncan was put in the back seat of a squad car. Roy oversaw the process, rivulets of sweat still coursing down the back of his neck. His eyes felt like someone was stabbing the from inside the skull. He dug his palms into his eyes to relieve the pain. A siren sounded as the squad car took off, driving Duncan to the station. Roy had a million questions to ask him, but it would have to wait. His watch said quarter past four, which meant he had hardly any time left before the press conference. As if on cue, his phone buzzed. He took it out and swore under his breath.

"Where are you?" Nugent's gruff voice barked.

"The view from Jacob's Ladder is really nice. You should try it sometime."

"Get your arse back in here. I don't care–"

"We just got Duncan Reid after his wife tipped him off. We also got a bag full of money that Duncan was taking for himself, I think. But the money belonged to Amanda's dad."

"Oh god." Nugent wheezed like an old horse being strangled.

"Makes me feel religious too, which is saying something. Maybe only He can help us now. Smoke another one, I'm on my way."

Roy hung up and got into his car. His body felt heavy, like he was wading through water. His radio chattered, and he recognised Sarah's voice. He answered as he drove, giving her an update.

"Copy that, guv. I joined forensics at the crime scene in the Fox Hagg woods. We found the boy's bike. Nothing on it. Waiting for prints. The woods are also empty, but there's one interesting fact from a local staying at the caravan park. There's a path through the forest that links Fox Hagg to Wyming Reserve. Do you want me to check it out?"

Roy mulled it over. If there was anyone, he trusted to supervise searching that route, it would be Sarah. "Would you mind? I have to get back for the bloody conference. Nugent will have my guts for garters if I don't."

Unexpectedly, Sarah laughed. Roy frowned. "That was funny?"

"Guts for garters, that's a northern saying. Pretty soon you'll be saying owt for nowt."

"And calling dinner tea. Alright, the hidden northerner in me is coming out, okay? Hope you're ready."

"Can't wait, guv." She cleared her throat and went silent, and so did Roy. He wasn't quite sure what to say.

"See you back at the nick," he followed up, then ended the call.

Meersbrook wasn't far from the South Sheffield nick, and in his mind, he still called it nick, but he wasn't sure what they called it up here. The media hordes were absent from the gates of the rear car park, because they were all in the press conference.

He parked the car and got out, half running, half hobbling to the canteen. He downed an espresso and went into the open plan office. He saw Nugent standing in front of his desk with a face like thunder, a woman fidgeting next to him. Nugent saw him and his lips twisted like he'd just eaten something with a horrible taste. "Now then. What happened to you?"

Roy hadn't stopped for a loo break, but he knew he wasn't a sight for sore eyes. His shirt was still sticking to his body, and his head felt like it'd been squeezed through a meat grinder.

Before he could answer, the woman stepped forward. She was a tall brunette, dressed in a nice charcoal skirt suit.

"I'm Donna, the MLO. We've got two minutes to make you look presentable. God, that bruise on your forehead. And your left eye." She got up close and peeked at him like she was watching the Rocky Horror Show.

"Are you always this charming?" Roy said, as Donna examined him. "Or do you really like what you see?"

Donna ignored him and turned to Nugent. "This doesn't look right. We can't present an injured officer to the national media. It gives South Yorkshire Police a bad reputation."

Nugent flapped his arms, cursed, and kicked a nearby chair. Roy said, "Don't you think not finding those two boys is worse for our reputation?"

Donna showed him a palm. "I'm not arguing that. But frankly you look terrible. Not the image we want to portray."

"The image?" Roy was incredulous. "We've got a crisis on our hands. Two suspects in custody but no sign of the missing boys. By tomorrow, our chances of finding them will be lower. Every passing minute goes against us, and you're worried about image?" Donna went to speak but Roy hushed her. "A TV and radio message helps us. You never know what a witness might have seen." He looked at Nugent, who was staring at him with something that looked distantly like newfound respect, he thought. Pretty distant still, as a sneer curled around his lips. "I've done this before, and it helped. Hundreds called Crimestoppers. I'm doing it again now." He turned on his heels and headed for the major incident room. Donna made a sound like a mouse squeaking and ran ahead of him.

"I need to brief the press before anyone goes in. If I tell the Chief Constable you're going to barge in there looking like… like this, she's going to have a fit."

Roy put his hands on his waist. Nugent was huffing and puffing behind him, catching up with them. "Donna, do you know what your problem is?" She opened her mouth and blinked at him. "Let me tell you," Roy offered. "You haven't seen the despair in Amanda Reid's eyes, or the terror in Clara Witney's. They won't sleep, or eat, or do anything really till we get some answers. Even if it's answers they don't want. These mothers want closure, even if that will be the worst news they ever hear, even if it breaks their hearts." Roy stopped and took a deep breath. He pointed at his face. "No one cares about this. To be honest, a beaten-up copper on TV might be just the jolt the nation needs."

"I hear you," Donna said. "I'm not heartless. I have children myself. But it'd be much better if Superintendent Nugent would handle the conference."

Both of them turned to Nugent, who went to speak, then failed. By now, Roy knew the signs. The geyser was about to pop. Nugent's cheeks were slowly turning crimson. "Chuffin' hell! You havin' a laugh? This bugger's done the arrests and now you want me to speak to them scallywags?"

The inner Yorkshire man in Nugent was clearly out now, and he didn't care about what he sounded like. Roy also suspected Nugent had a fear of the press. Maybe he'd been strung up by them in the past, and he wouldn't be the first senior copper to suffer that fate.

"I couldn't put it better myself," Roy said, for once on the same side as Nugent. "I'm the SIO, and my senior officer's just asked me to do the conference. Now, if you want to apply some blusher, I'm happy with that, but otherwise I'm going in."

He stepped past Donna, who wasn't having any of it. Roy actually respected her tenacity, but she was getting this wrong. He wondered how much she actually knew about the case. He glanced at Nugent, who was still seething. Was Donna aware they had Duncan in custody? Roy didn't think so, and, unless it was really necessary, she didn't have to know.

Donna fished out her phone. "Let me speak to the Chief Constable."

"You know what," Roy said. "I don't have time for this. Get someone else to do your bloody conference. I have suspects to question."

He turned on his heels and walked the other way. Despite her heels, Donna was quick. She pulled on his sleeve, stopping him.

"Okay, fine." She was a little breathless, spots of red appearing on her cheeks through the make-up. "I'll speak to the media before you go in, and explain you were injured while apprehending suspects."

"That works," Roy nodded. "If you do that now, I'll have a word with the DS here and then join you backstage."

Donna puffed out her cheeks, then scurried off. Roy watched her go, then shook his head. Image. This wasn't some publicity stunt for the police force.

"Gets on her high horse, that one. She would've kept fighting, too. She's probably calling the Chief Constable as we speak," Nugent said.

"She can call the King as far as I'm concerned." He piped down and glanced at Nugent. His small blue eyes were darting around, but they stopped when he hooked eyes with Roy. "Sir, I don't want to tell the media about Duncan Reid. Just mention the two arrests without any names. But I should tell them about Eddie Hearn."

"Yes, I agree. Did you ask the parents if they wanted to make an appeal?"

"Amanda declined, she said Johnny was too young to be aware, by which she meant her kidnapper wouldn't let him watch TV. I think she's right, but parents have been in appeals before."

"Just get it over and done with," Nugent growled.

CHAPTER 37

The incident room had been prepared for the conference. A large poster of Johnny hung on either side of the platform, and it had recently been joined by a smaller photo of Eddie. Donna and her assistant stood to the side, just out of reach of the cameras. Nugent stood next to them. Roy was seated on the platform, three cameras pointed at him. The reporters listened as he explained what had happened so far.

"Two local men are under arrest. They are being questioned and we will keep you updated. In the meantime, we would like to appeal to anyone who has any information, however insignificant it might seem to them, about the boys, to please come forward. Time is of the essence in our investigation. All contacts to the police will be treated with complete confidentiality. Please help us find the children and return them to their families."

Roy finished, then looked up. "I will take questions now. We have ten minutes, no more." He pointed to the young lady in the first row.

The woman said, "Libby Purves, from the Sheffield Herald. What are the names of the men under arrest?"

"I cannot disclose that. Please wait till our investigation is concluded."

Roy pointed at one of the men who had practically hit him with his microphone in Wyming Reserve.

"Rob Gore, from the National Herald. Do you have any clues as to where the boys are?"

"There are a number of channels we are investigating right now. When we have a conclusive answer, we will let you know."

The questions continued, and Roy continued to block them to the best of his ability. He was exhausted after almost an hour and grateful Donna sounded the bell that declared the end. Several hands shot up, then a cacophony of questions were hurled at him. He got up and left as quickly as he could manage.

"That wasn't too bad," Donna said. She was next to a man sat at a folding table by the curtain, his open laptop displaying footage from the conference, clearly meant for Donna's benefit. "You looked okay on camera."

Roy indicated Nugent, who was deep in conversation with a PC. "I'm more photogenic than him, which isn't exactly difficult. Your choice was limited."

He said goodbye and went into the office. It was past six, and the office was thinning out. It had been a long and bruising day, and he needed to get his head around all of it. He rang Sarah, who was on her way back from the Fox Hagg camp site.

"Go home," Roy said. "I'll tell the others as well. We have to wait to question Duncan and Burgess, and hopefully by tomorrow the DNA matches will be back."

"There's something from the Fox Hagg campsite. Three of the campers said they'd seen a man in a dark coat and jeans walk around the outside boundary, near the car park. They also saw him standing by the gate, but he turned and walked away when they got closer."

"Description?"

"IC1 male, middle aged. Slim build, average height to tall. Wore a farmer's peaked cap. No glasses. That's about all we got."

Roy thought about it for a while. "That's an important witness statement. Any other sightings?"

"I asked around. No one else, but we can start again tomorrow."

Oliver said, "Have we questioned Duncan? He's had a chat with the duty solicitor."

"Let's do that now. I need another tea first." He turned to Rizwan. "Get hold of Brian, Amanda's dad. We need his statement."

"Oliver," Roy indicated to Oliver, who perked up. "You come with me to question Duncan. Rizwan, you stay and update Sarah when she comes back. She might be a while though; I gave her some time off to pick up her son from school and drop off to her mother's."

"She told us," Rizwan said. "I'll be upstairs, it'll be reyt."

Roy frowned. "What?"

A flicker of a smile played on Rizwan's lips. "Be reyt. As in, all will be alright. You must've heard that expression, guv. Common in these parts."

"Learn something new every day," Roy said. "In fact, I have heard it before, just not for many decades."

They walked towards the canteen for a quick cup of tea, which also gave Roy a few minutes to catch his breath. It was ten past five already. He had to charge burgess and Duncan, otherwise he couldn't keep them here any more than twenty-four hours. And even if charged, he had to let them go if they got bail, which Burgess probably would, as he had the CCTV evidence to prove he was in the garage when Johnny went missing.

Duncan had no such luck, and a judge would have to think twice before allowing him bail. Roy finished his tea and rubbed his eyes.

"Rizwan," he told Rizwan. "Chase up the DNA matches. I know it's early days, but they should be able to rush it for us, given the case. Get an e-fit image for the man seen in Fox Hagg, and send it to everyone, and everywhere. I want it up in the city centre, public libraries, buses, internet, you name it. Make it viral on social media if you have to."

"I'll put it on the SYP social media sites, guv. And speak to the city council."

"Good." Roy's eyes flicked to Oliver. "Did either of you two ask Amanda where Duncan was yesterday morning?"

"He went to work," Rizwan said. "That's where I caught up with him. Maybe they've got CCTV, I'll check. I've got his car's reg number, we can ask traffic to check their cameras, see if they can spot him."

"CCTV at his work would be easier to verify what time he started, if they have it. Also, lean on Dobson. Apart from the boot prints, which could've been planted by Duncan, we have no other forensic report. I want one, by the time we're finished interrogating."

"Got it," Rizwan said, draining his cup. They parted company, Oliver and Roy heading down to the custody chamber, Rizwan going back to his desk.

"Who's the lawyer?" Roy asked as they went down the steps.

"Duty solicitor. James Keenan. He's been around for a while."

They signed their names at the notebook on the custody sergeant's desk. The interview rooms were arranged next to the custody cells, and Duncan was at the second one. Roy went into the side room first and watched Duncan and the solicitor through the glass box.

Duncan was restless. His hands moved; his feet tapped on the floor. He looked around the room like he was searching for an escape route. He turned to look at the glass screen, his eyes round, haunted, with hollows under them. The look of a trapped man, Roy thought. He walked out into the small passage that separated the two rooms, followed by Oliver.

CHAPTER 38

Duncan sat up straight when Roy entered the room. His eyes remained on them as they sat down, and Oliver pressed the red button on the machine. He spoke on the machine and introduced everyone.

Roy kept his face impassive, but sat upright, his eyes on Duncan. Keenan, the solicitor, wore a cheap, dark suit that had frayed edges, and he had an expression on his face not dissimilar to the tired appearance of his attire. He was in his fifties, with hair getting sparse on the top, and two-day white stubble on his cheeks. Duncan was shifty, and he kept looking around, but eventually he caught Roy's eyes.

"Shall we start then?" Roy said calmly. His face was carved in stone, only his lips moved.

Duncan's Adam's apple moved, and his breathing increased slightly. Good, thought Roy. He stared at him for few seconds, letting the silence deepen.

"Do you mind if I call you Duncan?"

Duncan's head moved a fraction downwards. Roy took that as a yes.

"Please tell us about your friendship with Keith Burgess." Roy deliberately kept the question open ended.

Duncan licked his dry lips. "I… I've told you already. He came to our house a couple of times, and I saw him at the pub. He was my sister's boyfriend."

"Did you know he had a house at Attercliffe?"

Duncan opened his mouth to answer, then stopped. Then he shook his head. He was struggling to keep calm. Wrong answer, Roy thought to himself.

"And yet, we have CCTV footage that shows you going into Burgess's house in Attercliffe twice last week."

Oliver took out an iPad from his bag and placed it on the table. He went to the relevant screen, then pressed play, and turned it towards Duncan. Roy thanked Oliver then focused on Duncan again.

"That's you, isn't it? Before you answer, please remember we have applied facial recognition software to identify you in the images." Roy glanced at Keenan whose face was now pinched, brows furrowed as he looked at the screen with his client.

"The software came back with a 98% match to Mr Reid's passport and driving licence photos", Oliver said.

"That's right," Roy said, remaining focused on Duncan. "That definitely was you, correct?"

Duncan's eyes widened a fraction, as he stared at the screen. Keenan squinted, then spoke softly in his client's ear. Duncan looked at his feet, hands twisting on his lap. "No comment."

Roy shrugged as if he didn't have a care in the world. "To be honest, it doesn't matter what you say. The evidence is there right in front of us. That close a match, it can only be you."

Duncan wouldn't look at Roy. His head remained downcast, and he only glanced at his solicitor, then at the floor.

"What sort of a father makes friends with a child molester?" Roy asked, the question directed at Duncan, but also rhetorical.

Duncan's head snapped up at that. His eyes glinted, then narrowed. "I didn't know that about him."

"He didn't tell you when you went to see him in Attercliffe?"

"No, he didn't..." Duncan stopped, realising his mistake.

"So, you did see him in Attercliffe," Roy said, with a plain face. He didn't smile at the small victory. There was no reward here, only repulsion at this sorry excuse of a human being in front of him. Barely a man, and not someone who deserved to be a father. Roy's skin itched with rage every time Duncan looked at him.

"Okay," Duncan replied in a shaky voice, his head still lowered. "Yes, I went to his place."

Keenan spoke in his ears again, and Duncan clammed up. Roy gave the solicitor an irritated frown, which Keenan responded to with a smile. Roy hated these lawyers with a passion. They thought they were doing their jobs when they were actually doing the opposite – obstructing justice.

He focused on Duncan. "Your son is missing. You were there when it happened. Three days before that, you went into the house of a convicted sex offender, drug dealer and armed robber. Burgess didn't even tell your sister he lived there. Yet, he told you. Why?" Duncan licked his lips. Roy didn't have time to waste. "You've got to answer."

Oliver said, "Silence looks bad. Only the guilty say no comment. If this goes to a court, a judge will look at the transcript."

"That's right," Roy nodded. "And there's every chance this will go to court once Duncan's charged, isn't that right?"

"That's right, guv," Oliver said.

Keenan cleared his throat and spoke for the first time. "Do you intend to charge my client? If you do, then let's hear it."

Roy smiled grimly. "Oh, I'm going to charge him alright. Don't you worry about that Mr Keenan. We just need more detail to shape our inquiry, that's all."

Keenan whispered something in Duncan's ears again, and the man looked at Roy briefly, then away.

"No comment."

He had cornered himself, and there was no way out. Roy decided to go for the jugular.

"Let me level with you," Roy relaxed back in his chair. He spoke softly, taking his time. Duncan swivelled his eyes, barely looking at Roy. "We got you on CCTV going into Burgess' house. You were at the crime scene when Johnny, your son, disappeared. We have Burgess in custody now. He's going to talk sooner or later, and he's going to want to cut a deal with us. You know the first thing he's going to do about his old pal, his mate Duncan?"

Roy hooked his eyebrows north and stared at Duncan, who swallowed, and then looked to the left, at the floor, like he could see the ground opening up.

"Yes, that's right," Roy said. "He's going to drop you like a piece of hot coal. He's going to blame you for everything. Say it was your plan to take his own son and make it look like a big kidnapping just to make money out of Amanda's dad."

Duncan's mouth fell open, and he looked like he'd been slapped across the face.

Roy continued his assault, raising his voice a few decibels. "Because that's what happened, didn't it? You lied to Brian and took the money because you were about to lose your job. You also wanted to leave Amanda. You were going to split the money with Burgess, and you kidnapped your own son for that." Roy shook his head. "Didn't you?"

Keenan was leaning towards Duncan, urgently whispering into his left ear. For once, Duncan stared at Roy, his chest heaving, cheeks mottling red.

"No," he whispered. "I didn't take Johnny. He's my son. And I didn't know Burgess was on the sex offender's list. I knew he was dodgy, and he'd done time before, but not for what."

"What plan did you make with him?"

Duncan was silent and Roy repeated his question. Then he said, "Duncan, I can charge you with kidnapping Johnny. Given the evidence we have, the charge will stick. Tell us the truth, and we can help."

Duncan lowered his head into his hands and remained like that for a while.

Then his defeated, dead eyes hooked with Roy's. "I don't know where Johnny is, or who took him."

Oliver cleared his throat, and Roy nodded at him to take over. "If you didn't, then why did you take the money and do a runner?"

"Because I wanted to keep the money for the kidnapper. I wanted to get my son back. I knew you would take it from me, and I wouldn't get my son back," Duncan said, a little conviction in his tone now.

Oliver asked, "And you have no idea who took Johnny? Or where he is?"

Duncan's face was colourless, his cheeks sunken in, eyes wide. He shook his head, then licked his dry, cracked lips. "No."

"How did you know where the kidnapper would be? He didn't specify time and location for an exchange, did he?"

"Yes, he had. I had the note on me, but it fell out of my pocket. My wife didn't see it."

"Really?" Roy allowed the scepticism to show on his face. "When did you get the note?"

"Early this afternoon. My wife told me it'd arrived. She picked it up before that policewoman at home saw it. Then she told me, and I knew then we had to do this."

So, Sarah the FLO hadn't seen the latest note from the kidnapper. That explained why no one knew about it.

"And you want us to believe you lost it? We need to see it, Duncan. Crucial piece of evidence, that."

Duncan moved his arms like a drowning man begging for help. "You lot chased me in the park. That's when it fell out. I can't help it."

"You ran," Roy reminded him. "You could've just given yourself up and saved everyone a lot of bother."

"And not get Johnny back," Duncan spat with venom. "I was going to take the money to the kidnapper and get my son back."

Roy pressed his lips together, a sudden thought niggling at the back of his mind. It was gone before it

262

arrived, and he chased it in his mind. He shook his head once. Nah, it was gone.

He asked, "Where was the drop off?"

"The man didn't specify. He said get the money and be ready, like. He'd let us know. And not to tell the bizzies."

"Bizzies?" Oliver frowned. "That's Liverpool. You don't sound like a scouser."

Duncan curled up his lips in a snarl and looked away. Oliver raised his eyebrows and Roy gave him a look that suggest he leave it. Roy turned back to Duncan.

He put his elbows on the desk and leaned forward. "You took Johnny. You put him somewhere, and you asked your friend Burgess to help hide him."

Duncan's forehead knotted together, and his nostrils flared. "I just told you I didn't."

Keenan sighed, almost bored. "Inspector Roy, my client has clearly told you what he knows. Is there any point in pushing this any further?"

"Yes, there is," Roy snapped. "We have not one, but two missing boys. Father of the Year over here says he didn't do it, but I don't believe him as far as I can throw him. What do you think, DC Oliver?"

"Not as far as I can throw him," Oliver echoed. "And that wouldn't be far at all. Like across the table, at the very most, and even that's a stretch. Well mardy, if you ask me."

Roy considered the use of "mardy" but wisely let it slide. He fixed Duncan with a stare but wasn't hostile. The layers were peeling off, and he could see a lot more of the man now. He was a snivelling, pathetic wreck, and one aspect of that worried Roy. Someone like the Lily Man would be a far tougher nut to crack. And yet, he didn't believe Duncan wholly. He was still hiding something.

Roy crossed his arms across his chest and exhaled theatrically. "So, there you have it. Do you really expect us to believe you planned all of this, were there when it happened, and yet, you don't know how Johnny was abducted? Come on. Pull the other one."

"I… I'm telling you," Duncan's frown got deeper, and he looked at Keenan frantically, like a schoolkid trying to get off detention from his teacher.

Keenan was still reclining on his chair but had a notebook open on his lap. He glanced up at Roy. His seasoned stare was starting to get harder. "Once again, Inspector. This is a broken record now. Time to move on?"

Roy ignored him and remained fixated on Duncan. That little niggle in his mind was growing, spreading across like ripples on a pond. He could now see the gaps.

Burgess couldn't have been there to take Johnny. Someone else had to. Duncan had to be lying. As much as Roy wanted to believe him, just for the sheer sake of the man being a father, logic dictated that Burgess wasn't the kidnapper. Ergo, it was Duncan. Unless…

unless… Damn it. There was a shape here, and he could just make it out, but it was dim, obscure, just out of reach.

"Duncan," he said aloud. Roy knew Nugent was watching from the other side, and for all he knew the Chief Constable, or one of Assistant Chiefs had joined him. Everyone knew the clock was ticking. For Roy, a crashing, bone jarring sound with the passing of every second.

He said, "With your wife, Amanda, you decided to give in to the kidnapper's demands, in the hope you get Johnny back. But," Roy paused and jabbed a finger at Duncan, "We don't know if you wanted to take the money and run, because run you did, as soon as you saw us."

Oliver said, "And only the guilty run. Isn't that right, guv?"

"Yes," Roy said, happy to carry on with the double act. "Only those who have something to hide run from the old bill. That's cockney for cops, in case you were wondering."

Oliver blew out his cheeks. "Bizzies in Liverpool. Old bill down south. Cops are just cops here, guv."

Roy shrugged, not taking his eyes away from a squirming Duncan. "What do you have to hide, Duncan? What are you not telling us?"

The man looked like a cornered rat, his dark eyes turning left to right, moving constantly.

"You were going to take the money and run anyway, weren't you? Your marriage to Amanda was over. You hated her father. You were out to diddle them anyway."

"Diddle?" Oliver frowned, glancing at Roy.

"Keep up with the lingo, son," Roy said, not taking his gaze away from Duncan, who didn't find any of it amusing in the slightest. "I'm not the Oxford English Dictionary. Diddle her dad out of a hundred-grand, which must be a good chunk of the old man's life savings. Then bugger off before we could get to you. Amanda told you we had Burgess, and you knew the game was up."

Duncan's mouth moved up and down without any sound, making an almost perfect impression of a fish out of water.

"But the real question is if you know who took Johnny, or where he is now. That would make sense, because you got the cash, now all you need to do is pick up your son, and off you go into the Spanish sunset."

"Hasta la vista," Oliver said. "Or maybe just Adios."

"Perfect. Now we're international." Roy rubbed his hands together.

"Auf Wiedersehn, Pet," Oliver said, then caught the frown from Roy. "Sorry. He's not going to Berlin, I guess."

"So, were you on your way to get Johnny?" Roy got back to business. "Is that why you were so desperate to get away from us?"

266

"No," Duncan said. "Once and for all, I don't know where the hell Johnny is." He covered his face with his hands, and his head lowered to the table.

CHAPTER 39

"He's not lying," Sarah said. She had some colour in her cheeks, and unless Roy was mistaken, there was a sparkle in her eyes.

They were sitting behind the closed door of the incident room that was now empty. Only a whiteboard with the photos and names of the suspects kept them company. Rizwan slurped noisily from his cup and looked over the rim, aware of his transgression. He caught barbs of dislike from Sarah and Oliver.

"Sorry," Rizwan said, lowering the cup. "It's the cream on top of the Mocha. I have to get it out."

"Use a spoon next time," Roy advised. "Plenty in the kitchen."

"And you won't sound like you're oral farting," Oliver pitched in, drawing a round of bewilderment from everyone.

"Oral farting? Isn't that just burping? Both sound disgusting, mind you," Sarah said.

"Nope, oral farting is different," Oliver insisted. "It's like farting but it comes out of–"

"That's enough," Roy said. "Let's get back on track here." He turned to Sarah. "You were saying?"

"He's too scared," Sarah said, taking a long, and silent sip from her teacup. "I watched the final bits of your interview. I think he bit off more than he could chew, then panicked. Bloody idiot, if you ask me."

"He's got no prior PCNs or convictions," Roy said, referring to the sheets of printout he held in his hand, courtesy of Rizwan.

Roy closed his eyes, digging the heels of his palm into them. It released the pain a little, but only a little. He needed some sleep, but that was a long way away. Instead, that vague shape he'd been thinking of was now firmer in his mind.

"What if Duncan was set up as the fall guy?" He murmured out loud. "What if Burgess was working with someone else?"

"A third guy?" Rizwan frowned. "That muddies the waters."

"Why not just use Duncan? Maybe he's lying after all, and this is all an act," Oliver said. "Duncan's making us believe what he wants us to believe."

Roy considered that. It wasn't a million miles from the realms of reason. Sarah said, "If that was acting, then he deserves a bloody Oscar. Looked like a cat on a hot tin roof!" She grinned. "No pun intended."

"Stick to the day job, guv," Oliver said. "That was terrible."

Sarah made a face at him, and looked at Roy, ostensibly for support. Roy shook his head. "Sorry, have to agree.

Terrible pun, even if it wasn't intended, which I think it was."

Sarah looked to the heavens in mock despair. "That's what I get for working with three blokes. Prayed for a female boss this time but didn't happen." She grinned at Roy to take away the barb. He shrugged it away.

Rizwan said, "I checked the CCTV from Duncan's workplace. I saw him checking in, and most of the morning he stayed in. He went to his car, that's when I caught up with him."

"So, he couldn't have taken Eddie Hearn," Roy mused. "Are there any CCTV blackspots in the workplace?"

"The outside area is three hundred and sixty degrees coverage and would've spotted him." Rizwan said. "And I was there by midday. He would have to grab Eddie around 10 am and get back in time, which would be quite a feat."

"But not impossible," Oliver argued. "And he would know if there were any CCTV blackspots. He could've slipped out. Just a theory, mind."

"Yes," Roy rubbed his chin. "Anyway, Duncan is here till tomorrow and then we either charge him or he gets out. That Keenan will make sure he does. He's an old salty dog."

"That Keenan is," Sarah said. "I would've told you so if I was here. Come across him before. Gets on my nerves."

Roy noted that. "I still think we can press Duncan for more. Maybe Burgess told him stuff that he's not blurted as yet. We can chat to him again early tomorrow."

Roy finished the rest of his tea and got to his feet. He winced as he put pressure on the left ankle. He got to the whiteboard and picked up a black pen. Under the photo of Eddie Hearn that Sarah had stuck on, he wrote down the number one.

"What did you find at the crime scene?" He asked Sarah.

She sighed. "A note with a white lily stuck to it. Same drill. Don't tell the cops, wait for ransom note. Handwritten in big black caps. Simple white paper and white envelope. It was left under the bike. With forensics now. No prints on IDENT-1, as far as I know."

"What about the man the residents saw?"

"I got descriptions from three of them. They saw the man once in the last two days, and once in the week before that. Each time was in the morning. They have barbecues in the evening, and there's light till late. A woman also saw a man of similar description, around 8 pm, two days ago. He was standing by the gates, watching. Then he walked off."

Roy looked at Rizwan. "How did you get on with the other past residents of the caravan park?"

Rizwan put his coffee mug on the table and pulled up his iPad. His eyes flicked over the screen. "I got twenty-four phone numbers for people staying over the last week. Contacted ten of them – none of them saw anything."

"That means this guy's only been active this week. But make sure we follow up all the leads."

"Will do, guv. Forgot to say I also asked for a new FLO to visit Clara Witney's house, where she lives with Eddie and Lucy. FLO's called Patricia. A uniform squad will patrol outside her house, too."

"Seems like the coffee's working," Roy said. "Good work."

"But no more oral farts," Oliver cautioned. "Or I might have to hit you with an ASBO." Antisocial behaviour orders were typically slapped on drunken louts.

"At least I do some work instead of swanning around like the Elliot Ness of Yorkshire Police," Rizwan said.

"Elliott Ness? That takes me years back. Showing your age," Oliver grimaced.

"Shut up both of you," Roy murmured. "What did scene of crime say about Fox Hagg?"

"No prints from the caravan apart from Eddie, Clara, and Lucy's. The bike was wiped clean it seems, even Eddie's prints are absent. No prints on IDENT-1 from the envelope. Handwriting is the same as on the notes left in Johnny's house."

"Notes that Duncan could've left, including the last one only him and his wife have seen. Of course, now he's

272

lost it, which is convenient." Oliver crossed hands across his chest.

"Uniforms should find it in the park," Sarah said. "Give them some time. I still doubt he took his own son."

"He's not clear as yet," Roy said. "At the very least, I think he knows where Burgess's dale farmhouse is. We need to press him for that." He clicked his fingers. "Anything under his name?"

Rizwan shook his head. "Nothing, but I've not looked under his two fake names. By the way, Dobson came back with a report on Wyming Reserve."

Roy raised an eyebrow. Rizwan coughed into a fist as his fingers tapped the keyboard of his tablet.

"Just like you not to read it," Oliver shook his head.

"He sent it to you as well, by the way. Have you read it?" Rizwan shot back.

"I was in interrogation with the boss," Oliver feigned shock on his face.

"Here it is," Rizwan frowned at the screen. "I needed to clarify one aspect. The boot print that Dobson found next to Johnny's shoes, the forensic gait analyst matched exactly to the boot I found in Duncan's car. The hiking boots he said he never used."

Sarah said, "Hang on. Does that mean Duncan made those marks to distract us?"

"Looks like it, unless he was wearing the shoes that day, which he might've been."

"That could be a dead end," Roy said. "Even if he put it there as a distraction, he could argue he was just looking for his son. Anything else?"

"A new set of fingerprints, and a piece of tissue. The tissue was found in the woods, close to where Johnny went missing. Getting checked for DNA, as we speak. Should be back by tomorrow, to see if there's a match with Johnny. The Dive Team came back with their report – nothing found in the reservoirs around Wyoming. They went into all four of the reservoirs, including the one near Rivelin Dam, the closest. They did say the reservoirs are big, and a drowned child's body should have floated up by now. Nothing's been spotted so far."

Rizwan threw Oliver a sideways glance. "Didn't look at the screen for that, did I?"

"Got to fill in your time between scrolling those dating apps," Oliver said.

"As if you have any luck," Rizwan grunted. "Anyway, I'll ask Dobson to update if he has any new info. He's on site at Fox Hagg still I think?" He turned to Sarah, and she nodded.

There was a knock on the door, and the balding head of Burns poked around the corner. "Not disturbing anything, am I?"

Roy waved him in. Burns leaned against a filing cabinet, which almost toppled over. He straightened himself and the cabinet, swiftly.

274

"Good recovery," Roy grunted.

"Thanks. Try and keep myself fit," Burns passed a hand over his scalp. "I just spoke to Duncan. He's emotionally labile, but I do sense he has the control imperative."

"English please," Roy sighed. "Are you saying Duncan's a fruitcake?"

"He cried a fair bit, and seems remorseful, but I also think he might've taken his own son. He shows all the signs of a classic emotionally unstable personality disorder. He opened about his childhood as well. His parents split up and he had a stepdad who beat him up regularly. Maybe even abused him. I don't know yet. Need some more time with him."

There was silence in the room. Sarah was the first to break it. "Do you think he would do it? I mean, kidnap his own son?"

"It's possible." Burns pulled up a chair and sat down. "He told me about his unhappy childhood the first time I went to the family home and spoke to him. He wanted to give his son a happier life. Exactly what that life entails, I don't know, but it seems he had his own plans."

"A life in Spain, it seems," Rizwan said. "So, Duncan colluded with Burgess, is that right?"

Burns pressed his lips together. "I'm not so sure. Did Burgess mention anything to you?"

"I spoke to him informally. No, he didn't," Roy said. He was thinking hard as he stared back at Burns. "Do you think it's possible Duncan's got up to this on his own? His friendship with Burgess, the visits to his house, it's just coincidence?"

Burns shrugged. "I don't know. He could've got ideas from Burgess, sure. But yes, maybe he acted on his own."

Roy glanced at Sarah. "Is Burgess ready? It's time to get his official version."

CHAPTER 40

Nugent accosted them as they filed out of the incident room. Roy was hoping he'd be gone by now, and he didn't bother to hide his disappointment. Nugent barred his way as he walked off towards the exit.

"Can I have a word, please?" He eyed the others, who sat down at their desks. "The rest of you stay here."

"You lot," Roy said, "go and get some breakfast if you want." He didn't bother looking at Nugent.

Sarah shook her head vehemently. "No way. I want to be here." She held Roy's eyes, and after a brief hesitation, he nodded. Nugent was glaring at him. He turned on his heels and stomped to his office, leaving the door open.

Roy went in and shut the door. The room smelled of cigarette smoke as usual, and the window was open, which didn't make it any less stuffy. Nugent sat down, making his armchair creak. He didn't invite Roy to sit, but he did so anyway. He enjoyed the look of faint disgust on Nugent's face. "You charged the father with kidnapping his own son?" Nugent barked. "What the hell were you thinking?"

"You've seen the evidence. He's still holding something back, I can tell. Burns also thinks it's possible. Happened before." Roy said quietly. Nugent seemed to calm down a little.

"Yeh, that's true enough." A few years ago, a mother had hidden her daughter with a relative and claimed she'd been kidnapped. She planned to split the money raised on the missing persons campaign when the girl was "found" again. "But that time," Nugent said, "no one like Burgess was involved. It has to be him. Maybe he's got a body double who posed for the CCTV at his garage."

"He looks right into the camera. That's not a body double, unless he's got an identical twin. Burgess wasn't there. If anyone, it had to be Duncan. Burns thinks so as well. Duncan might have a personality disorder. He was kicked around by his stepdad when he was younger."

Nugent chewed his bottom lip for a while. "The Chief Constable's not happy. He wants to know where the boys are. There's too much pressure from the press now. Have you seen Facebook? There's hundreds of find Johnny and Eddie campaigns now. Not to mention Twitter and all the other crap I don't even look at. And the last thing we want," Nugent locked eyes with Roy, "is to lose another child. If that happens, we're shafted."

"Then let me crack on. Let's see what Burgess has to say." Roy got to his feet. He stopped at the door when Nugent spoke again.

"The CC wants to put up signs in public places and schools. That will spread panic, but he thinks we should do that rather than face the backlash if another child's abducted."

Roy turned and took his hand off the door handle. "Not sure if that's necessary as yet. A panic is exactly what the Lily Man, or whoever this guy is, wants. He wants his name to spread."

"If it is the Lily Man, why do you think he's back, after all these years?"

The same thought was tormenting Roy for the last twenty-four hours. "I don't know," he sighed. "Maybe it's a copycat. Whoever it is, it's time we caught him."

"Get me something by tomorrow. I mean the boys' location."

Roy nodded, then opened the door and walked out. Sarah was waiting for him. Rizwan and Oliver weren't around and were hopefully at the canteen.

"His lawyer's briefed and ready. Shall we go?"

"In a minute."

He went to his desk and rummaged around in his coat pockets. He found some Nurofen tablets. The throbbing in his forehead was back. He had tolerated it this long, but as the day dragged on, the worse it got. He filled up a plastic cup from the water machine and popped a couple. He swallowed, then stretched his spine, massaging the back of his neck.

Roy didn't show any of the turmoil inside him. He had faced Burgess three times already yesterday. He had to look past that horrible evilness somehow. He couldn't allow the dark shadows to reach long fingers into his throat and squeeze all the words dry. Every time he saw the bastard, he wanted to smash his face in, pulverize it till there was nothing left. Rage was the only antidote to the anguish within him, and he couldn't let that rage surface today.

Because he knew. In the pits of his soul, where the sleepless demons laughed at him, he knew.

Burgess was the Lily Man.

He was the right age, and, so far, he had escaped justice. But this time, he had slipped up. Pairing up with Duncan had been a mistake. Roy had to make him pay. This time, there would be no escape.

He turned to find Sarah standing behind him.

There was curiosity in her eyes, mingled with concern. "You okay, guv?"

"Having the time of my life. Let's go."

CHAPTER 41

The interview room was next to the one where he had seen Duncan, but it was a carbon copy. The same grey lino floors, the same wooden chairs with their metal legs screwed into the floor. Sarah went in first, and Roy took a moment, then entered.

Burgess was dressed in a blue scrubs t-shirt courtesy of SYP. His thick biceps flexed under the half sleeve when he saw Roy. The corners of his blue eyes crinkled, and his lips thinned out. The man sat next to him was dressed in a pinstripe suit. His hair was meticulously gelled back, and he had a haughtiness about him, like he was doing everyone a favour by being present. Jeremy Dickinson, Roy had already been told. An Oxford educated lawyer who loved to poke holes in police cases. A royal pain in the arse.

They introduced themselves, and Sarah spoke into the machine. Roy sat down, opposite Sarah. The rectangular black mirror on the other wall stared at them, and Roy knew Nugent was probably there, along with the two DCs.

Roy knew it was pointless to ask where Burgess had been at the time of Johnny's abduction, but he did so regardless. Burgess didn't know they had the CCTV footage from the garage, but it didn't take a genius to figure that out. He had to ask, for the sake of routine, and in the vain hope Burgess would reply with something different.

"In my garage. My employees will know. And look at the CCTV." Burgess allowed a smile to spread across his lips. The smile remained as he locked eyes with Roy. Roy stared back at the demon in the guise of a man.

"What did you do after work that day?"

"I went home, put my feet up, and had a takeaway. I can show you the receipt on my phone, but I'm sure you've checked already."

"Which home? The one you rent under your real name, or the false name?"

The smile slipped, then returned, a little forced. "Just a second name. Not a crime, is it?"

"It is when you enter that name into an estate agent's database. They do all their checks, which means you must have a bank account under that name. To get that you have to falsify documents, which is a crime, you will find."

Sarah said, "And that's not the only false name you have, Mr Burgess. You have financial, council registration and electoral documents with two other names, all of which you can be charged for."

"There you are," Roy said calmly, but squaring his shoulders just a little. "Nice to get the facts straight, isn't it Keith? Do you mind if I call you Keith?"

Burgess's eyes flashed once. He was an entirely different kettle of fish from Duncan Reid. So far, he showed no sign of nervousness. Not surprising from a man who'd done time and had more than a few scrapes with the police.

Dickinson stirred to life. Roy ignored him till he spoke. "My client is not here to answer allegations of fake identities. Indeed, he was going out on his boat when he was assaulted and apprehended. Can we please get back to the reason why we're here?"

Roy kept staring back at Burgess, then slowly, patiently, slid his attention to Dickinson.

"Assaulting a police officer. Possessing indecent images of children. Resisting arrest. How many reasons do you want?"

Dickinson sighed. His cheeks were marble smooth, flies would slip on them. His brown eyes were flat and cold as dark ice on a morning road. "You have no proof it was my client who assaulted you in Attercliffe, Inspector. Just because my client happens to live there–"

"His fingerprints were found in the half-eaten pizza box next door, and on the laptop."

"That doesn't mean you can accuse him of assault, when you didn't identify him. Anyone could have entered his property and done that to you. Please can we be sensible about what you accuse my client of."

"The sensible thing would be to wait for the DNA results from my nail scrapings to come back," Roy responded sweetly. "The skin cells from my nails, which belong to my assailant. If they show a match with your client, then we have conclusive evidence. That should be ready first thing tomorrow."

"The DNA lab have confirmed that," Sarah said. "Just a matter of time." She smiled at Roy, who smiled back. They both looked at Burgess, who definitely wasn't showing any signs of mirth. Neither was his solicitor.

"So," Roy made a show of pulling out some papers from the envelope that Sarah handed him. They contained photos of the laptop, and of the houseboat. "Can you please confirm that these belong to you? I mean, this is a routine question, because we found your fingerprints on the laptop, and we got you while trying to escape on the houseboat, which is registered to one of your false names. Carl Magnus." Roy turned a piece of paper bearing a fake driver's licence with Burgess's mugshot on int. "Nice name. Did you think of that yourself?"

Burgess merely stared at Roy, then flicked his eyes down to the table, at the papers laid out in front of him.

"All yours, right?" Roy repeated. Burgess moved a fraction, angling his neck towards Dickinson. The solicitor nodded, and his client confirmed.

"Excellent," Roy said morosely, settling back in his chair. Sarah picked up the papers and put them back in the envelope.

"Tell us what you did the day after? I kind of know, because of this," Roy pointed to his forehead stitches. "But would like to hear in your own words."

"I got up and went to work at the garage. My mechanics can vouch for me."

"That's right," Roy said. "And later on, you were on the houseboat where we met, with our friends," Roy smiled, the mirth not touching his eyes. Burgess didn't even blink. "When did you leave the garage?"

"Around 11 am. The boat needed some work, so I did that. And I was going to test it when you and the others assaulted me and caused an accident."

"Which could've endangered lives, if the boat had collided with another," Dickinson chimed in. "I hope you're aware of that, Inspector."

"But nothing happened. Your client has endangered far many more lives, and also been charged with GBH in the past." Roy stared at Dickinson but laid out his right-hand palm towards Sarah. She didn't miss a beat. She pulled out some A4 papers from the envelope and gave them to him. "Ah yes, here we are. The charge sheets for armed robbery, GBH and assault." He waved the papers at Dickinson. "Have you seen these?"

"He has represented Mr Burgess before," Sarah said. "So, I'm sure he's familiar with them."

"Who, him?" Roy pointed a finger at a clearly irritated Dickinson.

"Yes."

"Your client's reputation precedes not just himself, but yourself as well," Roy said, taking a huge amount of joy in the wave of crimson that swept up into Dickinson's cheeks. "Shame you couldn't save him from a prison sentence. Anyway," he raised a hand as Dickinson snarled and went to say something, "I was asking Keith when he left the garage?"

"You know already, so why are you asking?"

Roy shrugged. "Because you said you didn't assault me in the Attercliffe house. Even though you left the garage around eleven, which would've given you about fifteen minutes to reach Attercliffe. And I arrived just after."

"No comment."

"Ah yes, I was wondering when you'd start to say the magic words. So, tell me, did you attack me because you were trying to pack away the equipment from your child porn studio, and I stumbled upon it?"

Something had changed in Keith. He was still relaxed, but there was a tightness in his jaws, a little stiffness in his spine. The earlier cockiness was replaced with being watchful. "No comment."

"I'd be saying the same if I were you. Wouldn't I?" Roy glanced at Sarah.

"Maybe. But I don't see the point, really. When the DNA results come back tomorrow there'll be a match. Correct?" Sarah addressed Burgess.

"I sense another no comment, coming," Roy remarked softly. "Well?"

286

Burgess sniffed once, and his teeth bared in a part smile, part snarl. "No comment."

Dickinson huffed and moved in his chair. Roy ignored him. "Then you ended up on the houseboat. But let's get back to this morning. What time did you arrive at work?"

Something subtle in Burgess's demeanour changed, a faint ripple under the surface, more felt than seen. Roy sensed it immediately, and it was followed by a hesitation. Burgess recovered quickly.

"Around 9 am. I'm sure you've seen the CCTV footage already."

"And you left at eleven. So, you were in the garage and didn't leave, all that time. Correct?"

"Yes."

Roy looked at Sarah. He nodded, and she reached inside the briefcase she'd carried into the room. She put it on the desk, opened it and pulled out an iPad. Then she put the briefcase down. She scrolled to the screen where the CCTV footage played and turned it so Burges and Dickinson could see it.

"As you can see," Sarah said, "You got to the garage at 8.50 am this morning. Then you went into your office and stayed there till 10.30 am. There were no CCTV recording of the rear of the garage this morning, the camera was switched off. Is that correct?"

"They're battery operated," Burgess said. "Sometimes they run out."

"So, there is no record of where you were between 9.03 am, which is when you entered the office, and 10.30 am when you exited?"

Burgess frowned, but there was now a relaxed air about him that Roy didn't like. "I was in the office, clearly. I was busy phoning suppliers, dealing with paperwork."

Sarah persisted, which Roy enjoyed. "Who saw you while you were in your office? The door remains shut till you come out of it."

"No one," Burgess shrugged, and again his ease of manner bothered Roy. "I have to run a business. I need time alone to make sure it's all in order."

"So, no one saw you, and you sat in your office for an hour and a half. There's a window from your office that leads to the rear. We know, because one of our officers went in the office. The window opens out to street level, ground floor. Correct?"

Again, that infinitesimal pause, that fractional shift. It was back. Burgess swallowed, his Adam's apple bobbing. "Yes."

"And the rear cameras weren't working, and no one saw you in that time. Isn't this all rather convenient?"

Burgess frowned, and the stiffness was back in his spine. "Convenient for what?" He looked askance at his solicitor, who was leaning forward, and frowning at Sarah.

Bravo, Roy thought. Well done. Now reel him in.

"Convenient to nip out to the Fox Hagg campsite, abduct Eddie Hearn, store him at your farmhouse in the Dales, and then return."

CHAPTER 42

Burgess's face was mottling into different shades of crimson. "I have no idea what you're talking about."

"You jumped out of the office window, because you knew the rear camera was out of charge. Then you drove up to Fox Hagg, like you were doing over the last few days, to watch the children there, Eddie Hearn in particular, the little boy who liked to roam around in his bike. You got lucky because Eddie was out biking with his sister. You grabbed him, rendered him unconscious–"

"No!" Burgess barked, a vein pulsing to life in his temple. "I never did that. I was in my office."

Sarah appeared not to have noticed. "Then you put him in your farmhouse, where you had planned to keep Johnny as well. Are both the boys there now?"

Burgess looked like a hyena just deprived of his meat. His hands gripped the edge of the table, snarling, almost frothing at the mouth.

"It's time you came clean," Roy said, loud enough for Burgess to slowly turn to him. "Although clean is not a word I would associate with you. Tell us the truth now and make it easy on yourself."

Dickinson restrained his client, who seemed almost apoplectic with rage. Roy felt the waves of ugly anger radiate from Burgess, and hackles rose at the back of his neck. His stomach coiled as strength gathered in his fists suddenly.

Burgess was the man who assaulted him this morning. He was sure of it. And by God, he wanted to smash his face in right now… he gulped, rose from the desk, and walked to the drinks machine. It was an admission of time out, and he needed it. He didn't drink but took the cup back to the table and placed it in front of Burgess, who snarled at him.

"I don't want no fucking water. Get me out of here. These idiots are mad," Burgess went to stand but Dickinson put an arm on his shoulder and whispered in his ear.

"We're not trying to get a rise out of him," Roy said, anticipating what the seasoned solicitor was saying to Burgess. "We know he did it. He needs to say it."

And say what you did to my brother, a voice whispered inside him. That same old lonely voice, banging around in the empty chambers of his heart. A little boy, whispering.

What did you do to me?

Roy looked down at the table, and screwed his eyes shut. He could feel Sarah's eyes on him. He reached inside his jacket and took out the black notebook. He thumbed to a page and clicked his pen, poised above a blank page.

"The farmhouse you own in the Dales. Where is it?"

"What?" Burgess crinkled his nose like there was a bad smell in the room.

"The farmhouse. Where you and Duncan planned to hide Johnny. Where is it?"

Burgess was fuming. Dickinson had a natter in his ears, and he seemed to calm down. "Hollow Meadows. Off the A57. It's a piece of land called Mile End. Near the dog kennels."

"The Centre Barks dog kennels?" Sarah asked. Burgess nodded, his nostrils flaring, eyes flashing. He ground his teeth together.

"You've got no bloody right to search my property. And you bloody well know it."

Sarah glanced at Roy, who nodded and spoke in the machine, informing it of her departure. Sarah left to give the others the address of the farmhouse.

"You won't find owt there!" Burgess called out after Sarah. "You can look all you like."

"Then why did you decide to hide Johnny there?" Roy asked. Burgess dragged his attention back to him. The snarl appeared again, cruel, hyena-like.

"For the last time, I have no idea who took Johnny."

"Tell us what plan you made with Duncan."

Dickinson exchanged a glance with his client, and Roy didn't miss the meaningful look. They had prepared for

292

this question, and that's why he'd left it right till the end. Burgess would know Duncan would sing like a canary in a coal mine.

"That pillock," Burgess spat. "He's so daft he couldn't tie his own laces. He thought he had a grand plan to make money out of his son's ransom. I told him right up it was bloody stupid. He ain't the type to listen tho'. I knew he'd make a right mess of it, and I was right."

"What do you think he did?"

Burgess frowned, like Roy had suddenly grown two heads. "Eh? How the fuck am I supposed to know what he did? Ask him. I'm tellin' you what happened. He asked me for advice, I told him it's daft, and there's nowt more to it."

If Burgess was acting, then it was a very, very good effort. He had shed his earlier composure; it was now raw and open. Roy had a problem now. Burgess wanted to keep his nose clean as far as Duncan was concerned, because he would assume that Duncan would grass on him. He was right, of course. Which meant, Burgess was probably speaking the truth now. And if he was, with the CCTV evidence, it wasn't possible that Burgess had taken Johnny.

Eddie was a different matter. Burgess was hiding something there. No way was he in his office for all that time. It was make your mind up time. Burgess was guilty, no doubt.

"You saw Duncan the day Johnny disappeared. You were in their house, and you knew they were going to Wyming Reserve."

"Yes, but when they left, I went straight to my garage. You saw the CCTV, for cryin' out loud." Burgess looked to Dickinson for help.

Dickinson exhaled and adjusted his glasses. "Inspector Roy. Either you charge my client, or you let him go."

Roy allowed himself a grim smile. "He's not going anywhere for twenty-four hours and you know that very well." He opened up his notebook, and wrote down Eddie Hearn, then put an arrow next to it. At the end of arrow, he wrote Burgess' office, and circled it twice. Then he looked up and met Burgess's glowering, hateful eyes.

"We'll be back tomorrow."

Roy gathered the papers, and the briefcase, then left. He saw Sarah rushing back as he went out into the corridor.

"Did I miss anything?"

He shook his head. "Nope. We have till tomorrow to charge him, but, given his offences I'm sure we can stretch that. Not sure about Duncan, but at least we have him till tomorrow as well." He stifled a yawn and looked at his watch.

"Time to head down to the farmhouse? Hollow Meadows, or whatever it's called."

"Two uniformed units are up there already."

"Good. Let's catch up with them."

CHAPTER 43

Oliver and Rizwan were at their desks. Rizwan was scrutinising his screen, and Oliver had his feet up on his desk, holding a sheaf of papers to his eyes. He scrambled to attention when he saw Roy and Sarah approaching.

"Any news from the uniforms about the farmhouse?" Roy asked.

Oliver said, "Just spoke to DI Booth, who's in charge. It was dark to see much. But the farmhouse is basically derelict, and he's sure there's no one there. They"ll go again today."

Roy sat down at his desk and asked switchboard to put him to the search team's radio. DI Booth, whom Roy had never met, came on the line.

"Ayup," Booth said, which was the Yorkshire It way of saying hello. "Nowt up there. Just bricks and ruins. A few foxes, but that's about it." Roy had him on the loudspeaker, and the others were listening attentively.

"How many rooms? Have you checked them all?"

"Four bedrooms gathering dust. Nothing was locked. I say we get back at first light and search the grounds as well."

"Yes. Thanks for checking it."

He hung up and slowly replaced the receiver, his mind buzzing. Rizwan was the first to speak.

"It kind of makes sense. If Burgess hid them there, he would know that we would get there eventually."

"Does he have any other houses under the fake names?" Roy asked.

Rizwan pointed to his laptop. "That's what I was checking. Nothing else. No caravans, or homes abroad."

Oliver said, "I'm looking at his bank accounts. He transfers money to Spain, but nothing major. He's got a timeshare flat in Marbella, but he's not been in the last six months. Not according to his passport, anyway, including the fake ones."

The silence weighed upon them. After all was said and done, they didn't know where the boys were. It was infuriating, Roy thought, flexing his jaws. There it was again, the shape that flashed across his eyes like a wild beast, too quick for his mind to grab it. What was it? What was he missing?

You're so stupid you can't see what's right in front of your face.

What did Burgess mean? He hadn't repeated it again, which was strange. Was he just playing games?

Sarah said, "If the boys aren't there, and neither of the two suspects know…" she couldn't finish her sentence, and when Roy looked at her, he saw the hunted look in her eyes, the paling cheeks.

297

"We've got to find them," he said, aware his words were hollow, and it only sounded like he was trying to convince himself. Sarah puffed her cheeks out and nodded.

"Be reyt," she said. "One way or the other."

Be reyt, Roy was discovering, was the Yorkshire way of dealing with every occasion.

"Okay," he stood, and stretched. "Home now, everyone. Back first thing tomorrow." His stomach gurgled, reminding him of the lack of dinner. "Any of you know a place round here I can eat? Or drop me off at the hotel and I'll find somewhere."

"I'll drop you," Sarah said. "Your hotel's on my way back home."

"You two got far to travel?" Roy asked Rizwan and Oliver.

Rizwan answered first. "Not too far at all. I live in Nether Edge, won't take long."

"I'm a bit further out, on the A57, in the Dales."

"'Cos you still live with your parents, eh shagger?"

Roy frowned. "Shagger?"

"Slang for mate, guv," Oliver laughed, and the other two didn't just join in, they had to stop themselves from rolling around on the floor, pissing themselves. Roy's face was a mask of incomprehension.

"You know what shagger means, er, everywhere, right? As in shagging?"

"Big difference between shagger and shagging, guv," Rizwan said, wiping tears of merriment from his eyes. Then he succumbed to another convulsion of laughter, along with the others.

Sarah wheezed and managed to catch her breath. Her cheeks were red. "Your face," she told Roy, between bouts of laughing. "You should check the mirror."

Roy raised his hands in the air and slapped them down to his sides. "Well, I should be a stand-up comedian. Easy job. Are we all shaggers now?"

Sarah said, "Not everyone says it. More of a bloke thing."

"Is not," Oliver said. "My cousin says it and she's eighteen."

Rizwan said, "It could be a dales thing. I got lots of mates who're from there, and more of them say it."

"Plenty of shaggers in the dales, obviously," Roy said.

Roy was learning new things, and it had only been his first proper workday here. He hadn't lived in this neck of the woods for so long, he'd forgotten what people were like, how they spoke. He was happy with his team. They were a good bunch, with the exception of Nugent.

They said their goodbyes, and Roy headed out with Sarah.

"How's your head feeling?" she asked as they walked into the car park and hunched against the drizzle that had started.

"Like it needs to grow a new one," Roy grumbled as he got in the front passenger seat. He was going to leave his car here; it was easier that way as he had to pay at the hotel car park.

"You should've gone home earlier," he said. "Your mother must be tired, looking after your son."

Sarah waved a hand as she drove. "She's fine. Mum's a tough one. Raised me and my brother as a single parent. It's only gone nine, as long as I'm home by ten she's ok."

"Do the school drop off tomorrow before you come to work," Roy said. He raised a hand when she tried to protest. "Just do it."

They drove in silence for a while. She asked, "When was the last time you saw your girl?"

Roy counted the days. "Been two weeks now and won't see her for another two weeks. Missing this weekend as I'm up here. Unless she comes up, which won't happen."

"Sounds like you're close to her."

"As close as a separated dad can be to a fifteen-year-old. No wait, that didn't come out right. I would like to see her every week. But her home is with her mother, and my work means it's every other weekend." Roy sighed wearily. "That's not enough."

Sarah turned to him and offered a sympathetic smile. "Know what you mean. Can't live without my little boy. I know yours is older, but still. What's her name again?"

"Anna. What's your boy's name?"

"Matt." The bland façade of the Premier Inn arrived, and Sarah pulled into the car park. Roy thanked her and got out. Sarah pulled down her window and called out to him.

"Call Anna. Girls need their dads."

Roy halted, then turned around. "Right. Yes, I think so too. Goodnight."

"Goodnight, guv."

CHAPTER 44

"What do you think of the guv?" Rizwan asked. Oliver was driving, and he took a few seconds to answer.

"He's alright. Likes to get stuck in, mind. Not that that's a bad thing."

"Yes, he seems quite driven. There might be another reason for it, though."

Oliver looked at him askance. "What do you mean?"

"I was looking at what the Lily Man did. Almost thirty years ago, he took three boys. Two were found in shallow graves. The third boy never was. His name was Robin Roy."

It took Oliver a while to catch on. Then he sucked his breath in sharply. "Shit. Is it–"

"I don't know. There's not much detail about the guv online, so it could well be a coincidence. Did stick in my mind though."

Oliver pressed his lips together. "Not the kind of thing you can ask him either. I wonder if Nugent knows."

"If he does, he's keeping it to himself."

Oliver got closer to Rizwan's house in Nether Edge. He lived in a house converted into two flats, three streets away from his parents.

"Do you think the boys are alive?" Oliver asked as he pulled up.

Rizwan unbuckled his seat belt. "I've been asking myself that. The ransom was a hoax. But I think the boys are still alive. The sick bastard who took them is probably having his fun right now. If he's hidden them well, I don't think they're dead yet." He shrugged. "Who knows. Alright my mate. See you tomorrow."

He got out of the car, and waved goodbye. Oliver did the same, then gripped the steering wheel. He watched the rain, drowsing through the black night, smudging the yellow streetlights. He turned the car around and headed back towards home. His parents would be watching TV, they never missed the BBC ten o'clock news. They were used to him coming back at all times. Mum would leave dinner out for him, and there would be proper nosh waiting when he got back home. One of the many perks of living at home.

The A57 had no lights save his own and the occasional oncoming car. Mostly, though, once he left the city, this stretch of the road was pitch black this time of night. His windscreen wipers fought the strengthening drizzle valiantly. He was coming up to Hollow Meadows, with the pet cemetery, and the dog kennels. Where Burgess had his farmhouse.

His last conversation with Rizwan came back to mind. Over the years, they'd become good friends although neither would admit it to each other. And as much as it pained Oliver, Rizwan did have a sensible head on his shoulders.

I think the boys are still alive…

Oliver pressed on the brakes and checked the mirror. No cars behind him. His headlights picked out the sign, and the dirt track that led up to Mile End Farm. There was one thing DI Booth had said on the phone that stuck in his mind.

Nothing here but some foxes.

Foxes.

Foxes were scavengers. They liked to hang around human habitation to pick up garbage and titbits. And rabbits of course, out in the fields. But why would they be in a derelict farmhouse, where no had cooked any meals, or put out rubbish?

Unless someone had… and the foxes had hung around or came back to sniff out some more.

He was now next to the sign, and he had slowed down enough to indicate and turn.

"Sod it," he muttered. "I'll be home in a jiffy. Might as well."

He turned into the dirt track, passing the sign that said Mile End Farm on a makeshift wooden board, with an arrow pointing down the track. His Peugeot bounced up and down as he navigated around potholes. The rain lashed down harder, and the watery glow from the headlights only showed the deluge of fat drops, and darkness beyond.

He drove slowly, eyes trying to pierce through the night, and failing. He kept the wheel straight, aware that on either side, down a divot, lay barren farmland. Finally, in the headlight glow, he saw the farmhouse emerge from the darkness like a hulking beast. Its outline was broad, and darker than the evening sky. It blacked out the sky, rising higher as he got closer.

The dirt track changed to a cobblestoned path. He could see the building fully now. The farmhouse was on his left, a rectangular shape that was two storeys tall. On the right lay a barn, its open door letting the rain in. He was in a courtyard, and right ahead lay another small out house, its door shut.

Oliver took out his torchlight, and checked he had the extendable rubber baton. In his days as a uniformed constable, he had used that for many purposes – from smashing window glass to cracking a skull.

He left the headlights on, and the engine running. He directed the flashlight beam to the barn first. The light only showed paved stones on the floor inside, the angle of the door casting a shadow. Wind whipped at his collar, and a sudden gust made the barn door move like someone was pulling it shut from inside. Oliver stopped and took the baton in his hand.

He got to the door and pulled it by the handle. It was an old oak door, ravaged by wind and rain, but heavy and sturdy. He had to pull hard to see inside the barn. He turned the light on, and it fell upon a pair of gleaming eyes. It was a fox, and it was frozen in the glare for a second, then it turned and bolted. Oliver moved the beam around the barn. There was an upper floor, the wooden platform there holding nothing but dust. Giant cobwebs fluttered in the wind like tattered shades. He stepped inside. There was a smell here, of stale urine, and something else – a deeper, pungent, unpleasant smell. He wasn't a farm boy, but many of his friends in the Dales had farms. This smell reminded him of wild cats that prowled around the open land at night. That worried him a little. Although these cats didn't normally attack humans, they could lunge if they felt threatened.

Along one side of the wall he found a row of rusty utensils – spades of various sizes, pitchforks, and other crap. The beam moved quickly across. The depths of the barn were lit up by the beam, and he saw more cobwebs and some old, rotting bales of hay. He went out, and pushed at the door, trying to shut it. It moved, creaking loudly. He stopped after a while, realising the futility of his efforts. No one lived here, and no one cared if the barn door was shut.

He went to the outhouse. It was also shut, but with a wooden beam across the two doors. The doors were smaller than the barns. He switched off the torch. Darkness suddenly enveloped him. Rain drummed on the hood of his jacket. The steel bar that lay across the doors was wet and he had to grip it carefully to lift it. With a grunt, he took it off and leaned it against the wood. The door creaked loudly as it opened, a triangle of darkness appearing behind it. He switched the light on, and the beam pierced through the clot of night.

A couple of old bikes and a motorcycle that had seen better days were illuminated in the beam. Nothing but old junk. The beam swept across a couple of old cupboards with broken doors, revealing nothing inside. He heard a sound, over the rain and the car engine. It sounded like footsteps, running across the courtyard. Panicked, he whirled around, flashing the light. The arc lit up the barn, shone on the cobble stones, the car, and then the large hulk of the farmhouse. But no human being. And yet…

Oliver patted his coat pocket for the radio and cursed. He had left it in his desk drawer as usual after work. His heart was thudding at a nuclear rate and a pulse roared in his ears. He swept the light around, lingering in the dark corners to make sure no one was hiding in the shadows. The crooked angles of the rotting woodwork looked like missing teeth. The broken glasses of the windows reflected the light from the torch, gouged out eyes that stared at him in silence. He felt the house was waiting for him, daring him to enter.

Oliver exhaled. The rain wasn't getting any lighter. He took one last look around him, then stepped towards the house. The porch was at ground level, and the boards creaked loudly as he trod on them. The door was open and opened further as he pushed. The light showed a reception area that was devoid of any furniture. Cobwebs hung like shadows from the ceiling, so thick in places he had to move them with his hand. He smelled the dust as it rose up from the ground, but another smell crept into his nostrils. Not just the damp rotting odour that was all pervasive. Something far more pungent, and thick, like a slime that almost lay on his skin.

He crossed the reception, his light flashing everywhere. Pockets of darkness hid from the light, he almost imagined movement a few times, but it was only the wind that whistled in through the cracks, trembling the cobwebs. His senses were on fire, but a fear lay packed like ice in his stomach. He clenched the baton tightly in the other hand.

He came to a landing, and there was another door that led to what looked like an old kitchen and dining area. There was a hole in the floor, the boards had collapsed into the sodden ground underneath. A rat scurried out of the hole, running away to hide from the light. The light picked up what the rat was gnawing on. It was a dead rabbit.

Oliver moved on. He shone a light up the staircase, then started to climb. He came to a landing on the floor above. Three doors opened up in front of him. He pushed the first one with his foot, then stepped back. Then he opened it fully and looked inside. It had a single bed, bereft of a mattress. There was also an old desk missing a leg and leaning to one side. A row of shelves were on the wall above the desk.

He frowned as the light picked up something on the shelves. He stepped further inside the room. Like downstairs, the wall had a light switch that didn't work. He got closer to the shelf and leaned in with the light.

A bunch of flowers. Not dry, but reasonably fresh. Breath hitched in his lungs, as cold tentacles of fear stabbed at his spine. The flowers were white lilies. They were of various sizes and tied with small ribbons.

He was too absorbed in his findings to hear the light steps behind. Gentle, like a cat's, making no sound.

"My flowers," a voice whispered behind him in the darkness.

Oliver whirled around, and his shoulders hit the shelf, slowing his movement. He saw a black, huddled shape in front of him that changed, getting bigger, coming closer like a giant's mouth engulfing him. He lashed out with the baton, but at the same time a blinding pain erupted on the side of his skull, like a volcano bursting from its crater. His eyes dimmed as he fell, and the world slipped into blackness.

CHAPTER 45

A combination of exhaustion, and a belly full of fish and chips, had lulled Roy into the depths of an inky, dreamless sleep.

He had expected the alarm to wake him at six in the morning, but when the incessant, staccato sounds burst through his slumber, it was his bleeper. He scrambled up on one elbow, dragging a hand over his face, then rubbing slumber from his eyes. He couldn't find the damn thing, and it made a huge racket, the high frequency bleating designed to cut through walls. The red numbers on the digital alarm clock said it was 4.30 am. The last time he checked the clock it was midnight, so he had some sleep.

He located the infernal object in his trouser pocket and checked the message. Instantly he was wide awake.

Officer down. Mild End Farm Hollow Meadows.

The rest of the message gave the location. That was Burgess' farm. Roy called switchboard immediately. Breath froze in his chest when he learnt it was Oliver. Inspector Booth was the duty uniformed SIO, and he called him through switchboard.

"Bloody heck!" Booth didn't waste any time in getting to the point. "I can't believe he went there without approval. Did he ask you?"

"No," Roy ground out, frustration radiating from him in waves, hitting the wall, and bouncing back. "But he lives close by. He might've decided to drop by on his way home, which is..." he checked his words, and gripped his forehead. "Where is he now?"

"Northern General Hospital. He took a heavy blunt force to the head and had a concussion. Lucky to be alive, actually. Had a brain CT scan, no internal bleeding, thankfully. He's sedated, but stable. Do you want to inform his family?"

"Yes, I will. Thanks for that. Patrols up around the farm?"

"All around. We blocked the road this morning, but it can get busy due to commuters coming into the city. We got a look around, but, like last night, found little. Roadblock now lifted."

Roy thought to himself. "I'll tell the others, then head down there myself. Thanks, Steve."

He showered and dressed, then drank the rancid coffee provided by the hotel. He took a cab to the nick and went to the office. It was deserted, the motion sensor lights above turning on as he strode to his desk. He eyed the small office he had at the rear, next to Nugent's. He took his laptop in there and opened it up to check his emails. He had typed up a report for Nugent before he went to sleep last night, and he sent that off.

He went to the car park and got into his battered VW. He half expected the old bugger not to start, but it came to life with an unaccustomed roar. Maybe a couple of days rest had done it good. He followed the directions on his phone to the hospital. The woman at the reception directed him to the correct ward. He walked in and found a uniformed constable standing at the door of Oliver's room. Roy strode past him to the end of ward, where the nurse's desk was situated. A blue uniformed nurse looked up at him. Roy showed her his warrant card.

"Oliver Walmsley is my Detective Constable. Can I please speak to the doctor in charge of his case?"

The nurse looked bright and sprightly, despite the morning hour. She'd obviously just started her shift.

"Hold on let me speak to her." She jabbed at numbers on the phone in front of her. Roy leaned against the counter, looking down the corridor. The young constable was looking around, and he saw Roy, then swivelled his head in the opposite direction.

The phone rang and the nurse spoke to someone. "Dr Mackintosh will speak to you now," she told Roy. He took the phone and introduced himself.

Dr Mackintosh was a lady, and she did the same. "I did a ward round at one in the morning. Mr Oliver is doing well. He should be conscious now, but he might be drowsy due to the morphine we gave him."

"The brains scan was normal I heard."

"Enhanced contrast CT scan, yes. The on-call radiologist reported it. He's got a contusion injury in the scalp, and possibly a hairline fracture of the skull,

312

but it could just be fluid. Only on the skull, not in the brain."

"What's the prognosis?"

"Bed rest for forty-eight hours, then he should be home. He's lucky he doesn't have a hematoma, which is a collection of blood that puts pressure on the brain. We would have to drain that out in the theatre."

"Right," Roy breathed, a weight off his mind. "He should be fine then? Can I speak to him?"

"Hmm, yes, but not for long. He needs the rest. No visitors until late morning."

"I won't be long, but I need to know who assaulted him, and he might have the information."

"Like I said, for a couple of minutes, no more."

"Thank you, Doc," Roy handed the phone back to the nurse, and thanked her as well. He strode to the room and showed the constable his warrant card.

The young man glanced at it, then nodded nervously and averted his eyes. "I've been told not to let anyone in, sir."

"I'm the SIO for this case, and the man inside is my DC. I'm not anyone." He moved to reach for the door handle, but the constable stepped in his way. He was a tall bloke, the same height as Roy.

"I'm sorry, sir," he licked his lips. "I've got my orders."

"And who gave you those orders... Constable Pickering?" Roy read his name badge.

"D Sup Nugent. He said no entry apart from the medical staff." Pickering glanced at Roy, and their eyes met for the first time. "He mentioned you as well. Said you might come around."

"Did he now?" Roy said, flexing his jaws. He got closer to Pickering, and to the constable's credit, he didn't back down. He stared straight ahead, and his upper lip trembled.

"Now you listen to me, son," Roy said softly in the young man's ear. "That lad in there, he's one of ours, right?"

Pickering swallowed and glanced at Roy again. Then he nodded.

Roy leaned in closer. "He was left for dead last night, and he's lucky to be alive. And I might just know who did it. More to the point, I need to make sure he's alright. I don't care what anyone says. Now you have a choice, DC Pickering. You either move aside, or I swear to God, I'm going to move you." Pickering breathed heavily and sweat glistened on his forehead. Roy said, "Did you hear me?"

"Yes, sir, I did. It's just that..."

"Just what, son?"

"D Sup Nugent said–"

"Do you see him here?" Roy stretched an arm down the corridor. It was still early, and only a nurse hovered by a patient's trolley. "I know you're doing your job. But I don't have time to play games. See this?" Roy pointed to the stitches on his forehead. He had reapplied the same dressing this morning after his shower. "I'll split this open again if I have to. Now you step aside, or never mind the D Sup, you'll have to explain to the Chief Constable why you stopped a DCI doing his job."

Pickering wavered, his whole body shuddering once. "I… I'm not sure-

"Last chance," Roy ground his teeth together, and lifted his chin to almost touching Pickering's face. "And I mean it."

Pickering exhaled, blinked once, then stepped aside. "Thank you," Roy said, and pressed on the handle. He went inside and shut the door softly. Two dim lights were on in the sides, and there was enough light to see Oliver sleeping on the bed. Intravenous lines were attached to his left arm, and the drip bottle on the stand was almost empty.

He didn't have an oxygen mask on his face, that was good. It meant he was breathing spontaneously. He was sleeping, and there was a white dressing around his head. The TV screen above his head showed squiggly lines of red, yellow, and green. Roy pulled up a chair and sat next to him.

He stared at Oliver's pale face for a few seconds, then lowered his head into his hands. A bitter storm of rage showered flints into his soul, making it hurt and bleed. But it was nothing compared to what Oliver had gone through. Roy got closer to his ear and whispered his name.

"Oliver. Can you hear me?" He repeated it and saw a flicker of movement. Oliver's right hand moved. The index finger held the clip-on oximeter, and it rose up in the air. Roy exhaled and stood straighter. "Oliver it's me. Rohan Roy. I'm sorry this happened."

Oliver's head moved a fraction, then his dry lips parted. The lips moved but no sound came. Roy looked around and found a glass of water on the table next to the bed. He put a hand very gently under Oliver's head, and raised it a fraction, and brought the glass of water to his lips. He took a sip, then Roy eased him back on the pillow. He waited. Then he touched Oliver on the shoulder. The man stirred.

His lips opened, and his tongue flicked out, licking them. "Guv…" he croaked.

"Yes, I'm here," Roy leaned over. A movement at the door caught his eyes. Pickering, looking over the screen on the glass panel. He moved away when Roy caught him, but Roy didn't miss the phone in his ear.

"I went…. I…"

"I know where you went. Burgess' farm. Did you see who did this to you?"

Oliver rested for a while. Then he shook his head. His lips moved again, without sound. Roy leaned closer.

"Lilies," Oliver voice was low, scratchy. "Upstairs... lilies."

The storm bulged against the cages inside Roy, rattling his ribs. He exhaled, but the tension didn't release.

"What else did you see?"

Oliver seemed tired by the effort. Roy felt awful for asking, but he had to know.

"Water?" he asked. Oliver grimaced, then nodded. He took another sip, and Roy moved his hand from under his head again, slowly.

"He said... those are mine... flowers."

"Did you see him?"

The door opened and a matron came in. It was a man, wearing a white vest, blue trousers, and blue borders on his vest.

"What are you doing?" he said, frowning at Roy. He was balding and wore spectacles. "You're not allowed to be here."

"One second," Roy raised a hand, and turned back to Oliver. "Did you see him?"

Oliver opened his eyes once, then screwed it shut immediately, frowning as if the little light hurt him.

"You need to leave, now," the matron said. He got closer, and Pickering entered the room as well. He had the phone in his hand and extended it towards Roy.

"Sir, D Sup wants to speak to you."

Roy ignored them, his eyes focused on Oliver. Slowly, Oliver shook his head. Roy understood. It was dark, and Oliver hadn't seen his attacker, at least not in enough detail to describe him.

CHAPTER 46

Pickering followed him outside into the corridor. "Sir?" He thrust the phone to Roy.

Roy took it and wandered down the corridor. "What are you playing at?" Nugent's raspy voice barked.

"Visiting my own team in hospital. Part of my duty, actually."

"He's been told to rest! Which part of that did you not understand?"

Roy gnashed his teeth but controlled his tone with an effort. "I spoke to the doctor before I saw him. He was alright to talk briefly."

Nugent breathed heavily down the line. "What did he say?"

"Not much. He didn't get a look at who hit him, which isn't surprising. But he did mention the lilies."

"Lilies?"

"Yes, as in the flower. The Lily Man?"

Nugent wheezed in silence for a while. "But Burgess is in custody."

Roy desperately wanted to ask the D Sup what sort of detective work he'd been doing for the last twenty years, but wisely, he bit his tongue. "I know. I'm trying to find out what happened. I'll be at the nick soon."

He hung up before Nugent could ask him anything more. He seethed in silence, anger building in his guts.

"Sir?"

Roy turned to find Pickering standing a few paces behind. When the constable saw the expression on Roy's face, he took a step back. "Uh… the phone, sir."

He gave Pickering the phone, and the young man put it in his pocket, then adjusted his cap nervously.

"I'm sorry… I mean I hope you don't mind I called the D Sup; I wasn't–"

Roy raised a hand. "It's alright. Carry on as you were." He turned away, then thought of something.

"Has anyone else been to see DC Walmsley? Apart from the doctors I mean."

Pickering shook his head; happier it was a normal question. "No sir. The doctors came around one in the morning, when I turned up for duty."

"And you've been here the whole time?"

"Yes sir… well I did take loo and coffee breaks, but the nurses kept an eye when I was away. No one else has been here."

Roy considered that, then nodded. "Ok. Time for you to go home soon, right?"

"In one hour, sir."

"Get some rest. Back again tonight?"

"Yes sir."

"If DS Botham or DC Ahmed come to see him, then don't stop them, okay? They're in my team."

Pickering's eyes darted sideways, then looked down. "If you say so, sir."

"I do. See you later."

He got back in the car and called Sarah as he drove. The VW didn't have hands free, so he had to drive with one hand, and handle the phone with the other. It was almost 7 am now, so she should be up. She answered on the first ring. Roy told her.

"Can't believe he went there on his own. I know it's on his way back, but still."

"He was stupid," Roy agreed. "But can't fault him for wanting to be thorough. I'd have done the same in his position. I'll see you after 8.30, at the nick?"

Sarah hesitated. "You sure? I could come now."

"No. Drop your boy off to school. See you later."

He hung up and slammed on the brakes. A truck pulled in ahead of him from the other lane. His head bounced against the seat headrest, and he cursed the driver. Then he realised it was actually his fault for driving such a decrepit car. He thumbed down the list of contacts, a wary eye on the road. He found Rizwan's number and called it.

"Can't believe it," Rizwan gasped, shocked. "On my way in."

Roy hung up, and Oliver's pale, drawn face flashed before his eyes. The storm burst inside him, flooding the banks. He roared, gripping the steering wheel till the car zig zagged on the road, then he beat his fist on the wheel, against the sides. His hands were claws, teeth bared. He lowered the windows, letting the morning air seep in. It was getting busier, but mercifully the traffic wasn't heavy yet. He drew in a deep breath, then repeated it, trying to calm down.

He had to think. Pinpricks of rage itched all over his skin. He wanted to scratch it till it bled. The old demons were coming back. Long nails were raking down his heart. He had used booze to drown the demons many, many years ago now. But the booze only added flames to the fire. He went down the long sinkhole of misery and heart ache.

Roy indicated and pulled over on a side street. It was quieter here. He got out of the car. There was a park next to him, and a jogger ran past. A couple of pedestrians walked in the distance. He checked his watch, then went inside the park. He found a bench and sat down.

His teeth clenched as he stared at the ground. The fingers flexed, the knuckles rock hard, desperate to smash into something, preferably Burgess' face. Separate his teeth from his mouth, then see how he smiled. Of course, that's exactly what Burgess would want.

Roy stood and stared resolutely at the horizon where the green trees swayed in a gentle breeze. His mind was made up. Sometimes, shaking the tree was the only way. He got back into the car and joined the morning traffic.

Near the nick, he saw a group standing near the main entrance, waving placards. He pulled up behind other cars and got out, staying well away. He went past them and heard the chanting first. It was bright and early for anything like this. Way too early.

"Free Duncan Reid," A woman shouted. She looked familiar, and he recognised her as Fiona, Duncan's sister. Others joined in, and the shouting grew louder.

The group was small, only about half a dozen, but already, a couple of reporters had gathered. One of them held a microphone to Fiona, and although Roy couldn't hear what she said, he didn't need to. He could well imagine the drivel she was spouting. Free a man who planned to kidnap his own son. A man who was friends with a known criminal.

He looked for Amanda, but she wasn't present, which made sense. She wanted nothing to do with Duncan anymore. He turned on his heels and went back to the car. He thought of why Fiona was here, and her relationship with Burgess. Did Fiona know more than she was letting on?

His spine snapped straight as a sudden thought occurred to him. He smacked his forehead. Why didn't he think of this before?

323

He waited as the barrier lifted and watched the group. A couple of them turned and pointed at him. He drove inside, parked, then went in.

Despite the early hour, there were people around. A uniformed Inspector stopped him on the corridor.

"Ei yup. You wouldn't be DCI Roy by any chance?"

"One and the same. Who's asking?"

"Inspector Booth. I led the two teams who searched the farm yesterday." He extended his hand and Roy shook it. "Sorry about Oliver. I can't bloody believe it," Booth shook his head.

"Not your fault," Roy told him. "You searched it well and didn't find anything."

"Obviously not well enough. I mean, how the hell was someone hiding there? We looked top to bottom."

"He was probably not there at the time, but came later." The timing had worried Roy. Did the attacker know when Oliver was going to be there? But there was no way he could, because Oliver didn't tell anyone he was going to stop there.

But Burgess had known. He had given them the address, and Sarah left the interview room immediately. It didn't take a genius to figure out she went to give the address to someone to check out.

And Burgess was allowed a phone call every day. Could he have called Fiona?

Roy frowned, his thoughts twisting, bending onto themselves. His mind tied itself into a knot, and it got tighter, till he couldn't see a way out. Not a way he liked, anyway.

"You alright mate?"

"Eh?" He looked up at Inspector Booth. "Sorry, I was miles away. What did you say?"

"I was saying we didn't search it right, although we looked in all the outbuildings, and all the three bedrooms in the place. Checked it all, really."

"It's farmland all around there, right? No other abandoned barn or outpost there?"

"Not that we saw. It was dark though, mind you." Booth said. "There wasn't any place he could be hiding. We missed something, like."

"I'm heading down there as soon as I've briefed the D Sup."

Booth nodded. "Some of the lads will be there all day. Dobson's there now too, with his team. I'll let them know you're coming down."

Rizwan came up behind them and said hello. "I saw them out there," Rizwan hooked a thumb behind him. "The free Duncan brigade. Daft buggers, the lot of them."

"I wonder if any of them know the connection between Duncan and Burgess, apart from Fiona Reid. His wife's not there, is she? That speaks volumes."

"Emily, the FLO said she doesn't want him back. I'm not surprised. She's probably getting the divorce papers ready."

"She needs her son back, first." Roy eyed Booth. "Do you have any female officers?"

Booth raised his eyebrows. "Any reason?"

"Yes. There's one woman waving a placard outside that I want to see. Fiona Reid, she's Duncan's sister." He switched to Rizwan. "Can you please work with the female officer to bring her in? Just say there's new information, and it's important that we speak to her. Bring her down to interview room one, I'll be there. Let's try it informally, first. If she kicks up a fuss, arrest her."

Rizwan looked surprised. "Really?"

Roy stared at him for a while, considering his question. Then he nodded. "Yes. I've got this sneaking feeling she's closer to Burgess than we think."

"She didn't know he was kiddy fiddler when we questioned her at her house."

"That could well be true. But you'd be surprised what a woman in love is capable of. She might genuinely want to help or protect Burgess. And she could also be one of those who think an armed robber is sexy. But she won't tell you that."

"I'm glad. Too much information there," Rizwan raised his eyebrows. "Shall I bring her in then? Let's see if we can do this without a lawyer, eh?"

"Sounds eminently sensible." Roy switched to Booth. "Thanks for the help." He set off quickly down the corridor, and Rizwan called out after him.

"Where will you be?"

"In custody. I've got an appointment." He raised a hand without turning around and missed the confused expression on Rizwan's face. Rizwan also missed the vicious snarl that now adorned his. Roy could feel his heart cannon-balling against his ribs as he descended the stairs. The custody sergeant was a short, plump man whose chest and belly strained his white uniform shirt. He stood as Roy steamed in, then his face changed when he saw the warrant card.

"Sorry guv, not seen you before, like."

"I'm new, so no worries." He signed his name on the clipboard briskly. "Did Keith Burgess make a phone call last night?"

The man looked at the diary, then nodded. "Yes. At 9.30 pm. He didn't say who to. Do you want me to trace the call?"

"Yes please, if you could."

"I'll ask switchboard."

Roy asked if Burgess was in his cell and the man nodded. Roy asked the man to open the door for him, then trace the call. He walked with the sergeant to the cell, then stood to one side. He gathered his thoughts together. His fists clenched, and the old fire spiked in his blood. The sergeant left him with the door open.

CHAPTER 47

Burgess was sleeping. That wasn't surprising, it was still early. Roy dragged in a chair and left the door ajar. He shook Burgess by the shoulder, and the man stirred. Roy shook him harder, and his eyes blinked open. Then a spasm of irritation twisted his face. He turned away, but Roy held his shoulder and forced him back.

Burgess sat up on his bed, and Roy went to the chair.

"You know this is police harassment, don't you? I could report you for this."

Roy dragged his chair closer and lowered his face closer. They were now separated by the bed on the floor. The musty smell from Burgess's body was revolting, but Roy forced himself to ignore it.

"Go ahead and try it."

Burgess glared back at him, then a shadow passed over his face, as if a thought had occurred to him. "Why are you here?"

"I'm asking the questions. Who do you have on the outside?"

Burgess rested his head against the wall. He didn't smile, or change his expression, but there was a smug look on his face that Roy wanted to remove with a pair of pliers. Slowly. "What makes you think I do?"

"Stop playing games. You're going in for a long time. Not long enough, as far as I'm concerned. Do yourself a favour, and cooperate."

"And if I don't?" A slow snarl replaced the smugness. "You know I wasn't there when the boys went missing. You've got CCTV evidence to prove it. You can't keep me here."

"Who was at your farm last night?"

Burgess blinked once, and hesitated. It was a mere fraction of a second, but Roy pounced on it.

"Don't lie!" he shouted, his voice taking over his brain. His eyes burned with fury, and he pointed a finger at Burgess.

"Who did you call last night after the interview?"

"I don't think that's any of your business. I can call who I like. And I don't know who was at my farm last night. Not me, I was here. Just like I wasn't there when the boys were taken." Burgess spoke calmly, the smugness flowing back, covering him like a sheet. He looked far too comfortable, Roy thought. Like he knew the next move. As if he had planned it all in advance.

That shape moved across Roy's mind again, large, and ponderous but vague, and just out of reach. What was he missing? The frustration dug sharp nails inside him, and he clenched his jaws.

"I swear to you, Keith, this won't end well for you. Tell me now who you've got on the outside."

A smile tugged at the corner of Burgess's lips, a deliberately, infuriating, know it all evil smile that Roy felt like a slap on his face. Something popped inside him without a sound. A wail of rage erupted from his throat, and he grabbed Burgess by the collar and heaved him to standing.

"Who? Tell me? Is it Fiona? You told her what to do, and she got someone? Tell me, damn you."

"Go on," Burgess panted. "Hit me. Do it. You're assaulting me already, might as well carry on, you fucking idiot."

Roy stumbled back, his hands shaking, a tremor moving his spine like a leaf in a storm. His pulse roared in the ears, drowning out the sound of his own breathing.

The custody sergeant appeared at the doorway. "Everything all right here?"

Roy grimaced and moved outside. Burgess was talking to the custody officer.

"That man just assaulted me. I know my rights. He can't just walk in here and start beating me up."

Roy lingered on the doorway as the custody officer glanced at him, then at Burgess. "I'll get you some breakfast," he told Burgess, then locked the door. "What happened there, guv? Was he kickin' off?"

"Don't worry. We've got an officer down, and he knows who did it. I'll get it out of him, somehow. Did you trace the call?"

"Yes. It went to the mobile of a Fiona Reid, if that means anything. Same last name as the guy in cell four, eh?"

"His sister, and Mr Burgess's girlfriend. With any luck, she'll be here soon." Roy thanked the sergeant and went upstairs. He stopped at the water machine and downed a glass of water. He felt someone behind him and when he looked, it was Sarah. He was glad to see her.

"Dropped Matt off to school? Got here early, then."

"Preschool club. I have to pay a small fee, but it's worth it. My mum's out for the day, so I'll need him to stay for a couple of hours after school. They give him food and it's in the school, so safe." There was a commotion at the rear car park entrance into the corridor and both of them glanced in that direction.

Rizwan was walking in with a female uniformed sergeant, and Fiona was sandwiched between them. Fiona was agitated, and when she saw Roy and Sarah, she screwed up her face. The trio came to a stop in front of them.

"What's going on?" Fiona demanded. "What new information do you have? Have you found Johnny?"

"Not yet, but we do need your help for a couple of matters," Roy said politely. "If you'd be kind enough to give us five minutes of your time? In private."

The grid of annoyance didn't leave Fiona's face. "Why can't you tell me here?"

"Because it's a sensitive matter pertaining to the case. We can discuss it downstairs, and then you are free to go." Roy raised a hand. "You're free to go now as well, but we thought you'd like to know what's been happening."

That did the trick. Curiosity won Fiona over. "Okay," she said. "Can I bring someone with me?"

"If it is someone already involved in the case, like Amanda, that's fine."

Fiona hesitated, and Roy glanced at his watch, then looked at Sarah. She didn't hesitate.

"Miss Reid," Sarah said. "We've got a crisis on our hands, and the case has taken a turn for the worse. We won't take much of your time, but we're pressed for time as well."

The conflict on Fiona's features gave way to acceptance. Sarah and Roy walked down with her to the interview room. Sarah sat Fiona down, then came outside and had a hushed discussion with Roy. He brought her up to speed and told her what he wanted. They went back inside, and Sarah spoke on the machine, and Roy got Fiona a glass of water.

"Miss Reid, I think you saw DC Oliver, who came with DC Rizwan, to your house." Sarah waited while Fiona took a sip of water. She nodded.

"Yes, I think I do. What about him?"

332

"He was assaulted last night, at Mr Burgess' farm in Hollow Mead. He was knocked unconscious, and he's lucky to be alive. He's in his hospital now."

Fiona's cheeks lost colour. Her mouth opened, and remained so, and her soft breathing increased a notch.

"We know Mr Burgess called you last night," Sarah continued. "What did you talk about?"

Fiona swallowed, then licked her lips. She took a sip of water. Her eyes flicked from Sarah to Roy. "Do I need a lawyer?"

"No," Roy said. "We're just having a friendly chat, that's all?"

"Then why are you recording it?" Fiona pointed at the machine.

"Just procedure," Sarah said. "Without your consent, nothing can be used in a court of law, so please don't worry. We just want to know what happened to our colleague. He's in a bad way. Surely you can understand our concern."

Fiona stared back at Sarah, then her finger curled around the plastic cup, and she took another sip. Roy could tell she was playing for time, and to formulate a response that might get her out of trouble. He didn't like what he was seeing. Burgess's words came back to his mind.

You're so stupid you can't see what's right in front of your face.

Sarah remained relaxed on her chair, which Roy appreciated. She was giving Fiona time. More time to dig herself a real hole.

"Keith's having a hard time here. He didn't do any of the things you're accusing him of. I know he's made mistakes in his life. He's paid for them, hasn't he? Now he's turned over a leaf, and he just wants to be left alone."

Interesting, Roy thought. Fiona had changed her tune to what Rizwan and Oliver had told him. Previously, she was shocked by his past life and feigned ignorance. Now it seemed she had known all along.

Sarah urged, "Carry on."

"He said you have CCTV from his garage that shows he was there when the boys were abducted." Fiona locked eyes with Sarah. "Is that true?"

"Yes. What else did he tell you?"

"That he just wants to be left alone. He wants to go home. He apologised for not telling me about his house in Attercliffe. He also said what happened with that other boy he was accused of… you know… he said the cops made it up and blamed him for something he didn't do."

"And you believed him?"

"Well, he's never done it again, has he?"

Roy had heard enough. "Tell me, Miss Reid, did Burgess tell you about his past criminal life when you met him?"

Fiona hesitated. "Yes," she said slowly. "Later on, after we got to know each other better. He told me not to tell anyone, that's why I didn't tell the detectives when they came to my house."

They let it sit there for a while, the admission of her lie gathering volume in the silence, growing into discomfort that was etched plain in Fiona's face.

Sarah asked, "Why didn't you tell us this before? I know he told you not to. Is that the only reason?"

"Yes," Fiona said, and her face lowered. She tucked a loose strand behind her ear.

Sarah said, "When you spoke to him last night, did he tell you anything about his farm?"

"And this time," Roy interjected, "please tell us the truth. It looks worse on you if we find out later on that you hid it from us."

Fiona closed her eyes and muttered something under her breath. "He told me you asked about all his properties. He mentioned the farm but didn't say anything more about it."

"And you didn't tell anyone else about this?"

Fiona frowned. "No. Why would I?"

She might be foolish for trusting an evil being like Burgess, Roy thought. But men like Burgess were charismatic and likeable, that's what made them into real monsters.

However, he didn't think Fiona was lying. She didn't have it in her. Sarah glanced at him, and he could tell she was thinking the same thing.

"One more thing," Roy asked, "do you know if Mr Burgess has a close friend? A man, about the same height as him, similar in age?"

Fiona shrugged. "He's got some friends, sure, he's talked about his mates. I've seen a couple of them at the house, and at the pub. To be honest, they're all his age, and about the same height."

"Do you know the names, or contact details of any of these friends?"

Fiona pressed her lips together and furrowed her eyebrows. "One's called Paul, and there's also Steve and Ryan. That's the three I've seen before. But I don't know them well, and I don't know their last names, or where they live."

Sarah said, "None of his friends have been in touch with you, or called you last night? Or in the last few days?"

"No. They don't have my number, as far as I know. I certainly don't have any of theirs."

"And no one came to see you last night?"

Fiona shook her head firmly. "No. I went to bed after our chat." She looked at both of them in turn.

"I'm free to go, aren't I?"

Sarah sighed then nodded. "Please stay locally. We might need to speak to you again."

"I'm not speaking to you again without a solicitor."

Fiona rose swiftly and made for the door. Roy opened it for her and thanked her. He spoke to her back, as Fiona walked down the corridor as fast as she could.

CHAPTER 48

Sarah joined him as he watched Fiona go through the double doors and disappear as she took a left turn.

"I don't think she's lying," he said.

"I'm not so sure," Sarah said. He glanced at her, and her sea green eyes were focused on him. "Once a liar, always a liar. I do think she's one of those who find dangerous men attractive. She protected him the first time, and still stays in touch with him. The difference now is that she's scared of getting into trouble herself."

"I got that impression too. She gave up his friends easily enough. I'll ask Burgess about them, but…" Roy exhaled, and shook his head.

"What?" Sarah frowned and stepped around from the side to face him.

"After seeing Oliver this morning, I was… well, in a state, frankly. I went to his cell and questioned him, and…" he shrugged, avoiding her searching eyes.

Sarah groaned. "You didn't hit him, did you?"

"I pushed him against the wall, and that's only because he was playing silly buggers," Roy protested. "I didn't hit him. The custody sergeant was there, he witnessed it."

"I guess that's something. Anyway, Burgess didn't cough up, did he?"

"Nope." Roy looked heavenward, but there was no inspiration up there. "Let's get cracking. I want to see the crime scene, then go to Fox Hagg campsite once again."

He made to leave, but Sarah stood there. There was a questioning look on her face, and he didn't know what to make of it. She folded her arms across her chest and seemed to weigh up the words before speaking. "Can I ask you something?"

Roy knew, then. It was always going to be a matter of time. Sarah, and the others, would look into the Lily Man's past, and one name was going to stick out like mud on a white wall. Robin Roy.

From the expression on her face, he felt she'd known for a while, maybe even before he turned up.

"As long as you're not proposing marriage, fire away."

She smiled, her large, open eyes twinkling, touching the redness of her full lips. A shade of crimson spotted her cheeks, and her eyes swept downward. "Nothing as bad as that," she said. "Been through it once, not again, thanks."

"Same here. I'd rather face a nuclear war than go through my divorce battle again."

"That bad, eh? Once bitten, twice shy."

"I wasn't bitten, I was mauled within an inch of my life. Anyway, what did you want to ask me?"

Sarah's eyes lost their sparkle, and she cleared her throat. "Well, I was looking through the records of the Lily Man, and what happened. Obviously, we don't know who he is, or what happened to him. But I noticed the names of his victims, and–"

"Yes," Roy said. "Robin Roy was my brother."

Sarah was flustered. Her cheeks were tinged with red, and she started to blubber. "I didn't mean to pry; I mean I just looked, and it seemed–"

Roy raised a hand. "It's okay. I was expecting you lot to find out sooner or later."

Sarah was quieter. She held his eyes. "I'm sorry. I can't imagine what you and your parents went through. How old were you then?"

"I was fourteen, and he was eight, so I pretty much remember everything." He inspected the tips of his shoes, and dragged his voice from a deep, dark place.

"Robin's disappearance destroyed my parents, as you can imagine. It left me feeling confused and guilty, and I still struggle with it. Counselling never helped. Neither did booze or tablets. I'm still under occupation health in the London Met. I speak to a psychiatrist every now and then. It's alright. I've learnt to live with it."

She touched his shirt sleeved forearm. "I'm so sorry. I can see now why this case is hard for you."

He sighed, a black tidal wave of regret expelling from his lungs. "Yes. Especially when I think that Burgess was that man. The man who took my brother. And yet, he's not taken Johnny, and maybe not even Eddie." Roy rubbed his eyes with his fingers. "It's someone else. That makes me wonder if they were always a duo, or a group of sick bastards."

He blinked, arms dropping to his sides. Sarah said, "What if it's not Burgess, and not the old Lily Man, but a copycat? That's possible too."

"Yes, and I could be wrong about Burgess. But I don't think so. He's the right age, and call it a sixth sense, or whatever you want, but I can see it in him. I just know." He started to walk, and Sarah followed.

"When can Oliver go home from the hospital?" she asked.

"He needs rest his doc said, so will have to check later. But he's talking which is good."

"Listen, I know it's not much," Sarah said, her voice dropping. It made Roy walk slower. "If you ever need to talk about stuff, then I'm here."

"Thanks," Roy glanced at her. "But I'm alright."

He and Rizwan went in the black Ford titanium CID car, which ate up the thirty miles in less than half an hour. Roy called Sarah to let her know. She said she'd meet them at the scene.

The entrance to the farm was blocked by a squad car, and blue and white tape. The car moved and waved them through. Rizwan drove slowly down the dirt track. Brown and green patches of farmland opened up on either side, rising to the hills that ringed the city. Last night's rains had relented, but moisture hung in the air, low grey clouds bumping their heads against the hills, saying hello. A uniformed constable raised a hand as he saw them approach and Rizwan slowed down further. The white scene of crime van was parked in one corner of the courtyard and a blue Tyvek coated and masked figure was unloading the van.

Roy and Sarah signed their names, then put on shoe coverings and sterile purple gloves. Dobson, the chief scene of crime officer, came up to them and lowered his mask. He smiled.

"Now then!"

Roy was getting used to the standard greeting. He was still confused by the combination of the present and past tense, because it was obvious it was now, and not back then. He stopped thinking about it. At least Dobson didn't say shagger, which was a relief. Roy said hello, then did a quick 360. The barn door was wide open, and he could see one SOC officer kneeling on the floor, taking samples. The main house was to his left, and another outhouse was directly in front. The doors of the outhouse were also open, and he saw a flashbulb pop inside.

"Any news so far?"

"We went upstairs first, where it happened, like," Dobson said. "Got some blood splatter. Technicians up there, now."

"Anything down here?"

"Some boot prints but not much else. The rain washed away some prints. Not easy the morning after, not with so many of us trampling around."

Roy thanked him and went upstairs. Sarah was in the barn; she came out and followed him. They stepped on the sterile boards that were placed on the floor. Roy looked up at the broken windows, like toothless gums, staring out into the cold countryside. The woodwork was rotting, exposing rusty nails. It looked like a haunted house, and before he entered it, a shiver passed through his body.

Inside the reception area, he knelt near the floor, by a footprint that had been circled in yellow. It was a large man's size shoe, maybe eleven. Sarah overtook him and looked around in the kitchen. Roy came up behind her. Sarah put a hand over her mouth.

"What's that smell?"

"Dead animals," Roy grimaced, pointing to the dead rats, where the kitchen floor had caved in. There was a scurrying noise on the floor, behind the cabinets. Sarah yelped, and ran past him, towards the stairs.

"I hate rats," she explained, when Roy caught up. "Horrible creatures."

"Funny that. A girlfriend of mine kept a pet rat called Stanley. It used to be in a cage."

Sarah looked at him in frank disgust. "Who would keep a rat as a pet? Eeew!"

They climbed the steps together. Roy said, "I've seen giant water rats in India. They look like cats. Their teeth are huge, like 2 inches, and bloody sharp. Imagine those gnawing at you."

He smiled at the horrified, open mouthed look on Sarah's face. They got to the landing, where two forensic officers were busy at work. One had a tripod set up and was snapping photos, and the other was brushing one of the floorboards. Roy and Sarah stopped in front of the room which had blue and white tape on the door.

"This where it happened?" Sarah asked one of the forensic officers, and he nodded. Roy stopped at the doorway. There was a broken bed on the floor, without a mattress. A collapsed desk joined it, and, just to match, one of the two bookshelves was hanging down at an angle.

There were clear signs of a struggle. It wouldn't take much to break up this old furniture. The room wasn't big, and Roy stepped carefully on the boards. He could see the circles where blood spots were marked. He crouched and looked under the broken bed. He searched for the flowers but saw none. Sarah was speaking to someone, and their voices grew closer. A short, sparse haired man with glasses, wearing a blue vest and jacket was standing at the doorway with Sarah.

"I'm Andy, the blood splatter technician," the man said. Roy got to his feet and said hello. He pointed to the marked circles of blood.

"What do you make of it?"

"It's low-pressure venous blood, that's why it dripped on the floor. Arterial blood would be sprayed all over the wall. The injured person was standing on the spot."

Roy moved to one side and Andy came closer. "Right next to the shelves, here."

Roy looked at the shelf that was hanging from one end. Is that where Oliver had seen the lilies?

"He was probably hit from the side and toppled over the bed. That's how he was found."

"Thanks Andy. This is all Oliver's blood, I take it?"

"I can't see two types. Must be his. The DNA samples should match with Oliver, but I'll let you know."

Roy thanked him and stepped outside. Sarah had ventured into one of the other two bedrooms. These had no furniture. Wind whistled through the cracks of the windows. In the second bedroom, which was larger, and probably the master, two of the bay windows were boarded up. Roy looked carefully at the floorboards. They were scarred, decrepit, with holes all over them. He had shoe covers on, so he stepped over them, trying to detect any that had recently been lifted.

"What you looking for?" Sarah asked.

"Anything hidden underneath the floorboards," he replied. "The uniforms can do it, under Dobson's supervision. I'll have a word."

They checked the second bedroom, which was similarly empty but smaller. This room had a broken single bed, gathering dust.

Roy came out on the landing and stuffed hands in his pockets. He didn't understand why this place bothered him, but it did. His phone rang, and he groaned inwardly when he saw the number. It was Nugent. He answered.

The growl interrupted his hello. "Get back here, now. That's an order."

CHAPTER 49

"You did bloody what?" Nugent looked like he was about to explode. His whole face was going purple, including his ears. His chest seemed to swell till his shirt buttons almost popped, and his belly started to quiver.

Roy watched in fascination, wondering if Nugent would come apart at the seams, and just blow up. Maybe an aneurysm would burst in his brain. The possibilities were endless.

"Cat got your tongue?" Nugent demanded.

"I pushed him against the wall. He's playing with us. He's guilty as hell, and he's got someone on the outside."

Nugent shook a finger at him, his breath literally smoking. "You don't know that."

"Then who attacked Oliver last night, at his farm? He saw the flowers there. How much proof do we need that Burgess has a hand in this?" Roy shook his head, controlling his own anger with an effort.

Nugent's lips moved, formulating words that didn't find utterance. His face remained like a purple balloon, and his fists bunched as he grunted. He paced the floor around his table like a caged animal.

"I don't care. We can charge him, anyway, with his laptop crap and the assault. But you can't go around beating people up. Got that?"

"I didn't," Roy said, hating he sounded so defensive. "The custody sergeant was there. If Burgess shows bruises, he did it to himself."

"I've spoken to the sergeant," Nugent scethed. "You grabbed Burgess by the neck and almost throttled him. He wants to press charges. For fucking police brutality." Nugent stabbed his forefinger to the side of his skull. "Have you lost your mind?"

Roy flexed his jaws, a heavy weight at the back of his throat. He tried to swallow, but it remained there, a craggy rock that would never shift.

"I was told about you," Nugent said. He wheezed, then succumbed to a burst of coughing. He hacked up a rack of phlegm, a disgusting sound that made Roy wince. Nugent went to the window, and actually spat out. He turned around and glared at Roy, who stood still as a statue. "Your boss, Arla Baker, told me about your brother. About your stuff." Nugent seemed a little calmer. His cheeks were still puffy and red, but the strident ring in his voice was gone.

Roy closed his eyes momentarily. It was all in his occupational health file anyway. As part of the process, Nugent would have access to it, even if Arla hadn't told him anything.

"Do you still see the counsellor?" Nugent asked. There was a gleam in his eye that Roy didn't like.

"Sometimes, but I don't really need to anymore."

Nugent stared at him, then made a huffing sound in his throat, that sounded like a bull frog croaking. "On current evidence, I'd beg to differ, like," he said, the gleam in his eyes intensifying. The rage was receding from his leathery cheeks, replaced by a more cautious, crafty look. Roy was starting to feel uncomfortable, but he did his best not to show it. "You almost killed that child trafficker before you came up here. Then there was Gary Hutchins, the Mason girls' abductor. You did a number on him, too."

Roy clenched his teeth together and averted his eyes. Nugent folded his hands across his ample belly. The strained shirt buttons rubbed against the edges of the table.

"But you can't go around beating suspects up. Gives the entire force a bad name."

"Whatever I did to Hutchins and the child trafficker was in self-defence. Burgess attacked me. The DNA from my nail scrapings, and his, will be back today. The match will prove I was the one who was assaulted first."

"It's not a tit for tat, and you know that. What I can't have is you giving South Yorkshire Police a bad name. What if his lawyer speaks to a reporter?"

Roy's mind was churning, wondering where this was leading to. He remained calm. "I doubt the press would believe a violent armed robber, who has clearly assaulted various members of the police force now, and in the past. Can you see the public having any sympathy for Burgess? I don't think so."

"Regardless. You need to remember something. This is my gaff. I don't want to look bad or have to explain myself to the Chief Constable over what you're doing. And, frankly speaking, I think…" his words dried out, but the snarl was back on his face. The bushy brows descended over his small, gleaming eyes. Roy waited. This was it. Nugent had been building up to this. "I think you should take a break. Get off this case. I can appoint someone else to become SIO."

Roy's heart dropped down to the floor, then kept falling, gathering pace. "No," he said quickly. "We're close to getting a result. We have two suspects in custody, and that's just a day's work. I think by tomorrow we can charge them and get the boys back."

"You're not listening to me."

"Duncan knows more than he's letting on. He colluded with Burgess. He needs to confess. He's done this to get hold of that ransom money. He might even know where Johnny is."

Nugent made a face like he'd swallowed the frog whose sounds he was making. "You expect me to believe he kidnapped his own son?"

"It's happened before, and you know it. Duncan was there. His marriage was ending, and he needed the money badly, he was about to lose his job. He wanted to escape with his son, and the money."

"And he told you all of this did he? Or did you beat it out of him?"

Roy rocked on his feet and looked skyward. "Please, sir. Duncan's not innocent."

"I know he's not innocent, damn it, but there you go again, blaming him for something he's not done."

"Why did he run with the ransom money? I'm telling you; he knows something about Burgess that we don't."

"I doubt that very much. He made a mistake, and he's going to pay for it. No need to make him suffer more than he has."

Roy frowned. "What do you mean?"

"Have you seen the idiots outside?" Nugent asked, crossing arms across his chest.

"The ones demanding freedom for Duncan? Yes, I have. What about it?"

"Emily, the FLO, has been in touch last night. Said she couldn't get hold of you. The family and community are pissed off about us grabbing the father. They think he's innocent."

"What about him being buddies with a known child sex offender? His sister's out there, and she should know better. We just spoke to her. She confessed to knowing about Burgess but covering for him."

"What's that got to do with Duncan? She might be his sister, and the girlfriend of Burgess, but as far as Duncan's guilt is concerned, it means nowt, and you

351

know it." Nugent pulled up a chair. He wiped his red face with a shirt sleeve. "We need to let Duncan Reid go."

Roy's spine jerked straight. "What? Are you joking?"

"No," Nugent's small blue eyes flashed a warning. "We need the community on our side. Can't annoy them by charging the father."

"Can't annoy them?" Roy repeated, feeling heat rise to his face. "Are we scared of them? They won't be our mates anymore?" His chest heaved; sparks of brimstone collided as he breathed. "I'm telling you; we need to investigate that family further. Fiona lied to us till now. Burgess spoke to her last night. Duncan's close to his sister."

Nugent curled his lips upward. "Have you charged Duncan?"

"Not yet, but I could. For theft and resisting arrest."

"He took the money to get his son back. That's not a crime, it's a mistake."

"Agreed, but he might know something about Burgess that he's not revealed yet."

Nugent swatted an imaginary fly from his face, or maybe he was just trying to brush off Roy's argument. He made the croaky frog like sound again, and wiped spittle from the corner of his mouth. He said, "I doubt that. He made a mistake, that's all. I don't think he's taken his son. And Burgess, well at the time of Johnny's abduction he was in his garage."

Roy shook his head forcefully. "But not when Eddie Hearn was abducted. We don't see him emerge for an hour and a half from his office, and he could easily have gone through the back window and driven up to Fox Hagg. He matches the description of the man the witnesses saw there."

"We don't have to let Burgess go. We still have time to charge him. But I don't think charging Duncan is appropriate, and we should let him go today."

"I think that's a mistake. Duncan's a flight risk. We should keep him here and charge him if necessary."

Nugent's lips curled upwards, and a snarl unfurled across his face. "You don't have the right to do anything. You're on thin bloody ice right now, Rohan."

It was the first time Nugent had used Roy's first name. They glared at each other.

"So that's it?" Roy asked, scarcely believing what was happening. "I'm out of the case?"

Nugent took his time to answer. He swung his ponderous bulk sideways, angling his chair to the left, not meeting Roy's stare. "I'm putting you on watch," he said finally. "Slip up one more time, and you're off the case."

Roy exhaled. He was still here, hanging on by the skin of his teeth. "Okay, sir."

"And let Duncan go. Do it today." He raised a hand as Roy went to protest. "I don't want to hear it."

Roy nodded, then went out, and shut the door behind him.

CHAPTER 50

"Ei yup," Rizwan said in his Yorkshire drawl. "You alright, guv?"

Roy didn't answer and walked past him to the back office. He slammed the door shut, then paced the room. He spared the chair, but sank his fist into the wall, and rested his forehead against it, then closed his eyes. Frustration and regret raged in his veins. A wrecking ball of unspoken words swung like a pendulum within him, the heavy weight destroying his senses. He put a fist in his mouth, then roared, his hand muffling the sound. His broad forehead hit the wall, and he winced as pain mushroomed along the stitch lines of the wound.

He didn't hear the knock on the door till it was insistent, and almost police like, shaking the woodwork.

"Yes, yes, come in." He shouted, ready to face whoever it was. He hoped it wasn't Nugent. He really bloody hoped it wasn't Nugent. If it was, he wouldn't be responsible for where his fist or forehead landed, so help him God.

Sarah's petite, lean form entered the room, and she shut the door slowly, like she was handling a grenade. She didn't say anything. Roy passed a hand over his face, letting out a shaky breath.

Sarah pulled up a chair and sat down. Roy remained leaning against the wall. Eventually, he said, "We have to let Duncan go. Nugent doesn't want to annoy the community, he says. Or whatever. I can't figure it out."

"If his only fault was to run with the money, then I can see why he said it. But Duncan hasn't explained why he was so close to Burgess, visiting his house in Attercliffe, in the days before Johnny vanished."

"Exactly," Roy sighed in relief, glad that someone was talking sense. "And Burgess didn't exactly tell people about that house. Only a few people knew."

"I would've kept him for as long as possible, but we would have to charge him sooner or later."

Roy sat down on the remaining chair, facing the desk with the laptop and phone. "Then we charge him. At least we get more time to interrogate him."

Roy shook his head. Nugent was using the threat of removing him from the case to get leverage, and part of him wondered if he should call Nugent's bluff. But then he would lose control of the case.

"Get Rizwan in here. We need to knock our heads together now, and sort this out."

Sarah went to get him, and Roy opened up his laptop. Rizwan carried a tray with three cups of tea and a plate of biscuits.

Roy thanked him, and gratefully sipped his tea. Nothing like a nice cuppa to calm things down.

"Right, so where are we? I'll check on Oliver again today and if you two want to visit him, just go ahead. I've told the constable on duty to expect you."

"See that mardy git? No thanks," Rizwan grinned. He sipped his tea, then opened up his iPad. "DNA results from yesterday are back. The skin scrapings from your nails match that of Burgess'. It's also his DNA in the bedroom and his fingerprints on the laptop."

Roy smiled at the first piece of decent news of the morning. "Now we can go ahead and charge him."

"But the bad news is that his lawyer wants to press charges against you for assault. For what happened earlier today." Rizwan looked at him askance. "I wasn't there."

"Bloody rich if you ask me, considering that picked a fight with me to begin with."

"We can charge him with the material on his laptop as well. He's got no hope of avoiding either of them."

Sarah said, "That leaves us with the man who assaulted Oliver, and the two boys."

Roy sucked his cheeks in, then picked up a biscuit and dunked it in his tea. "I think Oliver was unlucky. The man was there, and he chanced upon Oliver. It could only be a trap if Oliver was expected. Fiona's not lying, and even if she is, it's not like anyone knew Ollie was going to be there."

He put his cup down. "But he is our man. He kept the flowers there. We don't know why he was using

Burgess' farmhouse, but it only makes the link between him and Burgess even stronger. It's clear to me that Burgess knows who this guy is."

"But he won't talk. And we can't make him," Sarah said. "However hard you try," she raised her eyebrows at Roy, then smiled.

Roy said, "He won't play ball, and why should he? I want to find his friends. Can we ask around at the pubs in Nether Edge he went to, where Fiona saw his friends? The pub will have CCTV, with any luck. We can see who he was speaking to. Let's re-check the CCTV at the garage as well. See if anyone came to visit him. Our man has to be someone Burgess knows, and others in the community know as well."

Rizwan said, "I've got in touch with the prison warden from when Burgess was at HMP Strickland. He's going to send me the list of his visitors. Expecting that soon this morning."

"Good. If we get that and see if there's any matches with his current friends or contacts. Also ask Fiona once again if she remembers anything else. We need to keep an eye on her."

"I heard from Emily, the FLO, this morning. Amanda wants to know if there's any progress. She's worried about Duncan too. She now admits their marriage is almost over, but he's still Johnny's dad."

"Tell her we should have more to go on later today. It can't be that hard to find who Burgess used to mix with.

Pull up all the CCTV footage on Burgess from anywhere in Sheffield. Something's got to give."

He looked at Sarah. "We should go and see Eddie's mother, Caitlyn. Did you call her?"

"Yes. She's expecting us now."

Roy stood, draining his tea. He clapped Rizwan on the shoulder. "Find that man, Riz. I know you can do it. Just think how much you can brag to Oliver that you didn't need his help."

"Now that," Rizwan grinned, "is the best motivational speech I ever had."

CHAPTER 51

Duncan Reid was let out from the side entrance that was at the far end of the police station. The entrance opened out into a street that faced the rear, and Duncan was glad that it was a quiet spot. The placard-waving crowd were at the front, and, although he hadn't seen them, he was told by one of the uniformed constables that he had a fan club waiting for his release. That was the very last thing he wanted. He had begged them to release him from a different entrance, and, thankfully, they had agreed.

Duncan hurried down the street, which was empty apart from a couple of women walking with a dog. He could hear the crowd chanting behind. Stupid fools. By making this racket, they had probably alerted the one person Duncan wanted to avoid for the rest of his life. That man was probably there now, asking questions, finding out when Duncan would be released.

Daft prats, all of them. The truth was, he felt safer in custody. Keith Burgess was in a cell a few doors down from him. He had nothing to fear while they were inside, because Keith would keep his mouth shut, or at least he hoped so. While Keith was scary, he was no comparison to the man Duncan wanted to avoid at all costs.

And Amanda... how could he go home now? She knew he had messed this up massively, and she wouldn't believe a word of what he said. Amanda would know the truth. He had tried his best to keep it from her, but it was now out in the open. He had failed. Most importantly, he had failed to be a father. Remorse overcame him, a palpable, immovable force that stopped him in his tracks, He leaned against a park fence, and his head lowered. His little boy, where was he now? What happened to him? Only that man would know... the man Duncan wanted to avoid.

Or maybe there was another way. Duncan wiped the useless tears from his eyes. He had to view this as an opportunity to get Johnny back. Atone for his sins.

He didn't know where the man lived, but he might find him somewhere in Attercliffe. That's where they'd last met. Duncan took a right turn that would take him towards the city centre. He heard a car speeding up behind him, but he was on the pavement, so didn't pay much attention. But the car screeched to a stop in front of him. The driver side window lowered, and Duncan's heart froze.

"Get in," the man spat.

A serpent of fear was baring its fangs at him, and his limbs were frozen in shock. "I've got nothing to say to you."

"Get in, or you know what happens."

Duncan's eyes bulged as he remembered the threat. Mess up and your son dies. "No, please."

"Then get in the car. Now."

Duncan looked around him. The road was deserted. "Last chance," the man said, inching the car forward. "Either you get in now, or it's all over."

Duncan had no choice. He got in, and the man drove off quickly. He took the back roads, and then came out on Ecclesall Road South. The dual carriageway started to climb, and they were leaving the city behind. Red and brown brick Sheffield suburbs receded into the background.

"Where are we going?" Duncan asked. A knot of panic hardened its grip on his guts, making nausea churn to his throat. His pulse boomed so loud in his ears he could barely hear the engine roaring.

"Where we can have a chat in private," the man said. "You need to tell me the truth."

"What do you mean?"

The man didn't answer. He ignored Duncan and stared straight ahead. The silence bothered Duncan. All of a sudden, he wished he had met up with the crowd outside. He'd have safety in numbers. It was too late now. For everything in his life, it was perhaps too late.

The car crested a hill, then took a sharp left, throwing Duncan against the door. He banged his head against the window. The car shuddered and swayed as the road became a dirt track. Trees loomed on both sides, darkening the path. The car came to a stop. It was very quiet all of a sudden. Duncan could hear the tweeting of some birds, but nothing else.

"Where's Johnny?" Duncan asked. He looked at the man, who rested one hand on the steering, and the other in his coat pocket. He ignored Duncan, who repeated the question.

"What did you tell the cops?" The man asked, still staring straight ahead. "I want the truth."

"Nothing," Duncan swallowed, his breathing fast and ragged. This guy gave him the creeps. He was so cold. So bereft of any emotion whatsoever. And always, always completely ice calm.

"Don't lie to me. Did you cut a deal with them?"

"No, I did not. I stuck to the plan."

"Then why did they let you go?" The man let the question hang in the air, and then he turned to fix him with a stare. Duncan squirmed.

"I… I don't know. There was a group outside, asking for my release. Maybe they put pressure on the police."

"The police don't care about things like that. They let you go for a reason. They didn't charge you with anything, did they?"

Duncan was searching for words, but his brain was a frozen desert. "Look, I'm telling you. I didn't say a word. Honest to God."

"Last night a police officer was at the Mile End farm. He was snooping around. I had to take care of it. Why was he there?"

The slab of fear on Duncan's chest was settling deeper, making breathing difficult. "I... I don't know. Honest to God."

"So, you don't know why the let you go but kept Burgess in. You also don't know why a copper was at the farm last night. In short, you know nothing. Is that correct?"

Duncan stared at the man. "Why don't you believe me?"

"Because I don't think you're speaking the truth. I think you made a deal with the cops. You told them about our plan, and also about the farm. That's why that cop was there, looking for the boys."

"Where is Johnny? What have you done to him?" Duncan asked, fear and revulsion paralysing him.

"You're a snivelling, worthless piece of shit." The man said it calmly, like he was making a comment about the weather. "And you, and your son, deserved everything coming their way."

"What do you...?"

Duncan didn't finish his sentence, because the man's arms were a blur of movement. The hand inside his jacket flashed out with a long, sharp knife blade. Duncan didn't get a chance to move. The knife plunged into his neck, burying itself to the hilt. Blood spurted like a geyser, an arc of red that splattered against the car's ceiling. Duncan tried to fight back, but it was too late. As he slumped to the side, the man pushing the knife in deeper, Duncan had one final image in his eyes. He saw Johnny and himself, walking on the hills on a sunny day. Then the vision faded, and Duncan saw nothing anymore.

CHAPTER 52

Rizwan was scrolling through the emails he had received. His phone rang, and he tore his eyes from the screen. It was the manager of the Swan Pub in Attercliffe. The drinking hole had seen its fair share of fights and hooliganism over the years. The manager didn't seem too happy to be speaking to him.

"Who're you, eh?" Came the gruff male voice. "What do yer want?"

"I'm detective constable Rizwan Ahmed of South Yorkshire Police, and I need to speak to you about a couple of your clients."

"What for? You bloody cops haven't got nowt better to do, have yer? Leave my punters alone, will yer?"

Rizwan ignored the unsolicited advice. "I need to speak to you about a Keith Burgess. He used to frequent your pub. He was friends with three men, and we only have their first names. Paul, Steven, and Stuart."

"Lots of people drink here, mate," came the sneering reply. "I can't keep an eye on all of 'em. Besides, you lot don't drink, do yer? And you don't go to pubs. If you did, then you wouldn't ask such daft questions."

You lot. Rizwan shook his head at the man's enlightened attitude. "Mr Miller, is it? If you have known criminals at your establishment, and you do not cooperate with us, we can search your premises without a warrant. Would you like that to happen this evening?"

The silence on the other end was pleasing. Eventually Mr Miller bristled down the line. "What do yer want?"

"We know that Keith Burgess and his friends drank at your pub. Do you have CCTV?"

Silence again, and Rizwan had to repeat the question. The low, rough voice answered. "Yes, we do, like. What for?"

"We need the CCTV footage from the last two weeks. Policemen are on their way to pick it up from you. I thought I'd give you some advance notice?"

Mr Miller was indignant. "Call this advance notice? I haven't even been downstairs this morning."

"We don't have time, Mr Miller. This is about the two missing boys. Mr Burgess is in custody, but we urgently need to find who he associated with. Do you understand?"

Mr Miller was quiet, and when he spoke, his tone was devoid of the earlier sting. "Aye, I do. Send your lads around."

"They'll be there in the next half hour. Please download the video footage for the last two weeks and have it ready."

Rizwan hung up and focused on the screen again. The warden from HMP Strickland had got back to him with the details of the visitor contacts from when Burgess was last there, three years ago. It wasn't a long list. Six people visited him often over the five years he lived at Her Majesty's pleasure. Two of them had the last name of Burgess, Rizwan assumed they were family. The other four names were unfamiliar. Rizwan made a note and sent it to the researchers to do some background snooping on all of them. The visitors had to put down their contact details, which helped.

The warden had also sent a list of the professionals that Burgess had contact with. Rizwan stared at the last name. His brows met in the middle as he stared at the screen. His jaws relaxed slowly as the implication hit him.

He made a note of the dates and times Burgess had met with that professional. He sat back in his chair, his mind running loops, and a horrible suspicion spreading, then growing into a conviction.

It couldn't be... but if it was... how could they have missed it??

Rizwan called the number, and waited, his pulse rate surging. The man didn't respond. Rizwan left him a voicemail to call back. He asked switchboard to try and got the same response.

He called Roy, his fingertips numb with shock, mouth dry. He remembered what Roy had said – Burgess's accomplice was someone well known, and he hid in plain sight. Too damn right.

Roy answered, and Rizwan spoke so fast his words jumbled.

"Easy tiger, slow down," Roy cautioned. "What's happened?"

When he heard, there was silence on the line. When Roy spoke, it was deliberate, measured with intent.

"Write down these names: Gary Hutchins. Charlie Allerton. Tony Dalglish. These men abducted the Bristow and Mason children. Find out the name of the professionals who dealt with them. And then chase them down."

"On it, guv."

*****

Roy put the phone down slowly, his eyes staring out the windscreen but not seeing anything. Gears shifted and clicked in his brain. Like a train emerging from a long tunnel, he could now see the whole, horrific picture.

"Pull over," he whispered. Sarah threw him a distracted look.

"Eh? What for? Was that Riz on the phone?"

"Just pull over."

Sarah did and swivelled in her seat to face him. Roy's hands shook as he took his phone out again.

"Have you got Stephen Burns' number?"

"Yes, I think so let me check. Why?" She got busy looking at her phone.

But Roy was already on phone, speaking to a person who could help him in times like these. His mentor, Arla Baker.

"Arla, it's me, Rohan. Listen, I'm going to keep this short. It's about the missing boys up here. Can you please ask your team to check if Stephen Burns was the forensic psychologist who did the profiling and treatment of these three men – Gary Hutchins, Tony Dalglish and Charlie Allerton?"

Arla was quick to catch on. "You found a link with same FP up there? He's a suspect now?"

"Yes. He told me he dealt with Allerton but kept the others a secret. Most importantly, he never mentioned Keith Burgess. From the prison records, it's obvious Burns and Burgess were in close contact."

"I'll call you back in five." Arla hung up.

Sarah was on the phone as well. She left a message and hung up. "Stephen's not answering. And Steve was one of Burgess' mates at the pub, correct?"

"Yes," Roy slapped his forehead and recoiled in pain. "Ouch. Do you know where he lives?"

"Not far as he drives home most days." She rang switchboard and got the address. "He lives off Lodge Lane, near the Rivelin River Valley." A deep frown creased Sarah's pretty features. "That's very close to the Fox Hagg campsite."

She thumbed the map, and zoomed in.

"Oh god," Roy breathed. "It's only a couple of miles from where Eddie went missing."

Sarah pointed down the map. "And there are walking paths that link it to Wyming Reserve."

"Go."

Sarah put the siren on, and the Ford Titanium screeched onto the road. Sarah drove expertly, dodging cars, while Roy spoke on the radio, asking all available units to converge at the address off Lodge Lane.

Roy held on to the grip above the passenger side window. Sarah's face was a mask of concentration. Her slight frame was hunched over the steering wheel. She wrenched the wheel savagely to the left as she humped a red light, and a woman with a pram appeared on the crossing. The woman screamed, and Sarah swerved, missing her but almost hitting an oncoming car. She squeezed through the thinnest of margins and swerved again to get the car back on track.

"Good skills," Roy shouted over the roar of the engine. Sarah's eyes were on the road, knuckles bone white on the steering. They came out on a busier road, and the traffic scattered as Sarah ploughed her way through.

They heard sirens behind them as other patrol cars joined in. Roy chattered on his phone again, telling them to cut the sirens and flashing blues when they got closer to the address.

Sweat trickled down Sarah's face as she drove. Another vicious turn to avoid a lorry almost made her lose control. The car's backside fishtailed out and crashed against the side of a car. Sarah didn't blink. She turned the wheel and got back on track, then zoomed forward. It was rush hour, and despite the siren, cars simply had nowhere to go.

"Half a mile away," Roy said from the map. "If traffic gets any worse, we ditch the car."

Sarah nodded in silence. They left the dual carriageway and entered the narrow single lane of Lodge Lane. Sarah cut the lights and siren. The black Ford now looked like every other car, barring the speed at which it travelled. Sarah kept pedal to metal, and only slowed down when they entered the street where Burns lived. This was a quiet and secluded area, with woods all around. Only a few houses were dotted along the road, with thickets of woodland between them.

Roy had two missed calls from Arla. He called her back.

"Yes, Stephen Burns was involved in all of those cases. In fact, it seems he took pains to be the psychologist in all the cases that you handled – Hutchins, Dalglish, and obviously now Burgess."

"But those cases were down south. What was he doing there? And why have I not heard about him?"

"He was attached to the forensic psychiatry unit that treated those men. These units don't have much contact with us. They are based in the prisons and psychiatry hospitals. Burns worked down here for many years, but the researchers dug up his past profile."

"And?" Roy was out of breath as he was walking fast, his long legs keeping pace with Sarah who was running.

"He's from Rotherham, South Yorkshire originally. Did his degree at Sheffield University, so he knows the area well. He came down to work here, twenty-eight years ago. Around the time the Lily Man began his abductions. He worked here for three years, not very long, and then he surfaces in Strickland Prison, where he's part of the forensic psych unit."

"Has he changed jobs? Why is he in the south Sheffield nick?"

Roy slowed down, and followed Sarah who sank to her knees, against the broad trunk of an oak tree. He crouched, and Sarah pointed to a detached, two-storey house on the opposite side of the road.

"He's now become a general forensic psychologist, not just one who deals with paedophilia and sex offences. Hence you saw him."

"Thanks. Can you please send all his records to DC Rizwan Ahmed at SYP?"

"I'll tell my team. Be careful."

"He's in that house," Sarah pointed. It was a detached property that had seen better days. It was large, with thick, brown wooden shutters on the windows and a sturdy, weather beaten door. Damp spread along the crumbling grey stone walls.

"I'm going in," Roy said. He checked he had the extendable baton and cursed when he realised, he left it at the office. He told Sarah, who handed him hers.

"I'm coming with you."

Roy shook his head. "You need to be out here to coordinate."

She didn't look happy, but agreed.

CHAPTER 53

Roy kept low and scurried out to the middle of the road, then sank down behind the blue Honda. He raised his head and watched the front entrance of the house through the car's windows. A wind blew across the trees high above. A bird called out in the distance. Then the road was quiet again. Behind the house, the land sloped down towards a valley. The Rivelin river valley, according to Roy's map, with the river at the bottom of the hill. His phone buzzed with a message from Rizwan.

Burns car seen in Wyming Reserve two days ago. And this morning, behind the nick, picking up another man. He drives a black Audi, LG20 TFP. Will keep you posted.

Two days ago, would be the day Johnny vanished. And this morning… Roy didn't have time to deal with this now, but a fear sparked inside him. Duncan was released by the rear entrance earlier today…

Roy observed the house for a little longer. He couldn't detect any sign of life. He went to the corner of the car and lay down flat on the road to observe the side windows. They were also shut, although he couldn't see the other side very well. On his side, which was to the right of the house, he noticed a ground floor window that looked open. He might just be able to reach it.

He signalled to Sarah, who remained hidden behind a tree trunk. She answered on the radio.

"I'm going in," Roy said. "Wait for my call."

"No units available to help, guv. Just you and me for the time being. I'll keep trying."

"Roger that."

Roy turned the radio knob all the way down to silent. He rose, then ran across the overgrown grass, and sank to his knees against the corner of the house. He moved when there was no sound from inside the house and came up to the window. He pulled the shutters, and they opened up. He had to jump to grip the ledge, and when he hid, he held on, feet dangling. He lifted himself up, inch by inch. He used his shoes to get support on the grey stones. Grunting with effort, he was able to hook an arm across the window ledge and manoeuvre himself inside. It took a few seconds for his eyes to get used to the darkness inside.

The bathroom was empty. He jumped inside, his feet barely making a sound as he dropped, then rolled on the floor. He was up swiftly. He opened the door and found himself staring at a stone-flagged passageway. The house was silent. A tap dripped in some invisible corner, the sound faint. Roy walked out into the corridor, baton in hand. Ahead, he could see the entrance lobby and front door. Behind him, the passage ended in a kitchen, with stairs next to it. He stole down the stone flagged passage to the kitchen. It was well kept and clean, but there was a rotting odour that assaulted his nostrils. It was a thick, heavy smell that hit him like a wave, surrounding him as soon as he stepped inside the kitchen.

The back door of the kitchen was locked, but the long garden beyond sloped down the hills without a boundary fence. Roy walked out into the hallway and turned left into a door that opened easily. It was the dining area, with a long table and several chairs. The room was empty, with a back door that led into the garden.

He made for the stairs, but a sound stopped him in his tracks. It came again, a soft, remote thud. It came from under his feet. Roy went down on the floor and put his ear to the cold stones. He could hear it better now. A muffled thudding, that went on for three beats, then stopped, and started again.

There was another door ahead of him, next to the bathroom. He tried, and it was locked. It had a glass panel, and he drew out the baton, extending it to its full length. He smashed the glass. He took his jacket off and wrapped it around his forearm, then reached in, brushing off the shards of glass on the doorframe. His finger found a door handle, and he pushed it. The door opened. It was dark, but he could sense stairs descending into the basement. His finger groped the wall till he found a switch. A naked yellow bulb's glow showed stone steps disappearing into a black void.

Roy went down slowly, his fists clenched, senses fire. He heard the thudding sound again, but it was weaker, and only twice. Then it fell silent. The bulb's glow faded, and he came to the bottom of the staircase. A door stood in his way, and it was locked. It was made of plywood and had seen better days. When he leaned on it, the frames creaked. Roy stepped back and hurled himself at the door. He did it three times before the hinge cracked, and the frame splintered. The door slammed open, exposing another area of darkness.

He flicked on his torch. Baton in one hand, torch in the other, he went inside. The stone steps were smooth, and he didn't smell dust. This place was used. The torch beam picked up old, broken chairs and tables. It was a long basement, and he had to go further inside. To his left, the space opened up, getting broader. It was chilly here, and dark as night. He heard a rustling sound and he stopped, hair standing up at the back of his neck.

He did a 360, but no one had come down the steps. He tried to use his radio, but it didn't connect. Only static answered his call. He went forward, beam flashing around. Then he came to an abrupt halt.

The beam lit up a cage. It was up to his waist height. The two steel doors had heavy padlocks on them. He saw two small bodies curled up inside. They weren't moving or making a sound. Roy rushed up closer. It was two boys, huddled close together. They embraced and hid their faces in each other. Their chest moved, and they were alive.

"Hey," Roy said, sinking to his knees. He took the light off their faces and pointed the beam upwards. He put the baton on the floor next to him. "It's okay. I'm a friend. I'm here to help," Roy whispered. "Are you Johnny and Eddie?"

The boy stirred. One of them lifted his head to look at Roy. The other one turned around. Their faces were grimy, cheeks marked with track marks of tears. Their thin, sallow faces stared at Roy in silence. His heart broke as he tried to reassure them. "I'll get you back home. Can you nod if you can walk?"

The boys observed in silence, not moving a muscle. Then one boy nodded and the other followed suit.

"Who's Johnny?"

The boy farthest from Roy raised a hand. Neither of them spoke. Roy heard a sound, and he flashed the torch beam down.

A tall man stood in the middle of the room. He wore a black ski mask, obscuring his face. He held a machete in his hand, and it glinted in the light as he raised it.

"My children," the man whispered.

CHAPTER 54

"Stephen," Roy whispered. Although his face was obscured by the mask, Roy could tell it was Burns.

"Show me your face," Roy said, his voice shaking. "It was you. All these years, it was you."

"Leave my children alone," Burns whispered.

"They're not your children," Roy raged, his words jagged, sharp. "I'm going to take them back."

"No," Burns said, stepping forward, gripping the machete.

Roy had to ask the question. "What happened to Robin Roy?"

Burns halted in his tracks. The lower half of the mask stretched, and it seemed Burns was smiling.

"Tell me," Roy growled. Burns looked down at the cage. Roy did as well, moving the light to the ground. He realised his mistake a split second later. Burns was a blur of movement, the machete a glint in the air, the swooshing sound terrifyingly close as the blade sliced through the air. Roy ducked, and the machete hit his back, ripping through the coat he had thankfully put back on after entering the basement. He tumbled to the ground, but the blade got into his flesh, and he grunted as the searing pain spread across his upper back and shoulder.

He also dropped his torch, which lay on the floor, pointing away from him. He lunged for it, aiming to get closer to the cage as well, where his baton lay. A heavy boot landed in his midriff, crashing him back to the ground. He heard the slice again, and felt, more than saw, the blade descending towards his head. He rolled on the ground and heard the machete hit the ground where his head had been a millisecond ago.

Burns grunted with the effort and the machete whished close to him again, and this time he couldn't stop it. The blade hit him in the back again, nicking his skin, and the sharp, tearing burn made him cry out. If he didn't stop this, he was a dead man.

He rolled on the ground a few times, then scrambled to his feet. He heard Burns rushing for him. He didn't look back and ran for the stairs. The jumble of old furniture lay to his left, and his eyes were now used to the dark, so he was able to spot the legs of a broken chair. He dived for it, crashing into the furniture, turning a table over onto himself. He was about to push it off his back, when he heard Burns scream, and the machete landed on the table with savage force. The force broke the table, and Roy lunged for Burns legs. He toppled the man to the ground, then tried to hit him with the chair leg in his hand. Burns responded by bringing the machete down on Roy and met the chair leg. The blade sliced the chair leg in two, and narrowly missed Roy's face. But Burns was on his back now, and Roy was able to thrust forward, and close his fingers around the arm that held the machete.

For the first time, he had an advantage. With lightning speed, his broad forehead slammed into Burns' face, and his left pressed the man's arm to the ground. Burns cried out as his nose got smashed to pulp, and Roy didn't hesitate to head butt him twice more. Burns twisted, but Roy wasn't letting go of him that easily. A fist slammed into his face, rocking his vision. He grunted, and felt dizziness overcome him. Warm liquid trickled down his forehead wound. Burns was desperately trying to free the machete, but Roy kept his hand firm on the wrist. With his left hand, he gripped Burns' throat. He pressed down, grinding Burns' head to the stones, and tried to sit up astride him

"Where's Robin? What did you do to him?"

Another sickening blow to his face sent a red explosion of pain reverberating through his skull, and his eyes darkened. The grip in his hands relaxed. Burns pushed him off, but before he could raise the machete, Roy had moved away. He got to his feet and scrambled toward the cage. His hands groped around and closed around a wooden object that was long and heavy – a table leg. He panted, blood dripping from his forehead wound, and tried to lift the leg. It was too heavy. The leg pulled him down to the floor. He fell to his knees and wiped away the blood blinding his eyes. A black shape loomed in front of him.

"Got you now," Burns cackled.

In the glow of the torchlight from the floor, Burns was a horrifying demonic figure, machete aloft in one hand, descending upon him with lightning speed.

Roy knew he had to do something. He had no time to search for his baton. He was on his knees, and the table leg was still in his hands. He slid an arm down the length of the shaft and leveraged the end close to him under his armpit. A roar erupted from his mouth as with one last manic burst of strength, he raised the table leg off the floor. Like a cannon, he aimed it Burns' rushing figure.

His thighs burned with the effort, but somehow, he raised himself to his feet. He swayed as the heavy wooden object trembled in his hands. But he wouldn't let go. Burns screamed as he rushed in, machete raised for the killer blow.

Blood blinded Roy's vision, but he bared his teeth and roared, pushing forward to meet Burns. The table leg was longer than Burns' arm. With every last ounce of strength in his body, Roy lunged ahead, forcing his aching shoulders to take the weight of the leg, coaxing his exhausted limbs to spend their last molecules of energy. He roared again as he increased his speed, slamming the heavy wooden object into Burns' midriff. Burns saw it coming and tried to step aside, but he was too late. The leg smashed into his ribs, driving him backwards. Roy grunted with the effort, but he pummelled Burns back, till the man fell to the floor. Roy didn't stop, he kept pushing, shoving, hitting

Burns with the leg, pressing it into his abdomen, pinning him to the floor.

Burns flailed with his machete, but Roy reached out one leg and kicked the hand away. With fearful strength, he lifted the leg a few inches, and brought it slamming down on Burns' abdomen, again and again, till the man stopped moving. Blood and sweat blinding his vision, body wrecked with pain, Roy collapsed on the floor.

CHAPTER 55

Roy's breathing was heavy, and his eyes were hazy, but he was still awake. He crawled on all fours, panting like he'd run a marathon. He located the machete and flung it as far as he could. Burns was unconscious. Roy slapped him on the face once, and the man didn't stir. He took the mask off. Then he stood, arms aloft, like a drunken man balancing himself. He managed to take a few steps, and get the torchlight, whose battery was almost running out. He shone it on Burns and identified him. He was stirring now, arms moving again.

Roy searched in his belt line and took out a pair of plastic handcuffs. Burn coughed, and then heaved a breath. He tried to sit up, and Roy fell upon him, punching him hard on the jaw. He did it again, and Burns' head snapped back. He lay still. Roy turned him around and handcuffed his hands behind his back.

Roy searched his pockets and found a keyring. Light was fading from the torch. He used the keys on the padlocks till one fit. Blood kept dripping down his face, and he put a hand to it, but it was no use, it poured between his fingers. He took his jacket off and held it to his forehead to staunch the flow. He almost wept when a key fit, and the padlock slipped off. He opened the cage door.

"Come on," he said to the boys. It was dark, and although his eyes were used to the dark, he could only make out their huddled shapes. "It's okay. The bad man's gone. I'll take you back to your mum and dad."

The boys didn't move. They were watchful and silent, and he felt iron fingers of sorrow curl around his heart and crush it to pieces. He wiped blood and tears from his face.

"You'll be alright. Come on."

There was a crash from above, and the sound of running footsteps. Voices shouted the word, "Police!" Roy got to his feet and stopped once to make sure Burns was still out cold. Then he went to the bottom of the stairs and called out. A face poked in from the top and shone a light down on him. Roy shielded his eyes from the light. The figure came down the stairs, and he recognised Sarah. No explanation was necessary. She could see it written on his face, and she simply flashed the light around. It stilled when it got to Burns, and then stayed on the cage. She muttered under her breath.

"Get the boys out, they're too scared of me," Roy said. Another person appeared down the stairs, and it was Rizwan. He shook his head at the carnage inside.

"Bloody hell guv, how're you still standing?"

"With great difficulty." Roy clapped him on the shoulder. "Get some more female officers down here please. Leave Sarah to it."

He almost followed Rizwan up the stairs, but then he hung back. Sarah was speaking to the boys, and they were actually talking back to her, which was progress.

Roy faced Burns again. He slapped his cheeks twice, and then shook him. Burns opened his eyes.

"What happened to Robin Roy? Tell me."

The ghost of a smile flickered on Burns' face. It chilled Roy's heart, and an icicle of fear plunged deep inside him.

"Tell me," He whispered.

The smile remained on Burns' face, but his eyes closed, and his head slid back to the cold stone floor.

CHAPTER 56

A hushed silence lay over Major Incident Room 1. Roy stood next to the projector screen. His left arm was in a sling, and every time he moved, his shoulder screamed with pain. Gingerly, he pointed the projector slider, and the view on the screen changed to Burns face.

"As you now know, Burns was effective at hiding himself as he was a member of staff. Twenty-seven years ago, when the heat was growing after the boys' abduction, he applied for a new job as forensic psychologist in Rotherham, and got it. He didn't abduct any more children, but he made friends with Burgess, who helped him. These two men went on to develop a ring of paedophiles, many of whom we're still trying to track down."

He paused. There was a film of sweat on his forehead, and the codeine painkillers were making him dizzy. He reached for a glass of water with his right hand.

"Emails from Burgess's laptop went to Burns, which he kept under a false name. They first met in HMP Strickland, after Burgess got done for molesting his neighbour's six-year-old son. Burns began to influence him, and they stayed in touch. Together, they planned the abduction of Johnny Reid. Duncan Reid was the foil, and he had become more trouble than he was worth. After his release, Burns picked Duncan up in his car, then killed him."

Roy paused, and drank some water again. Sarah and Rizwan sat next to Nugent, close to the lectern where Roy stood. They faced the assembled forces of South and North Yorkshire Police, and also Derbyshire Police, who managed the eastern parts of the Peak District.

Sarah stood, and picked up the thread. She said, "By then, Burns also knew he was in trouble. He had assaulted DC Walmsley already, the night before. He didn't know that Oliver would be there, but Burgess had told him he gave us the address of his farmhouse. Burns used that farmhouse a lot, because it didn't have his name on the title deed."

Roy nodded at her, and took a deep breath. "And we found a bed in the basement of that farmhouse. DNA from discarded bedsheets were match with the missing boy, Robin Roy. His DNA was also found in Burns' own home. It's clear that the boy had been in close contact with Burns, but he's still denying everything."

It had been two days since the event, and Burns was now incarcerated in HMP Strangeways, one of UK's Category 1, maximum security prisons. He would never be a free man again. Burgess was also there, but the length of his sentence depended on the outcome of his trial. The trial date was set at four months from now.

Nugent coughed, and spoke up. "We still need to continue the search for Robin Roy." He looked at Roy, who nodded at him, grateful for once.

Nugent said, "While we can assume that Robin isn't alive, it is an assumption as Burns won't talk. Neither will Burgess. Hence, we keep searching."

CHAPTER 57

The lanky, slightly stooped man stood outside the gates of the police station. He watched as Rohan Roy, and some other officers walked out into the sunshine. DCI Roy's left arm was in a sling, but the man knew it wasn't an arm injury. The laceration to his back was the reason his shoulder was immobilised. The man knew a lot about Rohan Roy, and what happened to him. A car stopped, and a man came out of it slowly. Rohan Roy and his team gave the man a hug. Detective Constable Oliver Walmsley. He still had the mark on his scalp from the stitches. The man smiled. Well done, maestro. You left your mark on them. Marks they would bear forever, even when the external scars had gone.

But their injuries didn't go far enough. Those wounds should have sliced Roy's head from his neck. The man felt rage bubble in his veins. Stephen Burns was now in prison, and he would probably be there for life. He would never see Burns again, and he would miss him like a desert missed the rain. Burns had helped him see sense, and seek retribution when everyone had failed him. Everyone, like Rohan Roy.

The man crossed the road, getting closer to the group of plain clothes detectives walking down the road slowly. How relaxed they looked. Congratulating each other on a job well done.

Did they have any idea what was about to happen? He would wreak havoc, make every waking hour a living nightmare for them. Hair stood up on his arms and neck as he got closer to Rohan Roy.

His nemesis turned, and smiled at him. The man smiled back, then nodded. He moved on.

Keep smiling, Rohan Roy. Smile now, because you don't know what's coming your way.

Want to know what happens to DCI Roy and his team next?

Click here for Book 2 in the series: *Suffer the Torment (https://geni.us/sufferthetorment)*

More books by ML Rose

The Arla Baker Series, in order (read for FREE in Kindle Unlimited)

The Lost Sister   https://geni.us/HFGU8

The Keeper of Secrets   https://geni.us/qXbvZ7

The Forgotten Mother   https://geni.us/cAeO

The Nail Collector   https://geni.us/g6XA

The Last Girl   https://geni.us/thelastgirl

Her Silent Obsession   https://geni.us/silentobs

The Forsaken Son   https://geni.us/forsakenson

The Vanishing Child   https://geni.us/vanishingchild

The Dead Voices   https://geni.us/deadvoices

To Die For   https://geni.us/todiefor

Last To Know   https://geni.us/lasttoknow

On My Skin   https://geni.us/onmyskin

AUTHOR'S NOTE

I went to school in Yorkshire, and some of my happiest memories are from that time. I remember going to Sheffield and the Peak District, and most of the landscape in the book is what I've seen and enjoyed.

At night, driving up the motorway, Sheffield really does look like a carpet of stars, down in the valley. Summer camping in the Jacob's Ladder area remains an unforgettable experience.

I hope you liked Rohan Roy, and the support crew of Sarah, Oliver and Rizwan. I also write the Arla Baker series, and Rohan Roy is a lot like her. Troubled, headstrong, damaged, but brilliant at his job.

There will be more stories to follow in the Rohan Roy series. Book 2 is out in a couple of weeks. Book 3 should be out later in June. I have a core group of beta readers, and an editor, but feedback is always welcome. My email is at the bottom of this page. Please let me know what you think about the books.

*****

If you read this far, I'm hoping you enjoyed this book. Would you please mind leaving a review? It takes two minutes of your time, but less than one reader in one hundred leaves a review. Will you be that person?

Just click here: https://geni.us/mybrotherskeeper

Thank you very much

ML Rose.

Please get in touch, I love to hear from my readers!

Email - mlroseauthor@gmail.com

Facebook - https://www.facebook.com/arlabake

Click here for Book 2 in the series: *Suffer the Torment (https://geni.us/sufferthetorment)*

Made in United States
North Haven, CT
26 November 2023

44555996R00243